Praise for *Gone to Earth*

'A fast-moving, clever book with
Highly recommend!' – **D**

'*Gone to Earth* explores conte_____ __sion
and empathy. A thriller full o_____ _____ and a climbing
detective, with her feet on the _____, steering the reader to a
gripping conclusion' – **Nicky Downes, author of *Her Perfect Girl***

'Jesmond's writing is full of tension, twists and surprises, and she
tackles the murky theme of people-trafficking with courage and
sensitivity' – **Susanna Beard, author of *The Perfect Neighbour***

'Fast-paced, perfectly plotted and agonisingly pertinent to our
times' – **Anne Coates, author of *Murder in the Lady Chapel***

Praise for *On The Edge*

'Jesmond explores the adrenaline rush of risky sports in this
original mystery… A promising debut' – ***Sunday Times***
(A Best Crime Novel of the Month)

'Intriguing… The landscape of Cornwall, with its history of
smuggling, makes a suitably mysterious backdrop' – ***Herald***

Praise for *Cut Adrift*

'Riveting… Jesmond's first novel marked her out as an original
voice in crime fiction, and the new book shows how the
conventions of the genre can be used to reveal a personal tragedy'
– ***Sunday Times*** **(A Best Crime Novel of 2023)**

'Jesmond's delineation of her characters as people with plausible
flaws and hot tempers adds depth and complexity to a story that
might wear its sentiments on its sleeves, yet which is trimly steered
and freighted with contemporary resonance' – ***Times***
(Thriller Book of the Month)

Also by Jane Jesmond

On the Edge
Cut Adrift
Her
A Quiet Contagion

GONE TO EARTH

JANE JESMOND

VERVE BOOKS

First published in 2025 by VERVE Books Ltd.,
Harpenden, UK

vervebooks.co.uk
@VERVE_Books

ISBN
978-0-85730-871-9 (Paperback)
978-0-85730-872-6 (Ebook)

2 4 6 8 10 9 7 5 3 1

Typeset in 11.4 on 14.6pt Garamond MT Pro
by Avocet Typeset, Bideford, Devon, EX39 2BP
Printed and bound in Great Britain by
Clays Ltd, Elcograf S.p.A.

MIX
Paper | Supporting
responsible forestry
FSC
www.fsc.org
FSC® C018072

For Oliver, for lots of reasons, and because he lives in Glasgow

PROLOGUE

Two months ago.
The English Channel off the north coast of France.

A moonless night and a calm sea. A smuggler's night, they called it. Not that modern day smugglers needed the dark, Basset thought. Even in daylight the gendarmes were rarely quick enough to stop them launching their overloaded vessels.

He steered the boat towards the beach, eyes searching the shoreline for the torch he'd told the Englishman to wave. Two flashes every thirty seconds, he'd said. There'd been nothing for at least three minutes.

Maybe it had been a mistake to use the English youngster to help. Basset would have preferred to co-opt someone from one of the migrant gangs. Someone strong and silent. But he needed to dump the man out at sea immediately. While he was still alive so, if the body was ever found, his death would look like another migrant drowning. The Englishman had been handy. Already up to his neck in this and heading back to Glasgow tomorrow anyway, his work completed.

Finally two flashes from the shore. Basset motored in as close as possible, dropped the anchor, then followed it into the sea himself and waded ashore.

They manoeuvred the unconscious body through the shallow waves and into the boat. Then sailed into the Channel. The

Englishman had given up asking stupid questions and was silent, crouched shivering on the deck next to the motionless man. The weight of the water stuck the clothes to his scrawny body and he'd stopped fiddling with the studs and chains that adorned his nose. Basset smiled. The youngster was smart enough, and mouthy enough when it came to technology, but faced with real life and its messy problems he was useless.

'*Ca suffit*,' Basset muttered when they were far enough out. 'We put him in here.'

He stopped the engine and lurched over to squat by the unconscious man. Waves sloshed against the boat making movement difficult. He cut the cord tying his feet and hands together and removed the rough gag he'd shoved into his mouth.

'What are you doing?' the youngster asked. A hint of panic brought his face to life.

'It needs to look like an accidental drowning. *Dieu le sait* there are many in this part of the sea.'

'Got it. Don't want the feds to get interested.'

'Feds?'

'Pigs. Police. What do you call them, Pierre?'

'*La Gendarmerie Nationale.*'

It riled Basset to hear his first name on the little *chieur's* lips. But the instructions from Glasgow had been very clear. Ronnie was only to be trusted so far and he'd only be there for a couple of days, so no full name and Basset was to use a hired car rather than his own. He wished yet again he'd told the youngster to call him Monsieur rather than Pierre.

'Who is he?' Ronnie jerked his head towards the unconscious man.

'*Policier infiltré.* I don't know the word in English.'

In all honesty Basset wasn't sure if the man was but the whispers about undercover British police infiltrating the smuggling gangs were more and more frequent and he couldn't afford to take any risks. Not with their operation so close to launching. Not with the prospect of real money finally in sight.

Heaving the body out of the boat was easy enough. It fell with a satisfying deep-noted splash as the boat rocked from side to side. The immersion in icy water half-woke the man. He tossed his head around and made feeble gestures with his arms as he sank. A few seconds later he surfaced. Now fully awake. His eyes fixed on the boat and he shot his arms out of the water, seized the gunwale and began to hoist himself in. The hull dipped towards the water. Basset picked up the anchor and smashed it into his hands. And again and again until the man let go and slipped back into the sea.

Basset started up the engine and headed away, aware of the youngster looking back.

'How long will he survive?' Ronnie asked suddenly.

'An hour perhaps. Probably less. The water is very cold and his hands are damaged.'

'He started swimming as soon as we left.'

Basset didn't bother to reply. They were ten kilometres from the coast. He would never reach shore. At least not alive.

The man swam in the direction the boat had gone. He guessed the coast must be that way. But after a while, he stopped and went back to simply keeping himself afloat and concentrating on breathing in between the waves washing over him. He thought he'd last longer that way because his only hope was a passing boat. The cold seeped into his muscles and fogged his brain but still he forced his limbs to move through water that was becoming thicker and thicker.

Some time later the moon rose and cast a cold light over the inky sea. The man no longer felt chilled but then he hadn't felt anything for a while. He knew his limbs were still working because his face stayed mainly above water. Enough to breathe from time to time. The moonlight revealed what he should have realised earlier. Waves rose and fell around him. He managed to rise to the top of the smaller ones but the larger ones defeated his muscles' fading strength and submerged him. Not that it mattered any more. All that mattered was that they hid him from all but the tallest boats. No one was going to find him. No one had ever been going to find him. This was the end of his story and he was never going to know how everybody else's finished.

One

Cornwall. Two months later.

My phone rang as I waited in the queue at Asda in St Austell. The summer season had begun and, for once, the sun shone here in Cornwall. The supermarket rang with the chatter of sandy children, sticky with the residue of salt water and sweets, clutching buckets, spades and plastic fishing nets that would rip the moment they snagged against a rock. Parents watched on, too lazy from the warmth to do much more than smile.

My first thought was to leave my phone unanswered. It wouldn't be urgent. Neither Rania nor Aya, the orphaned children of an old Libyan friend of Ma's who now lived with us, had appointments in the next few days with the array of doctors, social workers and counsellors who were supposed to be helping them recover from the trauma of their mother's death and flight from Libya. So, if the call was another change to the timing of one of these, it could wait.

I hoped it wasn't because it would piss Ma off even more. The horror of the crossing from Libya to Europe in a sinking migrant boat had stopped Aya speaking for months and she'd only recently started talking again. Just a word here and there. But her recovery was fragile and she needed each day to be the same. To get up at the same time, eat the same breakfast, see the same faces, go for the same walk to the lighthouse and so on. It would have been funny to watch my impulsive, new-agey mother stick to a rigid schedule if I didn't think some of her free spirit had been extinguished by the awfulness of the last few months.

'Her phone's ringing.' The small boy sitting in the trolley in front of me waved the lolly he was sucking in my direction. His mother smiled. He opened his mouth to tell me, revealing teeth startlingly white against his purple-stained tongue. I pulled a face at him as the ringing stopped and he giggled.

It could be my brother Kit calling. He'd left Cornwall and gone to London with his wife and daughter almost as soon as Ma and I had returned with the girls. He'd gone for work, although he'd felt bad about leaving us. He didn't need to. Someone had to earn money and he was paying rent for my flat, even though I'd told him he could stay there for nothing. I knew he was sending Ma money too.

A collective sigh rippled down the queue as the cashier explained to a man who'd forgotten to weigh his carrots that he'd have to go and do it himself.

My phone rang again. This time I pulled it out of my bag. I might as well answer. I wasn't going to be reaching the checkout any time soon.

It was a Spanish number.

The noise of people chatting and trolleys rattling disappeared. A wild hope pierced my thoughts as sharp and painful as a shard of glass.

Nick?

Was it Nick?

I abandoned my trolley and headed for the exit. But my phone had stopped ringing by the time I got outside.

No message.

It didn't matter. I had the number. I could call back. Just needed a moment. A few seconds to collect the thoughts ricocheting around my head.

You fool!

You might not have a moment.

This could be a call Nick had snatched from a moment of safety. A few seconds in the middle of whatever undercover mission he was on.

I called back. And then I glued the phone to my ear and screwed my eyes tight shut. Only the heat bouncing off the tarmac and the smell of diesel reminded me of where I was.

It went straight to voicemail and a male voice fired rapid Spanish at me.

Shit, shit, shit.

He'd called someone else. Why hadn't I answered straightaway?

I went to my car. I'd go back later and buy the fish fingers and oven chips that were the only things Aya would eat for supper and the harissa paste Rania daubed her meals with and the pearl barley Ma ground to make flour for dumplings for her. Aya had turned her back on any food that reminded her of Libya but Rania couldn't get enough of it.

I drove to the church and walked through the scattering of graves to the back where I sat on a bench provided in memory of someone loved and lost. It was the only place I could think of that wouldn't be overrun with tourists. Should I try the number again? If Nick was still undercover somewhere, was I risking his safety?

Except the phone number was Spanish. Surely that meant he was home. Back in Alajar, the little Andalusian village he lived in.

But still I hesitated.

My gaze ran over the gravestones. Most so old that hidden movements underground had shifted them so they leaned at random angles.

My phone rang again. A Spanish number. The same number.

I answered it. My voice croaked a hello.

'Jen?'

13

'Yes.' And in case I wasn't clear. 'This is Jen. You're speaking to Jen.'

But as the words tumbled out of my mouth, I knew it wasn't him. It had taken a few seconds for my brain to register the voice. It wasn't Nick's.

'Jen.' The voice was slow.

'Who is this?'

'It's Angel.'

Angel. One of Nick's Spanish cousins and his closest friend. I remembered the last time I'd seen him. In the bar he ran in Alajar, sitting at the counter doing his accounts, the half-moon glasses he was wearing incongruous with his shaved head and tattooed arms.

'Angel. Have you got any news?'

Silence. I wondered if I'd spoken too quickly. Angel's English was very good but it was difficult when you couldn't see the person speaking.

'Do you have news? News from… your cousin?'

Some fear for Nick stopped me from saying his name on an open phone line.

'Yes. I am sorry. I am very sorry.'

I knew what was coming before he said it as though the thought behind the words travelled faster than the actual words themselves. Like the lag between where a plane is in the sky and where the roar comes from.

'Jen. Nico is dead.'

Two

I dumped the shopping on the kitchen table. The one in Tregonna's old and battered kitchen, the only part of the house Kit hadn't renovated. Rania looked up from the coloured threads and beads she was intertwining.

'I made another bracelet.'

Ma had bought a kit for making so-called friendship bracelets in a charity shop in St Austell. Rania loved making them. I suspected she'd have loved some friends to give them to, as well. We had to do something about that. It wasn't normal for a thirteen-year-old to be so alone.

I smiled.

She waved her hand still clutching the bracelet towards the shopping.

'You bought the pearl barley?'

I nodded.

'Fantastic. Morwenna and I are going to make *bazin*. We're going to practise until it tastes like my grandmother's.'

I managed to nod. My brain had been blank since I'd spoken to Angel. Blank while I'd redone the shopping and driven home. Finally a thought now flickered into life. Rania's top was grubby. Her dark hair needed a good brush. And there were more holes in her jeans than material.

'I shall make you a bracelet.' Her bony face lit up.

15

I knew I should show some enthusiasm but numbness blanketed me.

Ma came in through the back. With Aya. Both of them were clutching loose bunches of wild flowers that swished and swayed in a gust of wind curling in through the open door. Ma's dress, equally flowery, wrapped itself round her legs and her long, wavy hair blew over her face. She spat it away. Aya giggled.

The three of us stared at her, waiting to see if there would be more. There wasn't. The little girl pushed the door shut, handed her flowers to Ma, then took off her backpack and hung it on the low peg I'd put up at the right height for a six-year-old. Exactly as she did every day. Each action measured and precise.

The psychologist had told Ma we shouldn't put any pressure on Aya to talk. In fact, we should go out of our way to make it easy for her to function without speaking. It was working. She said little but her presence became more solid every day.

Normally Ma chattered away on Aya's behalf when they came back from their daily walk to the lighthouse, after a stop in a small cove where Aya lost herself for an hour or so playing in the sand and pools. Today she was quiet.

'And what did you do today, Morwenna?' Rania said, puzzled by Ma's unusual silence.

Something had happened, I thought, as Ma now told Rania how she and Aya had seen cormorants diving for fish, how Gregory, the retired lighthouse keeper, had made tea for Ma and how he'd bought the chocolate biscuits Aya liked, and how Aya had eaten two of them and drawn a picture of the sea for him. But a streak of some unconnected emotion ran under her words.

'Supper in half an hour, Aya,' she said. 'You can watch Scooby.'

Aya trotted after Ma into the little room beyond the kitchen that had been colonised since we returned with toys and games.

Something was definitely up. Ma rarely parked Aya in front of the television.

She came back in.

'Is something wrong, Morwenna?' Rania had noticed. But she was hyper-alert to any sign of disruption in her life. The skin over her sharp nose and cheekbones looked more stretched than normal. I wished she wasn't so skinny.

'Not at all.'

Ma sat down at the kitchen table and started sorting through the pile of wildflowers as I put the shopping away.

'I shall press them,' she said. 'And make pictures with them. The craft shop in St Austell told me they sell really well.' She looked up at me.

I realised I hadn't spoken since I got back.

'Good idea,' I managed to say.

We had supper. Fish fingers and chips for Aya. Last night's stew, jazzed up with *bzaar*, a Libyan spice mix, for the rest of us. Only Rania ate it.

Afterwards Ma put Aya to bed and Rania disappeared into the back room to plait more bracelets.

'Is something wrong?' I asked when Ma came back down.

'No. Yes.'

She sat at the table and sorted the wildflowers into colours while I washed up.

'Which is it?'

She sighed but, for once, came straight to the point.

'Mr Penrose rang while you were shopping. Your father's solicitors have been in touch.'

Mr Penrose was Ma's solicitor. We were locked in a family battle over Tregonna, the vast house we lived in. Ma loved it. It was her home, her refuge and the place she'd brought us up in when Pa had walked out on her. But it still belonged to Pa and he wanted to sell it. Ultimately he was going to win. It was just a question of how much he'd have to give Ma in recompense.

'Your father has made a very good offer. Half of the money from Tregonna after the mortgage has been paid off and sales costs and so on. Mr Penrose says it's more than a court would give me and he advises me to accept it.'

Really it was good news. Ma would have plenty of money for a house and maybe some left over. But the thought of trying to find Ma somewhere to live on top of everything else was overwhelming.

'We knew it was going to happen at some point,' I said.

'I could do without it now.'

'It won't sell quickly, Ma. We've got time. Who'd want to buy it?'

'Lots of people according to Mr Penrose. He thinks developers will snap it up and convert it into flats. Apparently that's what everybody wants, especially in a setting like this.'

I suspected Mr Penrose was right and I was wrong. There were new developments mushrooming along the coast.

'It will mean more disruption for Rania and Aya,' Ma said.

'We'll deal with it.' I tried to sound comforting and strong but the thought of the weeks and months ahead was depressing. It would be like trudging up a low gradient slope of a vast mountain, endlessly placing one foot in front of the other but knowing it was going to take forever to reach the top.

'We'll deal with it,' I said again.

'Aya is doing better.' Ma spoke as if she hadn't heard me. 'I can feel the words just waiting to pop out of her. It's Rania I'm concerned about. She can't sleep. She says she wakes up in the night and her head is full of thoughts that stop her from sleeping again.'

Rania and Aya had both slept huge amounts when we'd first got to Tregonna. As had I. It wasn't surprising that, now the initial exhaustion had passed, Rania was struggling.

'Doesn't it worry you that she never talks about her mother? It's always her grandmother.'

'She'll find her own way through. There's no fixed pathway for voyaging through your grief.'

Ma was right but I still wondered if we should be doing something.

'I said she should come and wake me to share her thoughts,' Ma added. 'But she hasn't so far.'

'She doesn't like to wake you.'

'I'm not asleep. I have my own thoughts that keep me awake. There's not enough time for them during the day.'

That was probably true. Her skin had the crumpled and chalky look of someone who was very tired.

'I think of Peter,' she said quietly. 'I try not to but he worms his way into my head. I got up last night and made jam. There was some rhubarb in the old kitchen garden. Anything was better than lying there wondering if I'd killed him.'

'Ma!'

'But it's true, isn't it? If he'd never met me, he would still be teaching English on Malta.' Ma seized a handful of flowers and wound them into a thick rope round her fingers.

She was right. Peter had been her lover on Malta but when someone had betrayed us to the people-smugglers, it had looked as though it was Peter. I'd reported him to Nick's boss and shortly afterwards Peter had died in a convenient accident. Too convenient, I'd thought at the time, and I still did. But I had no way of knowing for sure if Nick's department had arranged his death to protect Nick.

It was only afterwards I'd learned someone else could have betrayed us. Ma knew too. And both of us were struggling to come to terms with what had happened. I thought we never would. In fact, I hoped we never would.

'It would be easier if I knew he'd sold us down the river,' Ma said. 'Then I could harden my heart and spit in his face when he walks into my head.'

'We'll never know. Not for sure.'

She twisted the flowers tighter. My words lingered in the air.

There was so much we'd never know. So much I didn't know. I began to wonder how Nick had died. Why hadn't I asked Angel? Why had I just listened to what he said and then let him go?

'What is it, Jen?'

I didn't have any words. There was a curious emptiness inside me. And around me. The water in the sink was hot but I couldn't feel it. Someone else's hands were bathed in it. Someone else wiped the grease from the plates and piled them up to drain.

'Is it Nick?'

I don't believe in the crap that Ma loves – the mystic stuff, the crystals, the aligning yourself with forces of positive energy and cosmic unity – but sometimes I think she is a witch.

She took silence as her answer.

'I felt he was in great danger,' she said, almost to herself. 'Great danger.'

I stared out of the window at the wall of one of the outhouses that littered the grounds. Ivy had dug its way into the joints. I should pull it out. Except its tendrils might be the only things holding the wall up.

'Jen,' Ma said.

I'd leave the ivy alone. It would be a real pain if the wall did come down. That particular shed was one of the few whose roof was intact and we'd need somewhere to keep the bike Ma wanted to get for Rania. Because a bike would give Rania a bit of freedom. And there wasn't room for one in the corridor by the back door.

I felt her hand on my shoulder and smelt the lavender essential oil she used all the time now. Good for grief, she said. Good for loss and stress.

The bricks and ivy blurred. A buzzing filled my ears.

Ma made me sit down.

Words arrived.

'Nick is dead.'

And the relief of saying it.

'Oh, Jen.' She dragged her chair round and put her arms round me. I felt the first stirrings of sorrow churn my gut. 'How?'

How? *I didn't know.*

'I don't know.'

'His job, I suppose?'

'I don't know. I didn't ask.'

She waited.

'Angel phoned me. His cousin in Spain. His best friend, really.'

She waited some more.

'He told me Nick was dead. I think he said, drowned. But I don't remember.'

She tightened her arms round me.

'He wanted me to go to the funeral with him.'

'When is it?'

'In a couple of days. I told him I couldn't.'

'Why?'

'Because of all this.' I waved a hand round the kitchen. 'Looking after the girls and taking them to their appointments and dealing with Tregonna and the solicitors. And...'

'And what? I can cope for a couple of days.'

'Because...'

Because nothing had ever been sure between me and Nick. We'd had a short time together in Alajar which had ended in a bitter argument when he'd left to go undercover. We'd met again

21

on Malta, both caught up in the same people-smuggling gang, and I hadn't trusted him. Until the end.

And now he was dead and I wasn't even sure how. There was so much I didn't know. I wanted to know. I needed to know.

'I have to call Angel,' I said.

Three

Nick's funeral took place in Scotland. Not Spain as I'd assumed. In Helensburgh, a small town stretched along the banks of the Firth of Clyde near Glasgow. It was where Nick's Scottish family lived and where Nick had been brought up.

It was a part of his life I knew nothing about. Nick had never seemed keen to talk about it.

Angel met me at Glasgow Airport. I barely recognised him. Partly because he was wearing a sharp suit that hid his tattooed arms but mainly because he looked shrunken and grey. Nothing like the confident and slightly fearsome master of the bar he ran in Alajar. If it hadn't been for his shaven head, I might have walked past him.

It took him a couple of looks to recognise me, too. I'd borrowed Ma's least flouncy dress, a navy blue linen thing with big pockets and an irritatingly tight collar. He flung his arms around me, which was a surprise. For a few minutes, I could have been in the bar as the doughy sweet smell of *churros* undercut by traces of beer rose from his clothes. I wanted to cry. But I didn't.

He did, though. He told me his plane had got in a few hours before mine and he'd hired a car while he waited. And tears rolled down his face as he spoke. We should go. Helensburgh wasn't far from the airport but we didn't have a lot of time before the funeral started.

'How did he die?' I asked as we hurried towards the car park.

'He drowned but that is all I know. Duncan, his cousin, phoned me. To tell me. To ask me to come to the funeral.'

'His cousin?'

'From his father. His father was Scottish although his mother was Spanish. You knew that, didn't you?'

'Yes.'

But that was all I did know about his family.

We reached the car and I snatched a look at Angel's face. He'd stopped weeping. It was fixed and grim, now.

'When did you last see him?' I asked.

'When you did,' he said. 'That night in the bar when you and Nico argued and he left to go undercover again.'

Angel didn't know I'd met up with Nick on Malta.

'I know some things,' I said. 'I'll tell you as you drive.'

He manoeuvred out of the car park, muttering under his breath in Spanish. What should I tell him? Everything, really. Nothing could harm Nick now he was dead, and, besides, he'd trusted Angel.

I told him how I'd come across Nick in Malta while Ma and I had been trying to stop Rania and Aya being sent back to Libya after their mother died in a fire at the refugee camp. How Rania had fallen into the hands of child-traffickers and Nick, despite the danger of giving himself away, had helped to rescue her.

And for a moment, I was transported back to the last time I'd seen him. On a beach in Calais, as I lay half-stunned in a pool of icy water, surrounded by darkness and confusion, hearing gunshots break through the noise of waves crashing onto the rocky shore and the low thrum of a boat waiting for the refugees to wade out and clamber aboard for the final stage of their journey to the UK.

'He left on the boat with the other refugees,' I said. 'But when it landed in the UK he wasn't on it.'

Neither were Leila and Yasmiin, the two young women refugees who'd also helped Rania to escape.

'I think maybe the smugglers killed him because he helped Rania. I think they suspected him. Life is very cheap to men like that.'

In my darkest moments I was tormented by images of all three of them in the inky black water, Nick, Leila and Yasmiin, rising and falling with the swell and desperately trying to keep their heads above the waves. How long would they have survived?

I looked over at Angel. His face was as grey as the sky.

'I shouldn't have asked him for help. It was too dangerous.'

'Nico would not have let danger stop him from helping an innocent child.'

I thought it was more complicated.

'You shouldn't blame yourself,' Angel added.

But I did.

Except if I could go back in time and never ask Nick to help, I wouldn't. Not if it meant sacrificing Rania.

'I saw the man who bought Rania,' I said. 'While I was waiting at the lighthouse near Calais for night to come so I could run along the beach in the dark to meet her. I saw him hand over money for her.'

I hadn't realised what I was watching until later and the memory was seared onto my brain. A large and untidy man with bouffant white hair disturbed by the wind.

If I ever saw him again, I'd kill him.

'I spent a lot of time not trusting Nick,' I said. 'I should have known him better.'

It was the closest I could get to apologising to him.

'He was, I think, very good at his job.' Angel voice was quiet. 'It didn't make him easy to trust.'

'I have to know what happened, Angel. If Nick's death was because of me. Where did they find his body?'

'Duncan didn't say. Drowned. That was all he said. Drowned. But we didn't talk for long. I was too...'

He broke off and started muttering to himself in Spanish once more. Sharp and passionate words full of pain. Some I understood. *Amigo. Hermano*, which I thought meant brother. But I didn't need to know the vocabulary to understand Angel's grief. The tears rolled down his cheeks again although his gaze was still fixed on the road ahead.

Despite the weeping, his driving was sure and deft. Just like Nick. Angel's hands on the steering wheel here. Nick's hands on the steering wheel in Alajar. Nick's hands holding me the night in the mountains when we'd gone to look at the stars and hadn't come back until morning. They all blurred into one.

Being with Angel had stripped the skin from my feelings. I swallowed and forced myself to concentrate on the here and now.

The road left Glasgow and the motorway and buildings behind. Trees on our right hid the hills that stretched into the clouds and to our left the River Clyde had widened to an estuary. A few specks I thought were raptors wheeled over the waters.

The crematorium was on a quiet stretch of road with a view across the Clyde to distant fields, one minute glinting in the sunshine and the next broken up by the scudding clouds. It was a beautiful sight. Half an hour's drive from Glasgow and it felt as though we were in the middle of nowhere.

A dark-suited man approached us as we drove up to the cemetery building. He bent down to speak to Angel through his open window.

'For Jamie Kincaid?' he said.

I opened my mouth to say *no* as Angel said *yes*.

'Plenty of parking down there.'

'Jamie Kincaid?' I said as Angel drove into a parking space and switched the engine off.

'Yes,' Angel said. 'Did you not know?'

'No, Angel. I did not.'

He'd called himself Nick Crawford when I'd first met him in Cornwall. In Malta, he'd been Brahim but I'd known that was an assumed name. In Alajar, they called him Nico. Nico Carrasco. I'd assumed that was his real name.

'He was Jamie Nicholas Carrasco Kincaid,' Angel said. He stumbled over the *Jamie*. 'Jamie is pronounced *Himay* in Spanish. When he was young, Nico hated it because it sounded so different. So he used his second name when he came to Alajar every summer. Carrasco was his mother's family name and Kincaid his father's.'

Nick Crawford.

Nico Carrasco.

Jamie Kincaid.

I'd been calling him the wrong name all this time. I hadn't really known Nick at all, had I?

'To me, he will always be Nico. *Mi hermano Nico*.'

I envied Angel. He was so sure of his relationship with Nick.

The feeling of not knowing Nick persisted as Angel and I took our places in the almost empty chapel. It was light, airy and quiet. Every shuffle or cough cracked the silence. They should have had music. Nick loved music. Or at least the Nick I knew in Alajar did.

The coffin arrived and I understood why the chapel was half-empty. It was carried and escorted by a horde of policemen, who waited in the aisle until it was placed on a covered stand, then filed into the rows of chairs.

The family followed and took their places in the front row. I caught a glimpse of an older woman, her face buried in a handkerchief, clutching the arm of a younger man with blond hair damped and flattened over his skull, but my eyes were fixed on the simple wooden coffin sitting alone in the front.

Nick. It was Nick.

Memories poured in. I saw Nick the first time I'd met him. On the road leading down from the lighthouse near Tregonna, when he'd got out of his car in the middle of a storm and let me drive it home.

I remembered our hands stretched out on the wall of the ramparts in Mdina, nearly touching, as he warned me of the danger Ma was facing.

And, once again, the night in the mountains above Alajar, when we stared at the star-filled night and talked about the universe shifting around us and I'd felt as though I was on the prow of a ship travelling through space with him.

It was hard to hold onto those memories as the service progressed. This was Jamie Kincaid's funeral and, as I listened to the celebrant, I realised Jamie Kincaid was a stranger.

Jamie Kincaid had been born in Helensburgh. To a Scottish father and a Spanish mother. His parents had both died while he was a child. His mother from cancer when he was six and his father, from unspecified causes, when he was sixteen but his extended family in Scotland and Spain had rallied round and Jamie had been a happy child despite these tragedies.

He'd done well at school, studied modern languages at London University but afterwards he'd gone into the police because he was fixed on following the family tradition. The celebrant read a short piece from one of his tutors at the Scottish Police College. Jamie had been an outstanding student. Academically gifted but also understanding and compassionate. There was little else said about his career and nothing about how he'd found his way into undercover work.

I'd always wanted to know about Nick but not like this.

The eulogy tailed away into platitudes about a young life cut short, so much promise etc etc. And then the coffin gave a little jerk, the curtains at the head of the platform it lay on parted, and it slid on some hidden conveyor belt through the opening until it disappeared and the curtains closed again.

And that was that. Jamie Kincaid's funeral service was over. Jamie Kincaid's life was over.

The family filed out but I wasn't ready to. Neither it seemed was Angel. We both sat and stared at where the coffin had been, as people slowly rose and followed the family out.

'Fiona,' Angel said suddenly. 'I was trying to remember Nico's family. One of his aunts is called Fiona. I think she is Duncan's mother. I remember now. Nico spent every summer in Alajar. At first he came with his mother but when she died, his father sent him and the Carrascos collected him at Malaga airport. Senora Carrasco talked of nothing but his arrival for weeks before. And when his father died, he came and lived with them. We were sixteen. His aunt came with him then. I think she wanted to be sure he was doing the right thing, moving to a little village in a remote part of Andalusia.'

'And was he?'

Angel smiled and tears came to his eyes again. 'I think so. I think there were no reminders in Alajar of his father's death and he wanted to forget. He never spoke of it.'

'How did his father die? They skated over it in the eulogy.'

'Skated?'

'They didn't say much about it.'

Angel cast a quick look around but the chapel was empty now.

'I only know a little. His body was found in a Glasgow canal. He was beaten and stabbed. They never found out who did it but everyone suspected it was a...'

'Gang? Organised crime?'

29

'I think so. Nico said his father had suspected someone in the police of being involved with criminals.'

'It happens.'

'In Spain too. Everywhere.'

'Excuse me.'

The man with the flat blond hair stood at the end of the row of chairs. He'd come in from outside where the wind had ruffled the very ends into curls.

'I'm afraid the next service is going to start soon. It's a bit like a conveyor belt here.'

Angel looked confused.

'We need to leave, Angel,' I said. 'The next funeral will be here soon.'

'You are Angel?'

He pronounced his name *ankle* but Angel understood.

'Yes.'

'I'm Duncan. Jamie's cousin. We spoke on the phone. So glad you could come.'

He held out a hand and Angel shook it awkwardly. Duncan turned to me.

'Jen Shaw,' I said. 'I'm... I was a friend of... Jamie's from Spain.'

I stared into his face, some part of me willing him to have heard my name before. For Nick to have mentioned me. But no flicker of recognition broke his heavy features.

Now that he was close the family resemblance was clear. Neither he nor Nick was tall and both were solidly built. Each had a confidence in their bodies as though they knew they'd work when needed. I suspected Duncan's hair curled like Nick's did when it wasn't slicked down. Duncan's was blond though and his skin had the pallor of the typical Scot whereas Nick's had been light brown. Duncan looked like Nick's ghost. A Nick who'd lost all the colour and energy that made his dark eyes glow and his mouth twitch with laughter. A faded copy.

Two dark-suited men appeared at the door.

'We need to go.'

'Angel and I know very little about his death?' It was a statement but it came out as a question. 'Could you... tell us how he died?'

Duncan looked unsure.

'Not here,' I said. 'I don't know what's happening now but if you could find some time for us.'

'I have questions, too,' Angel said. 'Practical things. I look after Nico's house in Alajar. What is to happen to it? And to his car?'

Duncan frowned then sighed.

'Aye, right. We should talk. We're going back to my mam's. Just the family and a few friends. Come too.'

We went back to the cars, through groups of policemen chatting to each other. I scoured their faces. Nick's boss who I'd met a couple of times wasn't here but maybe there were others who'd worked in his department.

'Are the police all local?' I asked.

'No,' Duncan said and pressed his lips into a tight line.

Four

We followed Duncan's car to a house on the outskirts of Helensburgh. An imposing granite building with wide steps leading up to a front door framed by white pillars and pediments. Duncan waited for us at the top.

'My mam has the flat on the first floor,' he said.

A large white sitting room looked out over the sea but it was barely visible through the people crowding in. Mainly family and friends, I thought, although a few police uniforms were visible. The noise of chat engulfed me as Duncan took us over to the two older women we'd seen in the cemetery and introduced us. They were Fiona, Duncan's mother, and her sister, Margaret. They sat together on one of the large squashy sofas and clutched each other's hands.

'Duncan, get them a drink.' Fiona patted the sofa next to her and we dutifully sat down. 'Angel, what would you like?' She gave Angel's name its correct pronunciation.

'Tea is good,' he said. 'Thank you.'

'Same for me.'

'I remember you, Angel,' she said. Her eyes were red and puffy and she dabbed them constantly with a handkerchief. 'You rode over on a battered bike to see Jamie, five minutes after we arrived. When my brother died and I took him to Spain.'

Her face disappeared into her hands as a bout of weeping overcame her.

'I'm sorry,' she said eventually as the storm calmed. 'It's all such a waste. The family wiped out.' She picked up a framed photo from the coffee table. 'My brother's wedding day.' Tears threatened to overwhelm her again. 'It was a beautiful day. And they were so in love.'

I barely looked at the photo, just enough to get an impression of a host of men in kilts and women in floral frocks. The bridegroom and bride were kissing so their faces were hidden. It was very hot in the room and the noise and emotion were suffocating.

'I still can't believe Jamie is dead. He was such a livewire as a child. He was happy, wasn't he, Margaret?'

Her sister nodded.

'Despite everything.' She picked up another photo. 'Look at him smiling here.' It was a photo of Nick and Duncan, both in police uniform, grinning at each other. So Duncan was a police officer too. 'That was at their graduation. I was so pleased that they went to college together. Now I wish Jamie'd done anything but follow in his father's footsteps. Why? Why Jamie? I can't believe it. I just can't believe it.'

She buried her face in her hands. A tall man in a police uniform, his hair a curious shade of grey flecked with faded auburn, came over and put his hand on her shoulder, then bent over her and said something. I stood.

'Have my seat,' I said.

This was pointless. I couldn't ask his aunts how Nick had died and the heat and noise were making me feel sick. I shook my head slightly at Angel and slipped out of the room. It was cooler in the corridor. The front door had been left open and a faint draught swirled in.

A police officer with a neat red beard and slightly less neat moustache came out of the kitchen, holding the door open for Duncan who was carrying a tray of tea and whisky.

'Are you OK?' Duncan asked when he saw me. 'You're very white. You should sit down? I'll turf someone out of a chair for you.'

'I'm better here where there's some air.'

'A glass of water?'

I nodded.

'I'll get it,' the bearded police officer with Duncan said. 'You give everybody their drinks.'

'I'll be back as soon as I can,' Duncan said.

I drank the water slowly when the police officer returned and felt a little better.

'Thank you. It's been a long day. I'm sorry, I don't know your name.'

'Xander. Short for Alexander. Never liked the name.'

'Jen. Short for Jenifry. Not keen on mine either.'

He seemed happy to wait here with me unless he was being polite. It was hard to tell. His face gave little away. He was younger than I'd thought he was. His beard added a few years to his age. I wondered how well he'd known Jamie Kincaid.

'I didn't think police were allowed to have beards,' I said.

'Sorry.' He was so much taller than me that he had to stoop to catch my words.

I said it again and he smiled.

'Provided they're tidy and don't obscure your mouth we are. I have Scottish skin,' he added. 'It burns even on a cloudy day. The beard helps.'

I wondered if he'd known Nick well.

'Did you know Jamie from work?'

'Not really. My dad did. Jamie had already been, er… seconded to London when I joined up.'

I understood that *to London* was as close as he was going to get to talking about Nick's role in the police.

'Not many of us knew him really, but he was still a brother officer,' he said. 'That's why we came to the funeral.'

I tried another question.

'Did any of his colleagues come up from London?'

'Aye.'

'Who?'

'Ach, they've gone already. Strange crowd.'

I gave up. He knew nothing. We watched as Duncan handed out drinks to the sea of people. Most took the whisky rather than tea. Even Nick's aunts were knocking it back. I sipped some more of my water.

Nick's aunt Margaret stood up suddenly and came out.

'People need refills,' she said. 'Better to put the bottles out.'

She scurried away and came back a few seconds later clutching two bottles of whisky. She offered me some but I shook my head. 'You're drinking water,' she said to Xander.

'I'm driving my parents home.'

'Aye, right, you're a good boy. Your dad is taking it bad.'

She patted his cheek and he winced, his skin blotching red. She plunged back into the room where she filled up her own glass and Fiona's, and put the bottles on the coffee table. Everyone helped themselves.

Xander sighed.

'I guess I'm here for a while,' he said. 'I came with my parents. My dad was a good friend of Jamie's dad. They trained together and he's stayed close to the family.'

He pointed out the older man, also in police uniform, the one with greying red hair who'd taken my seat next to Nick's aunts. His back was turned to us so I couldn't see his face but the height and the breadth of his shoulders marked him out as Xander's father. He was a powerful-looking man as was Xander.

'Dad said Jamie was a chip off the old block.'

The roar of chatter grew even louder.

'Dad told me Jamie had drowned,' Xander said. There was a query in his voice.

'That's what I heard.' I wondered what else Xander might know. 'Did he tell you where?'

'France, I think. I'm sure someone said Calais.'

This wasn't what I wanted to hear.

'And Nick… Jamie's colleagues from London, did they tell you anything about his death?'

'Nick?'

'Jamie, I mean. He was Nico in Spain.'

'Not really.' He hesitated. 'They hinted he might have gone off-brief, though.'

'Off-brief? What does that mean?'

'I don't know really.' His pale skin flushed again. 'I was wondering if you did.'

'No.'

I thought I did. I thought Nick's colleagues were referring to the help he'd given me. And I couldn't help myself. Tears pricked my eyes and a couple spilled out. I wiped them quickly and looked away from Xander.

'You're not from round here, are you?' he asked after a while.

'No. Cornwall.'

'But you knew Jamie from Spain?'

'Yes. But not well. Not well at all.' The anger I felt every time I realised how true this was flickered in my voice and Xander stopped asking questions.

Angel looked over at me. He was an island of stillness in the talking and gesticulating horde around him. I didn't want to talk about Nick any more so I waved for him to come over and join us.

'It is very loud,' he said. 'Not at all like in Spain.'

'What do you do in Spain?' Xander asked. I guessed he was glad to change the subject too.

'We bury the body. Then a few days later all the friends and family meet for a *rosario*. Where we share memories of the... dead person. But it is a quiet thing. Not full of noise like this. Noise and anger. The aunt is very angry.'

'Fiona?'

'Yes.'

He was right. Her face was red and contorted and the man Xander had pointed out as his father seemed to be the recipient of her fury.

'It's the whisky,' Xander said. 'A Scottish failing.'

'Nico didn't like whisky,' Angel said.

'Nico?'

'Jamie. He didn't even like the smell of it. And after today, I don't think I will ever drink it again.'

There wasn't anything we could say to that so we stood in silence staring at the people. Nothing could express how weird and horrible today felt.

Fiona's voice, her words indistinguishable, rose above the din. Her face was tight with anger as she spat words at Xander's father. Behind him, a slim woman with a bob of polished, black hair and a beautifully cut grey linen dress watched with no expression. I guessed she was Xander's mother. They weren't at all alike but she shot him a cool glance and gave him a barely noticeable shake of her head. He stood a little straighter and his hands whitened on the glass he was holding.

Xander's father stood up abruptly and headed towards us. I was startled. Angel looked grief-stricken and grim but this man was consumed by his emotion. It scored deep lines into his loose and open-pored skin and dragged down the curve of his mouth. I realised it wasn't grief. It looked more like anger.

'We're away,' he muttered to Xander as he pushed past us. His wife stopped, though, and shook her head as Xander started to ask what had happened. Some unspoken communication passed between them.

Xander gave me a quick smile and followed her outside.

Duncan came out holding an empty tray. 'Did they leave?'

'You mean Xander and his parents?'

'Yes.'

I nodded.

He swore under his breath.

'Mam just let rip at him. At Xander's father, I mean. Sandy. He encouraged Jamie to go into the police so she's decided it's all his fault. But she's lashing out at everyone.'

Angel looked confused. I wasn't sure if he was struggling to follow Duncan's choice of words or if he was as bewildered as I was by all these complicated emotions.

'But you're a police officer, too.'

'Mam isn't thinking very straight. She accused him of pulling a few strings to make sure his own son got a safe and cushy job while encouraging Jamie to go into danger.'

'Xander? What does he do?'

'Cybercrime. Look, it's quieter in the kitchen. Let's go and talk in there.'

'What is cybercrime?' Angel asked.

'Anything that happens on line or with computers. Identity theft, internet scams, phishing and so on.'

It sounded very dull.

'Ach, it's the fastest growing form of crime,' Duncan said as we went into the kitchen. He nodded at a woman washing glasses in the sink and gestured for us to sit at a table in a small alcove at the rear of the room. We carried on a stupid conversation about cybercrime while he made tea and waited for the woman to leave.

I only half-listened as Duncan droned on about the dark web and how criminals used it in the same way that we used the normal web. Apparently it was much bigger than I'd thought – if I'd ever thought about it, which I hadn't.

Duncan handed us our tea. I took a cautious sip of mine and gagged. It was very strong, very milky and very sweet. Finally, the woman finished drying the glasses and left.

I cut straight to the chase before someone else interrupted us.

'How did Nick... Jamie die?' I asked. 'We both know what he did. His job, I mean. So you can tell us everything.'

Angel nodded.

'No point in secrecy now,' Duncan said. 'Jamie was on an assignment in France. He drowned. His body was found in a fishing net in the Channel, in French waters. He'd been dead for a long time. They identified him from dental records and informed us. I went over and brought him back. Mam didn't want him to come home alone. And neither did I.'

It wasn't what I wanted to hear.

'Is that all his department told you? That he drowned.'

'Aye.'

'You said he'd been in the water a long time. Did they say how long exactly?'

Duncan fixed his eyes on me. They were the same deep grey as Nick's. 'I didn't ask. I knew he must have died on some operation. What does it matter when it happened?'

It did matter. I needed to know if Nick had died on the boat. If he hadn't, there was at least a chance his death was nothing to do with me.

I looked at Angel. I'd run out of things to ask.

'Where was his body?'

'In an undertakers in Calais. They organised all the transport home.'

'So he wasn't at a police station?'

'A gendarme from the local station was in attendance when I went to the undertakers. There were things to sign.'

I remembered Leila and Yasmiin had disappeared too.

'Was his the only body they found in the nets?'

It was a stupid question. Even if they'd all died together, the sea would have separated them.

'I didn't think to ask.'

Duncan took our mugs of undrunk tea to the sink and poured them away. He'd had enough of our questions. He didn't have any answers. Angel asked him what was to happen to Nick's house and possessions in Alajar.

Duncan wasn't sure. The family was too upset to make any big decisions. Could Angel keep an eye on the house and send any bills to Duncan? He and his mother would come over and deal with everything as soon as they could face it.

We left shortly after that, asking Duncan to say goodbye to the aunts, and drove back to the airport in silence. There was nothing to say. I'd learned a lot about Jamie Kincaid and a little about how he died. None of it was good.

'What now?' I asked after we'd dropped the car back at the hire place. 'We still don't really know anything for sure.'

'I don't know,' Angel said. 'I'm going home. I need some time to think. I'll call you.'

Five

It was late when I got back to Tregonna and the house was quiet. I felt shattered but sleep when it came was patchy and light. Just after two am, I woke. My room was flooded with moonlight.

Shit.

I turned over, banged my head back into the pillow and shut my eyes tightly, willing myself to go back to sleep.

But straightaway, my head filled with pictures of a night sea, and people clinging to the sides of a boat that soared and dived in the swell. The lines of a childhood poem ran through my head. *They went to sea in a sieve, they did. In a sieve they went to sea.* The waves hurled the boat into the air, dislodging a couple of people. Their hands slithered over the wet rubber as the sea dragged them away. Their eyes flared with fear as they sank. One of them was Nick and I stretched out arms to seize him but I was too late. Nothing but water ran through my fingers. I screamed.

And woke up again.

I was wide awake and wired.

I paced around the room trying to shake off the clinging dregs of the nightmare. But it lurked in the dark corners the moonlight didn't reach.

'Jen?' A knock on the door. Rania's voice. 'Is that you?'

'Yes. Come in.'

Her face gleamed in the cold light.

'Are you all right?' she asked.

'A nightmare. Sorry if I woke you.'

'I was awake anyway.'

I reached over to turn the light on as she came in. Nothing. I tried the bedside light. Still nothing. A power cut? Or some fault in the house wiring? I hoped not. Kit had spent a fortune having the whole place rewired.

'It happened yesterday, too. Morwenna went to the big box in the kitchen and pressed something and it came back on.'

I suspected Ma's success had been more luck than judgement.

'OK. I'll go down in a minute and play with it. Why can't you sleep?'

She hesitated. 'It doesn't matter now.'

'It does, you know.'

'I thought you might not come back.'

'Well, I have. Didn't Morwenna tell you I wouldn't be gone for long?'

'Yes. But when I go to bed I worry you won't.'

She'd lost so many people. Her father. Her grandparents. Her mother. It was hardly surprising she needed to keep tight hold of the people she did have.

'Did you find out about Yasmiin?' she asked.

'Yasmiin?'

'Morwenna said you had gone to Calais to find out about a friend. I thought it might be Yasmiin.'

'It wasn't Yasmiin. I don't know what happened to her.'

I'd forgotten how closely Rania had clung to Yasmiin after Rania's mother died. I guessed that Yasmiin, the young woman travelling alone from Somalia to Europe, having long lost her family and friends in the fighting there, had been someone who instinctively understood how Rania felt, despite the age difference.

'Yasmiin was a good friend to you, wasn't she?'

'Yes.'

I wondered whether I should encourage her to go back to bed and sleep now she knew I was home, but she looked as though she had something else she wanted to tell me.

'I keep thinking I can smell smoke. Just as I'm falling asleep. It wakes me.'

I had the sense to keep my mouth shut and wait.

'It's because of the fire, isn't it? When Mama died.'

'I expect so.'

Was she going to talk about her mother's death? If so, I had no idea how to deal with it.

'Have you told Meghan?' I asked.

Meghan was the psychologist Rania saw.

'She says I'll never forget the fire and Mama dying and I shouldn't try to push it away. But sometimes I do want to forget. I want to turn my thoughts off like Morwenna turns the television off when she thinks we've watched enough. Do you think that's wrong?'

'Not at all,' I said. I felt the same but I wasn't sure I had the words to explain. 'It's not wrong. We can't spend all our lives being unhappy.' Was that the right thing to say? I was floundering in a sea of ignorance.

'I don't want to forget Mama completely. Just sometimes…'

'You won't. I promise you. Just with time I think the memories won't be quite so painful.'

God. I so hoped this was true. I remembered what Ma had said. 'You can talk about your mother to us, you know. Even if it makes you unhappy.'

'Aya is forgetting, though. Morwenna asked me to make her a book. Full of everything I remember from before. Every little detail. She says Aya doesn't have the words to seal the memories in her brain and someday she'll want to know.'

I wondered if this was Ma's effort to help Rania think about her mother.

'I think Ma is right.'

'Do you? Because Aya is forgetting everything. If I speak to her in Arabic, she ignores me. She only does things if I ask her in English.'

I suspected it was something other than forgetting in Aya's case.

'Or maybe she doesn't want to remember.' Rania had the same thought as me.

'Perhaps,' I said. 'The brain is very complicated.'

'Sometimes it is happening to me, too. Our grandmother used to peel the skin off an apple in one curl for Aya and I tried to remind her about it but I couldn't remember how to say curl. In Arabic, I mean. It was like it had vanished from my brain. I could see Jiddah, with a big smile on her face, holding up the curl and Aya laughing and holding her hands out for it. But the word wouldn't come.'

A huge feeling of inadequacy overwhelmed me. This was about so much more than forgetting a word. It was about all the things the social workers kept on saying to us. Things like cultural heritage, roots and identity. Things I knew nothing about. How could I help Rania? She stood and walked over to the window while my brain raced. The cold light made her look more like a skinny fairy than ever. She was always so patient. So well-behaved. Was that a good thing? I thought some more. Two ideas came to me. The first was, I thought, quite sensible.

'We'll find someone or a group you can talk to in Arabic. Or arrange for lessons. I don't know quite how we'll do it but we will.'

'I think I'd like that.'

'OK.'

My second idea wasn't so sensible but it felt right, although I couldn't explain why.

'Would you like to learn to climb?'

A smile lit up her face as she turned round.

'Like we did when we climbed off the beach?'

Rania and I had escaped the tide in Calais by climbing a rain-soaked cliff.

'Well, sort of. But properly. With ropes.'

'You'll teach me to climb?'

'I will. But there are also groups you can join. Friends of mine run them and I think you'd enjoy it.'

'I'd like that. I'd really like that.'

And then because I am madder than a treeful of monkeys.

'Shall we have a go now?'

'Now. In the night?'

'Why not? The moon makes it almost as light as day. You'll see. Besides you can't sleep. I can't sleep. What else are we going to do?'

'What will Morwenna say?'

I laughed. If there was one thing I knew for sure it was that Ma would wholeheartedly approve. In fact, if I woke her up and suggested it, she'd come with us.

'Morwenna will be fine.'

'OK.' I heard the excitement in her voice as she looked out of the window. 'You're right. It isn't really dark.'

It would be good for her, I told myself. She needed a bit of joy. A bit of fun. And the fresh air and exercise would help her sleep. I pushed away the thought that I needed this too.

'Oh.' Her gasp pulled me out of my thoughts.

'What is it?'

'I saw someone. Running up the drive and into the woods.'

I joined her at the window. The grey gravel of the drive glinted in the moonlight that bathed the rustling leaves in silver. A dark shape slipped across the ground. A cloud.

'There's a bit of a breeze,' I said. 'I think you probably saw a cloud. Moonlight is tricky.'

I grabbed some kit and took her to the place where Pa had taught Kit and me to climb. An outcrop of granite rising out of the grass at the far end of the Tregonna grounds. It wasn't very high but a fall would be enough to hurt, even though the ground at the bottom was soft and thick with clumps of sea thrift, now flowering pink. We stood among them and stared up.

'What are they?'

Silvery lines roamed over the rock, lit up by the moonlight. Ma used to tell us they were where the fairies slid down.

'Snail marks,' I said.

I climbed up to fix a top rope, then abseiled down. Maybe it was a mistake to have come here. The sea was less than a hundred metres away. Far less. And the cliffs that plunged down into it lured me. Just an hour or so climbing. That was all I wanted. An hour of thinking of nothing but the next move. Of feeling my muscles stretch and contract. Of rough textured rock beneath my fingers. Of hearing the waves whisper beneath me.

No. I'd come here for Rania. I shut my eyes and laid my face against the granite for a few seconds, breathed in its warmth and felt its caress. The urge faded.

Rania put her harness on. I checked and tightened it and tied the rope on, then picked up the other end.

'Go for it,' I said and pointed out the route I wanted her to take.

'But how? Aren't you going to tell me how?'

I laughed at the confusion on her face.

'There'll be time for all that later. Tonight you're going to try and figure it out for yourself. Just climb. I'll stop you falling if you slip.'

She'd learn so much more by having a go on her own and afterwards when she was taught the technique it would make sense because her body had searched for it.

'I'll give you one tip,' I said. 'Climb with your feet rather than your hands.'

'What does that mean?'

'You'll see.'

After an hour or so of experimenting, of learning the rope would hold her, of losing her fear, I thought she had the first glimmerings of understanding. A couple of times she instinctively used her free limbs to balance herself and she'd stopped clinging to the wall and started giving her body space to move. But she was getting tired and in the last few minutes, she'd misjudged a couple of moves she'd mastered before.

'That's enough,' I said. 'The moon is about to set. I'll take you to the climbing gym in Plymouth and sort you out some lessons. If you still want to learn.'

She nodded and opened her mouth to say something. Then shut it and suddenly started crying in barking gasps.

'What is it, Rania?'

'Mama,' she said. 'I thought about showing Mama and then...'

I held her tight and rocked her back and forwards. There were no words. I knew there were none.

After a while, her breathing calmed and I felt the moment when she wanted to detach. When she'd had enough.

'I'll go up and get the ropes now,' I said. 'Then we'll go back. But I'll go up the route you used. Watch how I do it.'

I climbed the face. I climbed it perfectly, emphasising the smooth transition of body weight as I moved from hold to hold, demonstrating the precision of each foot and hand placement. It was the easiest thing ever and it was hard. Easy to climb but hard to do it slowly and perfectly.

At the top I untied the rope. The moon was setting now and I was high enough to see it sink beneath the sea casting a silvery net over the water. I watched it leave then leaned over to warn Rania I was dropping the rope down.

She wasn't alone.

Even in the dark, I could see a figure towering over her. Hands reaching out to seize her. I half-fell, half-scrabbled down the rock and landed in a heap on the grass.

The two figures had become one. The tall stranger's arms were wrapped around Rania in a tight embrace. They separated as I stood up.

The stranger was Yasmiin. Yasmiin from the refugee camp on Malta who'd escaped with us and tried to help Rania. Yasmiin who'd left on the boat at Calais with Nick and Leila and who, like them, had disappeared before it landed near Dover.

I had a brief impression of a face marked by bruises, a swollen lip that forced her mouth out of shape and a half-healed cut above her eye before she crumpled into the grass.

She was out cold. And she was cold. Her hands were icy. The nights were still cool. Yasmiin wore nothing but a pair of cotton trousers and a T-shirt. By the look of them, she'd worn them for some time too. I pulled off my jumper and wrapped it round her shoulders. Where had she come from? How had she found us?

'Go and wake Morwenna,' I said to Rania.

Six

Between us we carried Yasmiin back to the house and into bed. Rania and Ma went to fetch hot water bottles while I tried to sponge the worst of the grime and dried blood from her face and hands. She surfaced a couple of times when I touched a recent bruise or cut but seemed happy to slip back into sleep.

'Should we call a doctor?' Rania asked after we'd put a variety of ancient hot water bottles in the bed.

Ma and I exchanged glances. It might be better to keep Yasmiin's presence quiet. I wasn't sure if the doctor would have to inform the authorities about her.

'Let's wait until morning,' Ma said. 'She's sleeping now.'

'We should all do that,' I said. Rania was stretching her arms and yawning

'Do you think it was Yasmiin I saw out of your window?'

'Probably.'

'We couldn't sleep,' Rania told Ma. 'So we went climbing. By the light of the moon and Yasmiin appeared.'

'It's nearly full moon,' Ma said. 'You should have woken me. I could have bathed in her light with you.' She rabbited on about the full moon being a time when the seeds of the new moon come into flower, a time of abundance and transformation.

'Yes, Ma,' I said but all I could think about was how long it would be before I could ask Yasmiin what had happened on the boat.

*

Ma was on the phone next morning when I yawned my way into the kitchen. I mouthed 'Yasmiin?' at her as I put the kettle on, but she shook her head and held up her hand. I guessed she meant to wait.

Normally Ma has two ways of speaking on the phone. If it's someone calling about something she thinks is unimportant, such as the bank about an overdraft or the council to complain about the bonfires she lights to celebrate the summer solstice, she barely listens and says nothing. There's no point, she once told me. They don't understand and they go away sooner if she doesn't speak. If it's a friend, though, she talks exuberantly, flinging her free arm around as she walks up and down the kitchen. This time she did neither.

She huddled over the phone, her face almost hidden by her hair, but interjected brief answers – mainly 'yes' and 'no'.

'Who was that?' I asked when she finally finished.

'Shona.'

'Shona from Malta?'

'Yes.'

'No way.'

Shona had worked at the refugee agency on Malta where Ma had been a volunteer. I hadn't liked her much. She shared the worst of Ma's hippy traits. Ma had adored her and asked her for help when we were trying to get Rania and Aya off Malta secretively. When someone had betrayed us to the people-smugglers I'd thought it was Peter, Ma's lover. But afterwards I'd learned it might well have been Shona.

I'd told Ma to steer clear of her.

'She knows Rania and Aya are with me,' Ma said.

'Here. At Tregonna? How?'

'I don't know. I couldn't ask. It was a tricky conversation. She wanted to know how we'd got here but I managed to avoid telling her.'

Not difficult. Ma was a master at deflecting questions she didn't want to answer. She looked at me with a question in her eyes.

'Maybe,' I said quickly. 'Maybe it means she's working with the smugglers. Maybe she was the person who betrayed us. But maybe it was Peter. She might only be calling because she wants to know how you are.'

'Well, I didn't give anything away.'

But I thought Ma might have. Her abruptness with Shona, so different from the effusive mutual adoration on Malta, might well have made Shona suspect we'd guessed her part in the smuggling.

'How's Yasmiin?' I asked.

'She was awake and she ate, but she's gone back to sleep. I think that's all she needs. Food and rest.'

Ma was right. Yasmiin needed to eat and sleep and she did exactly that for the next couple of days. In between she told us scraps of her story. She'd been in London but she didn't want to talk about it. At least not in front of Rania.

'I thought I'd found some people I could trust but I was wrong,' she said. 'So I decided to come to you.'

She'd taken a coach to Exeter where her money had run out, then walked the rest of the way, sleeping where she could, remembering enough of what Ma had told her about Tregonna when they were together on Malta to locate it. It had taken her nearly two weeks as far as I could tell and she'd used the mobile phone, her one possession, to find the way, turning it on only when absolutely necessary, to save the battery. Her food had run out somewhere before Plymouth. She'd been beaten up there, rummaging through a bin outside a restaurant for something to eat.

Some of her injuries were older than that but she didn't talk about them either, setting her cracked lips in a line and staring at the wall. I remembered the Yasmiin who'd railed at the situation she'd found herself in in Malta as a migrant, who'd ripped up the letter refusing her full refugee status and spat syllables of rage into the sea air.

That Yasmiin had gone.

On the evening of the second day, she got out of bed and ate with us. Afterwards, I suggested a slow and short walk in the evening sun. She nodded, pulled on one of the many old coats hanging in the kitchen and we slipped out while Rania was watching television and Ma was bathing Aya.

She was ready to sit after a few hundred metres. Tiredness still gouged lines in her face and her limbs trembled a little from the exertion.

'You can stay here for as long as you want,' I said to her. 'Take all the time you need. And when you're feeling better we'll talk about the future.'

'Thank you.' Her voice cracked.

'You tried to save Rania from the traffickers. But you'd be welcome anyway.'

And then because I couldn't wait any longer, the first of the questions I'd been desperate to ask burst out my mouth.

'What happened on the boat from France to England? You all left on it but you'd gone by the time it landed in England.'

'Leila and I jumped off and swam ashore as soon as we were close enough to England. Brahim told us to.'

It took me a few seconds to remember Brahim had been Nick's alias.

'Brahim told you to?'

'The police were waiting for the boat when it landed. I think Brahim knew they would be.'

I nodded. He might well have.

'We were still in the water when the boat landed and we saw police run towards it. We swam away and crawled onto the sand behind a sort of fence running down into the water.'

'A groyne.' I said.

'Leila and I waited until they'd gone.'

'And Brahim?'

'Brahim wasn't with us.'

'What?'

'He left the boat while we were still near France. He swam back to the beach there.'

'Why?'

'He went back to find you and Rania. He told us you were in danger. The traffickers were still out on the cliffs and if they came across the two of you, you'd be in trouble. He didn't find you, then?'

'No. I think he didn't make it. His body was found in some fishing nets. Drowned.'

Yasmiin swished her hands through the long grass while she thought.

'I'm sure he didn't drown then,' she said. 'We were still close to France when he left. The boat was very slow. Leila and I watched him swim. We saw his head from time to time and his arms left white streaks in the dark. He was a strong swimmer.'

I hadn't known that. I thought of his Aunt Fiona's flat overlooking the sea in Helensburgh. The young Jamie Kincaid had probably learned to swim as he was growing up. To swim in rough, cold seas.

'I can't be sure but I thought I saw him wade onto the beach.'

What had happened to him when he reached shore?

Yasmiin closed her lips tight over her mouth. She'd had enough, I thought. Tiredness had once again flattened the skin to her face.

'Go back,' I said. 'We can talk another time.'

I stood and brushed the pollen and grass seeds off my jeans, then helped her to her feet.

'I need to go for a walk, Yasmiin. I need to think. Can you get back to the house on your own?'

'Yes.' She twisted her hands through the dress Ma had lent her. She must have wondered what the connection was between Brahim and me but she didn't ask.

I strode off through the undergrowth. I didn't really know where I was going. I just needed to move. And move fast. To smash my hands through the tall grass and kick the ground and, as soon as I reached the coastal path, to run. And run and run.

Nick had come back for us.

If he hadn't, he'd be alive.

If I'd never met him, he'd be alive.

He'd be alive and maybe driving his battered car into the square at Alajar and sauntering into the bar. Saying 'Hi' to Angel and dropping into a conversation about local matters.

Angel.

I had to let him know what I'd discovered.

Now.

He was silent as I poured out what I'd learned from Yasmiin and said nothing when I'd finished.

'Are you still there?'

'Yes. I'm thinking.'

'There's nothing to think about. Nick came back for me and Rania. Even though he knew the child-traffickers were still out on the cliffs. They must have got him. If he hadn't come back, he'd be alive.'

'You can't be sure of that.'

'How, Angel? How can I not be sure of that?'

'Your friend said he reached shore. Maybe he couldn't find you on the cliffs and then he learned you were safe. Maybe he was given another job to do. Duncan didn't know how long he'd been dead.'

'Another job in France? Not very likely.'

'But you don't know.'

'In case you hadn't noticed, we don't know very much.'

He sighed.

'If only,' I said. 'If only I knew *when* he died.'

'I'm going to Paris.'

'Paris?'

'Yes, Paris is the nearest airport to Calais.'

'You're going to Calais?'

'Yes. I'll get the name of the gendarme he saw from Duncan. I'm going to ask the questions Duncan didn't ask.'

'I'm coming with you,' I said.

Seven

I took a cheap flight to Paris and met Angel at the airport. We hired a car and drove through the evening to Calais. Duncan had given him the name of the gendarme who'd been at the undertakers in Calais and the small gendarmerie where he was based. It was long closed when we arrived, so we found a hotel and then went to a cheap restaurant nearby where we ordered omelette and chips from a tired youngster who was the sole waiter. A beer for Angel and water for me. The chairs and tables were claustrophobically close to one another but as the place was empty it didn't matter.

'You never drink, do you?' Angel asked.

'If you mean alcohol, very occasionally.'

He raised an eyebrow, inviting me to expand but I wasn't in the mood for talking about my past problems with alcohol and drugs. I fancied a beer, though. It would take the edge off my jumpiness. But one beer might lead to another and before I knew it, the little voice in my head would start telling me what really would make me feel better. And the more beers I drank, the harder it was to resist the voice's soft reasonableness.

Something must have shown on my face because Angel reached out a hand and grasped mine briefly.

'You can come to Alajar any time.'

The threat of tears made me blink. The waiter put our food on the table and asked us if we were on holiday.

We looked at him blankly and then I said, 'Yes'. It was simpler than trying to explain.

He needed no further invitation. He told us we should visit the lace museum and the war museum housed in an old German bunker. He drew us maps while we ate, explaining he was a student studying law at the campus in Calais. He had to learn English. All lawyers did, so he was happy when English clients came in to the restaurant. It gave him a chance to practise. It was easier to let him chat than brush him off. In fact, he was a welcome distraction.

'I saw many rocks on the sides of the road and the roundabouts when we came here,' Angel said as he finished the last of his chips – hot, crisp and salty – and pushed the remains of the dry omelette to one side. 'Are they from the war?'

I'd noticed them too. White rocks placed too evenly on the grass verges and centres of roundabouts to be natural. Were they some kind of memorial to the people who'd died defending the town against the Nazis?

'They are to stop the migrants camping.'

I ate a few more chips but I no longer felt hungry.

'No one can stop them,' the waiter continued. 'The gendarmes try. They clear them from one place but they camp somewhere else and, when the gendarmes move them on again, they go back to the first place.'

'That must be difficult,' Angel muttered.

'The tourists don't like them. And we need tourists.' He gestured round the empty restaurant. 'Some gendarmes were stoned a few weeks ago when they tried to prevent a boat leaving. They were lucky not to be shot.'

'Shot? Is it safe here?'

'So long as you don't interfere with the migrants and the men helping them. It's big business.' He rubbed his fingers together in the universal sign meaning money. 'They all have guns.'

'And the police?' Angel persisted.

Our waiter shrugged. 'The *flics* don't try so hard. They keep away.' He rubbed his fingers together again. 'Money buys a lot of looking in a different direction.'

He shrugged again.

'Could we have our bill?' I asked and once the waiter left, 'Why are you asking all this?'

'Trying to understand what it is like here.'

'You don't want to. It's too depressing.'

Next morning, we went to the gendarmerie planning to spin a story about the Spanish authorities needing paperwork and armed with useful French phrases. We needed none of them. The police officer at the desk listened to my halting explanation in French that we'd like to talk to someone about Jamie Kincaid's death, took our names, made a phone call and told us *le Capitaine* would see us shortly. He spoke immaculate English.

There were a couple of chairs in the white-painted space that served as a reception area so we sat while we waited. Angel went back to studying French phrases on his phone, peering through the glasses he needed to read. He was wearing a long-sleeved shirt that covered up his tattoos despite the warmth.

'You should keep your glasses on,' I whispered to him. 'They make you look respectable.'

'Why are you whispering?' he asked. 'There's no one here.'

'I don't know,' I said in a normal voice. But I felt edgy and last night's omelette and chips stirred in my stomach.

The gendarme from the front desk reappeared and beckoned us. Angel thrust his phone into a pocket and we were escorted to another bland room, with nothing to break up the walls but glass-fronted shelves containing files and books and stacks of paperwork. The Capitaine himself was on the phone looking out of the window. He turned as we entered and nodded, waving us to the seats on one side of the expanse of desk that dominated the room.

As he turned round, a wave of nausea gripped my guts.

He was white-haired and tall but bulky with a beaky nose, although his jaw was soft with loose flesh and I suspected his body, beneath the blouson jacket he wore, was slack. Despite his flabbiness, he exuded a soft power. This was a man who was used to being obeyed and felt no need to ingratiate himself. His face was unlined and blank as his eyes flicked over us and met mine.

Sweat prickled under my hair.

He gave a slight smile as he held out his hand and introduced himself. 'Capitaine Basset. Pierre Basset. I believe you wish to know more about Jamie Kincaid?'

Unlike Angel he pronounced the name correctly and his English was good.

Angel nodded.

The Capitaine cast a quick glance at a piece of paper on his desk. 'You are Angel Carrasco and Jen Shaw. May I ask why you wish to know?'

Angel explained he was Jamie's cousin from Spain and flourished his identity card.

'Monsieur Kincaid was Spanish? It was the British police who reported him missing.'

I stared at my hands as Angel answered Capitaine Basset's lengthy questions about Nick's nationality, why he lived in Spain and a stream of other polite queries. Angel managed to duck the inquiries about Nick's job although he made Nick seem like something of a drifter. I said nothing.

'Monsieur Kincaid was a lucky man,' the Capitaine said when he'd satisfied his curiosity. 'Spain is a wonderful country. Now, tell me how I can help you?'

'We understand Jamie's body was found by fishermen near here,' Angel said after a pause. If he was surprised by my silence, he didn't reveal it.

'That is correct. Tangled in the nets of a... a *chalutier*? A boat with big nets.'

Angel gave me a chance to speak then continued.

'Where?'

'Let me see.' He tapped on his computer, muttered some French under his breath then found what he was looking for. 'I can give you the coordinates if you want to know exactly but I would say around ten kilometres from Calais.'

'How long was it in the water?'

'I cannot tell you exactly but several weeks.'

'Was there an autopsy?'

'Monsieur. Many dead bodies are found here. In the water or on land. You understand we have many migrants trying to cross the Channel. Many die in the sea. Most are unidentified and the ones, like Monsieur Kincaid's, that have been in the water a long time are unrecognisable. Not even their mothers would know them.'

'Nico – Jamie had no injuries then?'

'We don't think so but, again, after so long it is not easy to tell. I can give you a copy of the report into the body but there is nothing in it I haven't told you.'

Angel thanked him and looked over to me.

I wasn't going to do anything to prolong this interview. Besides it was clear Capitaine Basset had little to tell us that Duncan hadn't already.

'Let's go,' I hissed at Angel as the Capitaine picked up his phone.

'*Dupont?*' he said. '*Une copie du procés-verbal de l'état du cadavre. Oui, du Jamie Kincaid. Pour Angel Carrasco et Jenifry Shaw.*'

We both stood.

'I'm sorry for your loss, Madame.' The Capitaine's voice was smooth as silk. 'Are you a member of Monsieur Kincaid's family too?'

I had no choice.

'No. I was one of his friends.'

'Were you on holiday with him when he went missing?'

On holiday – was that what Nick's department had told the French police?

And to my horror, tears leaped to my eyes and I had to turn away from the Capitaine and shake my head at his proffered tissues.

I pulled myself together.

'No,' I said. 'I wasn't on holiday with him.'

'He was alone, then?'

'Yes,' Angel said. 'He was alone.'

'I see. We wondered why no one reported him missing earlier. Your police, Madame Shaw, told us he'd been missing for weeks and asked for details of any unidentified bodies.'

Angel looked confused. I wasn't sure he'd understood everything.

'No one was sure where he was,' I said. 'Jamie could be very uncommunicative.'

Capitaine Basset nodded and moved round the desk to open the door. He towered over Angel as he shook his hand and wished him a good day. He proffered his hand to me and I had no choice but to take it. I was expecting damp skin but it was dry and warm.

'Are you OK?' Angel said as soon as we were outside the gendarmerie, clutching the police report.

I nodded.

'We learned nothing,' he said.

'Oh yes, we did.'

'What?'

'Not here. I need to get away from here.'

I ran to the car.

'What did we learn?' Angel asked again once we were inside.

But now I wasn't so sure. Was I mistaken?

'I need to go somewhere first,' I said.

'Where?'

'The lighthouse at Cap Gris-Nez. It's very close.'

By the time we reached the car park at the top of the path leading to the lighthouse, I was glad I wasn't driving. I felt as though I was only half in the car with Angel. The other half had travelled back in time to the night all those weeks ago when I'd arrived in Calais after chasing the people-smugglers across Europe and found their minibuses in the lighthouse carpark. I'd known then that I'd caught up with them.

'What are we doing?' Angel's voice was gentle.

He'd not said anything to me while we drove.

'Stay with me,' I said. It was all I could say. I was locked in the past and I didn't want to leave. I needed to be sure about what I'd seen and this was the only way.

I turned without a word and retraced the footsteps I'd taken all those weeks ago along the path down to the lighthouse, vaguely aware that I'd started running. I heard Angel call my name a few times as he ran after me. But when I got to the lighthouse, it was all wrong. The midday sun blazed down on its glaring white paint. The vibrant green of the grass matched the Channel's blue and in the distance the white cliffs of Dover sparkled, clean and sharp over this, the narrowest stretch of sea between England and France.

I shut my eyes and reached back to the chilly evening when I'd last been here. When the watery sun had lit the Dover cliffs orange and pink as it sank beneath the horizon and I'd been waiting for the tourists watching its descent to leave so I could climb unseen down the cliff and run along the beach below to meet Rania.

A faint breeze now curled round my neck bringing with it a briny smell of seaweed and I heard the restless sounds of the coast. Nothing was ever still by the sea. The waves washed against each other and against the rocks and sand while the long grass whispered in the wind.

And I was back in my memories of that night.

I'd hidden in the grass by the cliff's edge, watching the tourists leave until only one figure remained. A man with a cloud of white hair. He hadn't been alone for long. He'd been joined by the people-smuggler who'd taken Rania. The two of them talked. Finally the white-haired man handed over an envelope of money. I'd watched as the smuggler counted it.

At the time I'd known something vile was taking place. It was only afterwards I'd worked out it was the exchange of blood money for Rania. The payment that sold her to the child-traffickers. The white-haired man had left and the night had descended into confusion and chaos.

I hadn't known who the child-trafficker was. But I did now.

I'd been sure as soon as he'd turned round from the window in his office at the gendarmerie but still I'd needed to come back here to check. The white-haired man who'd bought Rania. The child-trafficker. He was Capitaine Basset.

Basset was a child-trafficker. Basset was a gendarme.

What did it all mean?

'Jen.' Angel's voice brought me back to the present. I was still staring at the lighthouse. 'What is it? Are you ill?'

'Give me a minute,' I said.

I needed to think. Follow this thread all the way through to its conclusion.

Basset had paid for Rania and she'd slipped through his fingers. Basset was a gendarme.

But for the life of me I couldn't make the connections.

'Jen?' Angel spoke again.

I dragged myself back to the present and told him about Basset.

'What do we do?' he asked when I'd finished and, again, I thought how like Nick he was in so many ways. Nick, too, would have cut straight to the nub of the matter.

'I could be mistaken,' I said, voicing all the doubts he'd been kind enough not to. 'It was a very confusing time and I was stressed.'

'But you're not, are you? I knew something was wrong as soon as we met that *hijo de puta*.'

'No, I'm not wrong. What shall we do?' I echoed Angel's question.

'We must tell…'

'Who? The police? No. At least not the French. It's a sure way to let Basset know we are on to him.'

'If he's not already.'

'I don't think so. He doesn't know I saw him that night.'

'Are you sure?'

'Completely.'

'Let's go back to the car.'

I trailed after him, wondering what we should do. Basset needed to be stopped. I'd have liked to kill him. I'd have liked to kill all the men like him. They were bottom-feeding scum. Crawling crabs feeding off the weak and injured, the vulnerable and the hopeless.

'Do you think he killed Nico?' Angel said as soon as we'd got into the car.

The question had been racing around inside my head.

'It's possible.'

'He was very happy to meet us. And he asked us many questions about Nico.'

It was suspicious. He'd wanted to find out about Jamie Kincaid and about the people who were asking questions about his death.

'Listen.' Angel picked up his phone and tapped the screen.

Basset's heavily accented English filled the car, as he greeted us and asked us why we wanted to know about Jamie Kincaid.

'You recorded him?'

'I wanted to be sure I understood what he said.'

Angel was right. Basset had asked a lot of questions. In fact, he'd probably learned more from us than we had from him.

I winced when Angel tripped up and said Nico rather than Jamie. I'd been too lost in my own thoughts to notice when we'd been at the gendarmerie. I gestured at Angel to pause.

'Did he react when you said Nico rather than Jamie?'

'I don't remember.'

'But he didn't say anything?'

'Maybe he already knew his second name was Nico.'

'It's only Jamie Kincaid on the death report.'

'He wasn't Nico or Nick when he was here, was he?'

'No, he was Brahim.'

It niggled at my brain as we listened to the last few minutes of the recording.

'All those questions about Nick's life in Spain,' I said. 'And what he was doing in France. Basset was trying to find out about him. Why would he do that if he didn't suspect something?'

And then I remembered. When Nick's boss had been interrogating me in the Calais police station. He'd been ultra-cautious to say nothing the French police could overhear. He'd never mentioned Nick by name. But I'd let it slip in an unguarded moment and he'd been furious.

I started to tell Angel but he wasn't listening. He was replaying part of the recording. The part where Basset had been on the phone to his subordinate. Speaking French. He played it over and over again.

'You can play it into Google Translate in my phone if you want to know what he said.'

'I understand the important part. Listen.' He played it yet again.

'Dupont? Une copie du procés-verbal de l'état du cadavre. Oui, du Jamie Kincaid. Pour Angel Carrasco et Jenifry Shaw.'

'I don't understand.'

'He called you Jenifry. How did he know that was your name? You told the man on reception it was Jen. You didn't show your passport. How did he know your name was Jenifry?'

I stared out into the car park and once again I was back in the dark of that awful night all those weeks ago. Walking back to the car in the rain. With Rania safe at my side. And remembering the sudden glare of torchlights blinding me and French voices shouting at us. *Police. Madame Jenifry Shaw.* They'd yelled. *You are Madame Shaw?*

Basset was a child-trafficker. Basset was a gendarme. Basset knew...

'Shit,' I said. 'Nick's boss got the police to pick me up here. The French police, I mean. They knew me as Jenifry Shaw.'

My mind raced as I tried to put it all together.

'And afterwards he interviewed me in great secrecy at a police station. Basset would have known about it. Plus the child he'd bought was never delivered. The same night his colleagues were asked to pick up a British woman called Jenifry Shaw, who was accompanied by a very similar child, and someone from a secretive department in the British police came over to speak to her. If you were a gendarme involved in something illegal, you'd have done your utmost to find out what was going on. And whatever Basset knew, the name Jenifry Shaw left a deep enough mark for him to connect it to Jen Shaw today and see us straightaway.'

'Does that mean he knows what Nico was?'

'I don't know, Angel. It looks like he might have. And we've probably confirmed his suspicions.'

'Basset killed him.'

'We don't know that.'

'He was involved.'

'Possibly. Probably. He must have been waiting on the cliffs for Rania to be delivered to him. I want him stopped anyway. And the people who help him.'

'I will stop him,' he said. 'I promise you, Jen.'

I understood exactly what he meant.

'You don't have to do it for me,' I said. 'I will do it myself.'

He leaned his face close to mine. He smelled of Alajar. Of the yeasty beer in the bar, of the musty layers of dead leaves and acorns lining the forest floors and the spiky scent of olives. For a moment he could have been Nick. For a moment, I wanted to bury myself in him. I lifted my face to his.

He jerked back and I wondered if he'd felt the force of my longing.

Shit. What was I doing? He breathed in sharply.

'First, I think we must try to do everything correctly,' he said. 'I have a phone number at home. One Nico gave me. To use in an absolute emergency. He said someone who knew where he was would answer. It must be his department. I think I will go home to call them and tell them about Capitaine Basset.'

He turned the engine on.

'What will you do?' he asked.

For a moment I thought about going to Alajar with him. The pull was strong. I loved the place and it was full of Nick. I turned to ask him but something in his face stopped me. There was a wariness that hadn't been there before although his eyes brimmed with kindness.

I'd nearly kissed him earlier. I thought he knew that. I thought it worried him. It meant nothing. It was a moment of confusion because he was the closest I could get to Nick but I didn't know how to explain.

I couldn't go to Alajar anyway. Ma needed me. Rania and Aya needed me.

'I'm going home,' I said. 'There's nothing I can do here.' I hesitated. 'Will you wait a minute? There's a place I want to go back to. Where I last spoke to Nick.'

'Take as long as you want.'

I climbed up the dunes backing onto the car park, my feet sinking into the sand between clumps of reedy grass. Little falls marked where I'd trod. I found the dip where Nick and I had crouched so we could talk and stay out of sight. It wasn't the last time I'd seen him. We'd passed later in the night in the chaos on the beach but it was the last time we'd talked. We'd come up with a plan to save Rania here. A crazy plan. A plan that had only just worked, thanks to Leila.

Afterwards as I'd turned to leave, he'd grabbed my hand and said, 'If I told you to be careful, would you take it the wrong way?'

'Yes.' I'd said.

'So don't be careful,' he'd said and I'd heard an echo of laughter in his voice. 'Run headlong into danger if that's what you want, but make sure you stay alive.'

He'd lifted my hand and kissed it, released it and walked away. We'd never said another word to each other. I wished we had. I wished I'd told him the same. 'Run headlong into danger if you must, but stay alive.'

Eight

Everybody had long gone to bed by the time I got back to Tregonna. Despite feeling shattered, I couldn't switch off. My head whirled with ideas. I got up and went out into the night and only came back as the moon faded into the brightening sky. I fell into a deep sleep then and, by the time I surfaced late morning, the house was empty. Ma had left me a note. She'd gone to see Mr Penrose, her solicitor, while Yasmiin had taken Aya to the cove. A hastily scribbled PS told me Rania had gone too.

Having Yasmiin here might well turn out to be a blessing if Aya was comfortable with her. Another person to look after the little girl who was happiest when her routine was the same every day. It would give me and Ma a little freedom. A freedom I might need.

I sat at the kitchen table and fingered the Coco Pops Aya had strewn far and wide in her enthusiasm. The morning was the only time of day the sun made it into the kitchen and it picked out the stains and gouges on the table's surface. And a cluster of tiny holes I hadn't noticed before. Woodworm? Probably, and fairly recent judging from the fine dust on the floor.

Beetles must have crept into the cracks and laid their eggs last year, probably fleeing the poison Kit had used to rid the house's old timbers of their presence and make sure they didn't come back. The old and cracked timber in the damp kitchen was an ideal place to lay their eggs. Once hatched, the larvae had burrowed into the wood and eaten it. It was only now that they were old enough to become beetles themselves that they'd pushed their way out leaving the telltale holes and dust.

Shit. The table was probably full of them, slowly eating it away from within. Yet another thing I'd have to do something about.

And my mind fled back to Nick.

And the rage that had haunted my thoughts throughout the night flickered into life again. I wanted Basset to suffer. I'd pictured myself killing him during the night. Following him until I caught him in some secluded corner and coshing him.

But Angel was right. We needed to expose him for what he was. A child-trafficker. Being caught and prosecuted would be the best punishment. I had some idea how policemen and offenders whose crimes involved children were treated in prison. I tried not to think what the future would have held for Rania if she hadn't escaped. And she so nearly hadn't.

If it hadn't been for Nick and Leila rescuing her.

Leila?

What did Yasmiin know about the mysterious Leila who'd saved Rania from the traffickers on the beach near Calais, and then left with the other migrants on the boat to England?

Leila had been travelling with one of the people-smugglers as his daughter. Except I now wondered if she had been. Would she know anything about Basset? It was time to stop slouching round the kitchen and do something. I grabbed a bottle of water and went to the cove to find Yasmiin.

She had tucked herself into the cliff and only uncurled and waved at me as I reached the sand. Aya and Rania were crouched over a rock pool, poking its inhabitants. They didn't see me. I took a quick photo of them with my phone. Another family paddled at the water's edge but no one else. You had to tramp over a series of fields to get here so very few tourists made it.

Yasmiin sat back down and screened her eyes from the sun as she looked towards Rania and Aya. She wore one of Ma's dresses, far too short for her, with what must be a pair of Kit's old sweat pants underneath, but she'd rolled them up her skinny legs. The cuts and bruises on her face were drying and fading but she was still far from the woman I'd met on Malta.

It occurred to me she might find sitting by the sea difficult.

'Are you OK here?'

'It is very different to the other beaches I have been on. Small and quiet. Besides it is day. Light changes everything.'

'After you left the boat and swam ashore – you and Leila – what happened? You said you watched the police run down the beach.'

'They seized everybody and took them away in vans. Even then, Leila still made us wait. She said other people would come. People we needed to avoid. She was right. Once the police had gone, they came down onto the beach. The boat was still there and they turned it over. There were packets stuck to its underneath and they tore them off and left.'

'What were they?'

'I don't know.'

'Drugs?'

'Probably. The smugglers transport anything for money.'

Of course they did.

'Then we walked to a town. It took a long time because Leila wouldn't let us go to the nearest one. She said we'd be too obvious. Then she looked for a bank with a machine to get money.'

'She had a bank card!'

'Yes. She said she hadn't used it for a long time and wasn't sure it would work. But it did. It looked like a lot of money to me but she told me it wasn't and she couldn't get any more until tomorrow. Then she bought us clothes. From a charity shop. They weren't new but they were clean. We left our old ones in a bin. Leila said it would be better not to wear them. That we'd stand out less in jeans.'

I was trying to make sense of the Leila who'd done all this. She seemed far removed from the shy young North African woman I'd first met, travelling as one of the smugglers' daughters. But then the risks she'd taken saving Rania had been utterly out of character too.

'The clothes she bought were nice,' Yasmiin added. 'Even though they weren't new. I was happy, you know. I thought I'd… I'd arrived.'

She picked up a pebble from the beach and hurled it out to sea. A flash of the old fury lit up her face. Then faded.

'Leila must have been here before,' I said.

'I think so. She knew what to do. Nothing was strange to her. And in the shop, when she spoke English, she spoke as fast as you do.'

Leila knew too much about life here – charity shops and cash card limits and so on. So what had she been doing with the smugglers?

'Who was she?' I spoke my thoughts out loud.

'She wasn't one of the smugglers.'

'I'd worked that out.'

'Brahim knew who she was.'

Nick had known who Leila was?

'Brahim knew her?'

'Yes. She said they came from the same place.'

Leila and Nick came from the same place? Spain? Britain? Or had Leila meant the place Nick as Brahim had come from?

'Where?'

'I don't know. She didn't say. They talked a lot on the boat before Brahim left. I couldn't follow all of it but I heard him say it would be better for her if no one knew she was back.'

'Back? Are you sure he said that?'

'He said back. Or perhaps he said returned. And then he told us to get off the boat before it landed.'

'What was she doing with the smugglers then?'

But Yasmiin didn't know. She'd been exhausted when they arrived in England and Leila was desperate to get far away from the coast quickly. They'd eaten and gone to a railway station where Leila had bought tickets. They'd gone to London together and then they'd separated. Leila had given Yasmiin the remains of the money and looked up the address of a shelter for homeless women for her.

'We didn't talk much,' she said. 'Leila was very nervous.'

'Do you know where she went?'

'Another station. Houston?'

'Euston, I guess. So she caught a train. Do you know where?'

'I don't remember. It wasn't anywhere I'd heard of but I only knew London and Oxford and, of course, Cornwall from talking to Morwenna.'

I tried to work it out. To make sense of what Yasmiin had told me. Euston. Yasmiin thought she'd headed to Euston. Well, that ruled out a few destinations...

'Yasmiin, if I give you a list of places, maybe it might come back to you?'

'Maybe.'

Her voice was as light and loose as the sand she was scooping up and letting fall through her fingers. I wondered about asking her what had happened after Leila had gone but she looked suddenly shattered.

'I'll look after the girls if you want to go home and rest.'

'I will.'

She stood up in one swift movement, still innately graceful despite her tiredness, and went.

I buried my hands in the sand and thought. Nick had known who Leila was. Leila said they came from the same place. And Nick had said it would be better if no one knew she was back. Surely that meant Leila was British. Except what was a young British girl doing travelling with a gang of smugglers? She knew how to handle a gun. It was hard to reconcile the shy Leila I'd met first of all with the resourceful and quick-witted one who'd saved Rania on the beach.

And then I saw her in a completely different way. She was a chameleon. A shapeshifter. And I knew someone else who was exactly the same. Nick. Nick who'd known who she was. Nick who she'd said came from the same place. What if Leila hadn't meant a country or a city or a town, but a workplace? What if Leila wasn't as young as she seemed? Wasn't shy? What if she'd been playing a role? Exactly like Nick had been playing the role of Brahim. What if she, like Nick, had been infiltrated into the gang? What if she too had been working undercover?

It made sense of everything. Perfect sense.

Nine

My head was still spinning with ideas when I got back to Tregonna with Rania and Aya. Yasmiin had gone to bed but Ma was there. Far more cheerful than she'd been for an age. In fact, full of excitement. She whirled around the kitchen throwing vegetables and grains into a bowl as she listened to Rania's account of the creatures they'd seen in the rock pools and how Aya had pointed out a sea anemone with whirling tendrils and said 'pretty'. Every now and then Ma gave the tinkling laugh that used to annoy me so much but now I was simply pleased to see her happy.

'What's up?'

'Lots of things.' She shot a quick look at Rania who was watching her as attentively as I was. 'Today the earth is bathed in energy. Can't you feel it? It was full moon last night and the wind is coming from the east bringing new ideas and inspiration.' Her bracelets jangled as she swooped her arms around.

'Lovely,' I said.

Clearly she didn't want to talk in front of Rania.

'And I've been asked to speak at a literary conference. An international one.' She passed me a letter.

Ma had written a book about her travels in India years ago. It had been a success at the time and she still received the occasional invitation to events.

'I can't go but it's wonderful that people remember my book.'

'Actually you could do it. It's online.'

And because I knew Ma wouldn't have a clue what that meant I spent lunch explaining how online events worked and trying to persuade her to give it a try. I knew she wouldn't but it was something to talk about as neither of us wanted to speak about the things that occupied us most.

After lunch I slipped outside to call Angel.

He still sounded a little wary of me so I cut straight to the important things.

'What did they say when you called the number Nick left?'

'Not much. They listened and said they would handle it.'

'Handle it. Did they tell you how?'

'No.'

'You have to call them back. Ask them. Or I will if you want.'

'No. I'll do it now.'

I paced up and down through the long grass that was supposed to be a lawn except neither Ma nor I ever had time to mow it. The afternoon sun was hot and I started to sweat.

Ma appeared and announced we were all going to pick more wild flowers on the cliffs.

'The girls will enjoy it,' she said quietly to me, 'and you and I can talk.'

I trailed after her to a cluster of rocks rising out of the swathes of long grass that used to be the garden. If you looked hard enough you could see the low stone walls that had demarcated the long gone flower beds – now a sea of grass and wild flowers only broken by the occasional shrub that had clung on to life.

'It's like wading through the sea.' Ma echoed my thoughts as she swished her hands through the stalks, sending up a cloud of seeds. Rania and Aya lagged behind, already looking for flowers.

'It's a mess,' I said. 'And always will be.'

'Maybe not.' She sat down and smiled up at me. 'I have a plan for Tregonna. The idea came to me in the night. Last night. The night of the full moon. My energy was high because of it. And my creativity.'

I waited. There was no point interrupting her.

'I saw you coming home.'

'What?'

'Very early this morning. I was moonbathing. Around the full moon is the best time for reflecting on intentions.'

'I went for a short walk,' I said quickly. 'I couldn't sleep.'

Maybe I should have told her the truth. I hadn't been walking. The lure of the cliffs with the waves splashing below had been too much and I couldn't sleep. Ma's eyes narrowed but she let it go and explained her great idea. She thought Mr Penrose was right about developers snatching up Tregonna and turning it into luxury flats but she wondered if she could have one of the flats. Not that it had to be luxurious.

It wasn't at all what I was expecting. In fact, it was quite a sensible idea although it would need a lot of thinking through. I was surprised she was prepared even to consider it as a solution, though. Especially after all the years of mystic waffle about Tregonna being sacred. Maybe the time she'd spent in Malta and the arrival of Rania and Aya in her life had opened her. It had changed us both.

'What does Mr Penrose think?'

'He thinks it's worth looking into.'

This was good news. Mr Penrose was a sensible man and unlikely to give Ma false hope. He knew her too well.

'The thing is…,' she said.

'Yes.'

'He said it might take a bit of time to find the right developer.'

'Sure.'

'I haven't got time. Your father wants an immediate answer or he's going to the courts for a resolution. Mr Penrose thinks it would be best if we spoke to him ourselves and explained everything.'

'We?'

'Well, you.'

'What about Kit?'

'You would do it better. Kit is too...'

I was curious to see what Ma would say but she shut her mouth and shook her head then added, 'And Kit agrees.'

No surprise there. Kit was always happy to leave anything tricky to me. Probably rightly so. However much of a mess I made of it, I'd do better than him. Or Ma for that matter.

'I'll give Pa a call but I'm not sure it will work.'

'I think you should go and see him.'

'See him? Go to the States?'

'No. Your father's over here. Kit told me. He's working on a film. He's in Glasgow at the moment but afterwards they're going to the Lake District – so you could meet him there. I don't expect you'll want to go back to Glasgow.'

'No, I don't.'

'The Lake District is spectacular.'

I was saved from replying by my phone. It was Angel.

'I have to answer this,' I said and walked away through the grass.

'I called Nico's department again,' Angel said. 'The number is out of service. I've tried several times.'

'What?'

'They don't want me to call them again.'

We'd been cut out.

I remembered Nick's boss's lack of interest when I'd told him about the child-trafficking in the first place. I was sure they'd do nothing about Basset.

'I think they're going to ignore Basset,' I said.

'But Nico worked for them.'

'Did you tell them Basset might have had something to do with his death?'

'No. Only the child-trafficking. We don't know for sure.'

'They don't care about the children.'

'Jen!'

'They don't operate like you and me, Angel. The job they do changes them.'

'Maybe,' he said. 'But Nico was not like that.'

'Of course not.'

But I wasn't sure. Not really. I didn't see how Nick could work for his department and not be untouched by their attitude.

'Then I shall go to Calais,' Angel said.

'I'll come with you.'

For a few seconds, I heard nothing except Angel's breathing and a faint clink of glasses. He must be in the bar.

'No. I'm going alone.'

Was he saying this because of some stupid idea that I should be protected from danger or because he wanted to keep me at arm's length. I wished yet again that I hadn't nearly kissed him. A brilliant idea crept into my brain.

Duncan. Nick's cousin Duncan. Duncan who'd been as close to Jamie Kincaid as Angel was to Nick. Duncan the policeman. If anyone could help us bring Basset to justice, it was Duncan.

'Duncan,' I said. 'Duncan's in the police. Duncan will help us. He'll know how to get something done.'

'I'll call him.'

'No. I'll go and see him. It will be better face-to-face. I'll go to Glasgow.'

I turned round and looked back at Ma.

'I've got something else I can do while I'm there.'

Ten

The weather was vile in Glasgow. A penetrating drizzle soaked my hair and my jacket as I ran the short distance between the railway station and the Grand Central Hotel where the film crew were staying. The city felt grey and chilly, with litter and suspicious stains marking the pavements. The hotel was a massive Victorian edifice that spoke of commerce and money and old-fashioned values like knowing your place. I didn't have to stay here long, I told myself.

I reached the hotel porch and sheltered for a moment, shaking the worst of the wet off me. A group of women, laughing, clattered past in heels and summer dresses, their legs golden with fake tan. A lone woman with a shopping trolley and a mackintosh said something to them as she passed and they stopped and chatted to her. I tried to decipher the banter but it was impossible. Their accent was so different from the soft, rolling Cornish speech I'd grown up with. A couple of men deep in conversation took shelter alongside me. They wore kilts. Kilts in a tartan of different shades of grey that looked as comfortable and as battered as the jeans I wore. Nothing like the gaudy pleated things people wear to weddings. I waited for a while to see if I could understand their conversation. Some of it started to make sense. By the time they headed off into the rain, I knew that they were going to see an old friend whose mother had died. He'd taken it bad and was drinking too much. Or at least I guessed that was what they meant by 'bladdered'.

Now, I quite liked Glasgow. First impressions anyway. Or maybe second impressions. It had seemed dirty and unwelcoming, full of traffic and noise, through the bus windows but here it felt different. There was a sense of 'what you see is what you get' about the place. An energy that made me feel at home.

The hotel receptionist thought Pa was out. Which was fair enough. I'd left him a voice message saying I was coming to Glasgow today and hoped to see him. Nothing more. She thought someone at the film company might know when he'd be back. They'd rented a suite of meeting rooms.

I rang Duncan again before I went up. I'd left him a message too, telling him I needed to see him, whenever and wherever suited him but as soon as possible. He hadn't called back.

A frazzled-looking woman, permanently on the phone, was the only person in the meeting room. She was on two phones – her mobile and the landline on her desk – both of which rang continually. In between fielding calls she typed on her computer and bit her nails.

I explained who I was during gaps in her phone conversations, then waited for her to finish a call about permissions to visit a disused railway station. A hand tapped my shoulder and a light voice with an American accent spoke.

'Jenifry?'

I turned.

A woman of my own height stood there. For a moment I thought she was also my own age but then I noticed the lines and softness of flesh in her face that not even the cleverness of her make-up could hide. The blonde hair probably owed a great deal to expensive hairdressing. She was fit, though. The gap between her jeans and crop top showed abs of steel and the arm she held out to me was muscled and firm.

'Isabel,' she said. 'Although your father calls me Issy.'

Shit. This was Pa's girlfriend.

I shook her hand and found a smile from somewhere.

'Charlie told me you might turn up. I'm just finishing a brochure and then I'll take you out to where he is.' She turned to the production assistant. 'Polly, we'll need a car in thirty minutes for Auchinstarry.'

She spoke with the authority of someone who didn't expect to ask twice. Despite being in the middle of a conversation about permits, Polly nodded, reached for a camera and took a photo of me while balancing the phone under her chin and continuing to talk.

'Polly will make you a badge,' Issy said. 'Come and look at the plans while we're waiting. I'm stealing Charlie's thunder but I can't wait to show you.'

I followed her without a word. And learned a lot over the next half an hour. She was a climber. That was how she'd met Pa. And now they were starting up a business in the US. In Yosemite to be exact – the national park that was every climber's mecca. They were building a magnificent and luxurious lodge on its outskirts and from there they were going to run all manner of climbing trips. Very expensive climbing trips as far as I could make out. Aimed at top businessmen and millionaires who would spend a fortune to get the very best. She showed me the plans. The lodge was huge. And the brochure she was working on was very classy, with the famous picture of Pa on the front. The lucky shot on top of a previously unclimbed Himalayan peak after he'd led the first expedition to reach its summit.

A huge smile of achievement curved his thin mouth and, in his goggles, you can see the reflection of deep blue sky and snowy rocks rising through the clouds. It was the image they'd used on the cover of *National Geographic* and it was trotted out every time a newspaper or magazine ran an article on climbing or exploring.

No wonder Pa needed to sell Tregonna. This must be costing a fortune. My surprise must have shown.

'You knew about this right?'

'Of course,' I lied. 'Just not all the details.'

'Charlie explained everything to Morwenna so she'd understand why your old house – what's it called?'

'Tregonna.'

'Why Tregonna needs selling and fast.'

So Ma had known. I guessed she'd decided it was irrelevant. It wasn't, though. I couldn't see Pa agreeing to wait for her to find the right developer. He clearly needed the money.

Our car arrived, complete with driver, and we headed off to Auchinstarry where the shoot was happening today. Only half an hour away according to Issy.

'I need to make a few phone calls,' she said. 'What with the lodge and the business and the wedding to organise there aren't enough hours in the day.'

Wedding? This time I did manage to control my surprise.

'Charlie gave you the date, didn't he?'

He hadn't but some latent family protectiveness stopped me from telling her the wedding was news to me. Kit must know. And possibly Ma.

Issy's voice, although quiet, was penetrating and she was one of those people who say a lot when a few words would suffice. I watched the scenery go by and wondered about the film. I asked Issy when she finished her calls.

'It's one of those absurd adventure films where the hero, who's never climbed before, miraculously does impossible things. Charlie was keen to do it and they were thrilled when he agreed to act as adviser even though he couldn't do any of the climbing sequences himself.'

'Why not?'

Pa wasn't exactly young but he was more than capable of doing a few climbing stunts.

'Insurance,' Issy said. 'On the loans for the lodge. The insurers wouldn't countenance your father doing any stunts even though he explained how safe it was. So someone else does the actual climbing. The film is out next year at about the same time as the company launches so the publicity will be perfect. Here we are.'

We stopped by security at a temporary barrier while our driver spoke to a man in a high vis jacket, flanked on either side by a couple of police officers who looked on but said nothing. A few spectators had gathered and were trying to see beyond the barrier. Some of them raised their phones and took pictures of us on the off-chance we might be famous. Issy and I showed our passes and security waved us through into a car park filled with a town of caravans and trucks. People sat or stood around. Drinking coffee. Chatting. Flipping through scripts. Someone checked a stack of ropes and harnesses mounted on a frame.

'They never seem to be doing very much,' Issy said as we got out of the car.

I followed her to a small loch at the edge of the car park dominated by a crag at the far side with a cluster of boats round its base and climbers above. Someone had rigged a platform about halfway up it. On the rock, the climbers either clambered to the top or were hauled up and then headed towards the vans parked there. One of the boats sped over to us, carving a deep furrow in the murky waters.

'Looks like they're taking another break,' Issy said. 'Charlie will be pleased to see you.'

I wasn't so sure. Not when he knew why I'd come. This probably wasn't the best time or place to plead for Ma. Especially with Issy looking on.

Eleven

The boat slowed as it reached the little dock. Pa was first off. His face was tight and his lips pinched.

'Hey, Charlie,' Issy called. 'Look who's here.'

He ignored the group of people waiting to speak to him and came over.

It had been a while since I last saw him in the flesh. I counted up the years and then stopped. Best not to think how long. I'd seen photos and videos in the climbing press and forums, so I knew he was still as lean and sharp as ever. The snow and sun had left its mark on his skin and his curly hair seemed coarser now but maybe that was the streaks of grey. Judging by the expressions of the people hanging around him, he still had the streak of charisma that made him seem special. He'd never had to persuade anyone to see things his way.

Except his family.

'Jen.' He nodded and tried to smile through his grim mood.

'Hey, Charlie. Lighten up.' Issy punched him gently but this only provoked the outburst that had been simmering behind his frown.

'The cameraman's a total waste of time. You'd think they'd have booked a specialist. Someone who's used to shooting climbers. Someone who can climb, at least.'

Issy looked bored.

'But they wanted someone local. Trying to save money. Well, it's going to backfire on them. Mark my words.'

He pulled his face into a neutral calm as the van that had brought everybody back from the crag drew up.

'Fergus,' he said in a conciliatory tone to a thickset man whose expression rivalled Pa's in grumpiness. 'A quick word?'

'I'm on my break,' Fergus said, undoing his harness and handing it to an assistant. 'Be glad to see the back of that,' he muttered.

'Just a few minutes.'

'Batteries need recharging and you'll be the first to moan if they're not ready when we start again.'

And with that he stomped off, weighed down with camera kit.

'What was that?' Issy asked. 'The accent is cute but I can't understand a word he says.'

'Nothing.' He turned to me. 'So, Jen, what brings you here? Your mother, I suppose.'

Clearly this was not a good time.

'Yes. But maybe later.'

'I hope you've come to tell us she's agreed to Charlie's terms,' Issy butted in. 'We've been more than generous to her in my opinion. Letting her stay in the house for so long and then sharing the proceeds with her.'

I gritted my teeth.

I particularly didn't want to discuss this in front of Issy and, judging by the shifty look on Pa's face, he didn't think it was a great idea either.

'Yes. Ma's accepting your offer –'

Another van swept in from the crag and stopped near us. A voice from inside yelled *Charlie*. Pa put up his hand.

'About time too.' Issy started speaking before I could add that Ma needed him to wait. 'I'll ring the agents and tell them to put it on the market straightaway.'

'No,' I said. 'Not yet. You have to wait.'

The man from the van called again. 'Charlie, you need to take a look at this.'

There was something familiar about the voice but when I looked its owner had bent to pull a box out. He put it on the ground and straightened, still with his back to us. Black curly hair cut short. Strong but square body.

He looked like Nick.

A stab of grief shook me.

'What do you mean, *Wait*?'

Issy's voice penetrated my consciousness but I only had eyes for the man still standing with his back to us, now listening to an assistant who was waving a clipboard at him.

Not Nick. It wasn't Nick.

But I knew him.

I felt Issy's hand on my arm, shook it off as the man turned and strode towards us.

'Charlie,' he said again. 'We need a plan.'

It was Vince. An old climbing friend. I'd thought he was in the States. Last time I'd seen him, his hair had been bristle-short. He'd let it grow and it covered his head in dark, wavy curls. So he looked like Nick. From a distance, anyway. Last time I'd seen him, at the height of my risk-taking games, he'd been angry with me but he flashed me a quick smile now.

'OK, Vince,' Pa said. 'Let's find a quiet corner and come up with a plan for the rest of the shoot. We've got nothing except a few close-ups so far.'

'No, Charlie.' Issy butted in again. 'I want to find out why Jenifry's saying we've got to wait to sell your house.'

Pa turned back to me. 'Yes, what is the problem? I suppose it's something Morwenna wants.'

'Let's talk about it later. I can see you're busy.'

'No,' Issy said again. 'I want to know now. The sooner the

house is sold, the sooner we can pay down some of the money we owe.'

So I told them Ma's plan.

It didn't go well. Neither my attempt at explaining, nor their reaction.

'No way,' Issy said as I tailed off.

I fixed my eyes on Pa. I wasn't going to beg but he needed at least to think about it. He looked at his watch.

'All right. I'll think about it,' he said. 'Right, Vince, we've got half an hour to come up with a plan to sort this mess and get some useful shots.'

Issy was furious and started to say there was nothing to think about but he cut her off with an impatient gesture and stalked off. Issy strode away in the other direction. She summoned the driver who had brought us here and left.

Shit.

Not that I particularly wanted to go back to Glasgow with her.

Vince still stood by me. He'd witnessed the whole conversation.

'That went well,' I said. 'Nice to see you, by the way.'

'And you, Jen.'

Pa shouted his name.

'Get a coffee in catering,' he said. 'Charlie's hugely stressed today. Talk to him later. He did say he'd think about it.'

I went and got a coffee and a bun, then sat at one of the camping tables to eat it. Thought about calling Ma except I didn't have any news for her.

'Jen.' Vince had come back over. 'Are you in a rush to leave?'

'No.'

'Well, we could do with another climber, if you were up for it. Charlie and I have an idea how to make this shoot work. What do you think?'

Why not? Especially if it involved helping Pa out of a hole.

'Sure.'

'I don't suppose you've got climbing shoes with you?'

'Of course.'

'Great.'

He didn't ask why I'd brought my shoes but, as the van drove us to the top of the crag, he explained they were doing general climbing shots without the actors who wouldn't be joining them until next week. Close-ups of arms and legs, hands and feet. Not facial stuff because Vince had been doubling as the hero. Now they wanted whole body shots from angles where you couldn't tell who was climbing.

Except, Fergus, the cameraman, wasn't keen on heights. No one had really explained what they were trying to do today and no one from the production company had thought to check before booking him. I gathered that the first no one – the one who hadn't explained – was Pa, despite all his protestations. So he and Vince were fairly desperate for the day's shoot to produce something useable.

'You'll be climbing alone on a fixed top rope,' Vince explained. 'And so will I, but there's no real climbing involved. It's just doing a few moves probably over and over again. Charlie's up top to manage everything. We're going to put Fergus in a bosun's chair so he feels more comfortable and I'll stay with him all the time to assist.'

He described a few moves they wanted to achieve. An assistant took my rucksack and coat and gave me a blonde wig and a helmet plus a baggy top and trousers to put on over the top of my harness.

'Am I supposed to be climbing without ropes?'

'We're not sure. We'll try and keep the ropes out of shot and you must keep your face turned away from the camera as much as possible. Even on a bad day you don't look much like the actor. He's got a beard for a start. You'll have to take the helmet off when we're shooting, though.'

Fergus hadn't looked like the kind of person who'd be keen on anything much and, I quickly realised when I joined him, he certainly wasn't keen on Pa or Vince. Getting anything shot was long and tedious at first. Fergus was nervous but trying to hide it beneath a crust of grumpiness and, despite Vince's brief, I wasn't really sure what they wanted me to do. But Vince was patient. He got me to demonstrate a series of moves until Fergus saw something he liked. Then he shot it. I gathered it looked good.

I learned how to repeat the same action over and over again, and concentrated on making my movements clear and sharp. Fergus, reassured by Vince's constant presence, started to make suggestions. In between sequences I joined them to discuss what to do next and gradually things got better.

Early on we started ignoring Pa's shouted instructions. He couldn't see from his position up top. In addition, he was continually breaking off to answer his phone, making Fergus mutter about his mind not being on the job. He had a point.

'Some shots of the lassie from below would be good,' Fergus said to Vince as I edged along a crack towards them after a sequence. 'Could she push herself away from the rock? So I catch the sky between.'

'No problem,' I called and eyed the face above them. 'I'll go up there. Save you changing position.'

'No,' Vince said. 'Stay where you are. We'll move. It's a bit chossy up there. There's a seam I don't like the look of.'

Vince shouted up to explain what we were doing, but Pa disagreed. He had another idea, although neither Vince nor I could understand what it was. His phone rang again.

'We'll have to wait,' Vince said.

'The light'll change soon,' Fergus told us. And then, 'What does chossy mean?'

'It means the rock's loose. Bits might fall off.'

'Oh aye.'

Solid as a rock is a stupid description. Because it isn't. Weather breaks it down over time. Water gets in cracks and freezes, making them bigger. Climbers damage it. Even modern rock anchors exert a strain. And when you've been climbing for a while you get a sixth sense about rotten rock and I trusted Vince. I rammed the helmet on.

'Wouldn't want you to hurt yourself.'

'Not me. I won't get hurt. I might peel off – fall – but the rope would stop me. The rock I dislodge might hit you, though.'

Pa finished his call and he and Vince started shouting at each other. A note of irritation frayed the edges of Pa's voice.

I sighed.

'Walkie-talkies would have been useful. Pity no one seems to have done any planning,' Fergus said. 'You go up and see what the big man wants, Vince. I'll be fine. The lassie can look after me. I think she knows what she's doing.'

Something that might have been the beginning of a smile cracked his mouth.

'The lassie has a name,' I said. 'Jen. Jen Shaw.'

I twisted round and held out a chalky hand. He shook it briefly.

'So you're the big man's daughter?'

'Yup.'

'Hmmm. Well, you don't blether as much as he does, I'll say that for you.'

His face cracked into a sardonic grin as Pa leaned over again and shouted something else. We got the gist of it. He didn't want to wait for Vince to come up, he was coming down.

And before either Vince or I could warn him about the choss above, he launched himself over the edge and came towards us, kicking himself off the face in a fast abseil.

For a second Vince and I stared in shock. Fergus was the first to speak.

'Is that not the bit you said –'

A lump of rock shooting past his head cut him off. Vince and I yelled *Below* at the same time and I pushed Fergus tight against the slab. The rock fell into the water beneath and its splash was followed by cracking from above. Sharp flakes rained down. A couple bounced off my helmet. Light as they were, the impact juddered through my body. Fergus gasped and Vince gave a short cry.

I forced myself to keep my face pressed into the crag until it was quiet.

I looked down first. The boats were moving to the middle of the water. Their occupants stared up at me and above.

I looked to my left. Fergus's face met mine. His eyes fluttered and his mouth was open. His tongue, shockingly wet and pink against the grey dust that coated his face, went to moisten his lips and stopped when it tasted the grit. He spat.

'Keep tight in to the cliff,' I said.

I leaned cautiously out and peered round him. Vince hung off the wall. His arms limp by his side and his head fallen forwards. His helmet was still on and intact as far as I could see but he was unconscious.

A noise from above. More rock fall but only a shower of grit. I risked a glance up.

Pa clung several metres above. His feet rested on a ledge encrusted with rock debris and they slipped as he fought to keep still.

Shit.

'Pa,' I called up.

No answer.

'Could you get him to move out of the way? That'd help for a start.' Fergus sounded more annoyed than frightened. This was good.

'Vince.' Pa's voice came from above.

'Vince is out cold,' I shouted up.

'Move out of the way,' Fergus yelled.

'I can't. Everything I grip crumbles. I think it might all come away.'

If Pa set off a big fall he would injure us. And if he fell off the ledge his body would smash into us. Break bones. Maybe necks. It might also rip our anchors out of the rock. I hadn't rigged them. I didn't know how much force they could take.

All this raced through my mind as I tried to decide what to do.

Fergus was wrong. Getting Pa out of the way was impossible. We were the ones who'd have to move. Once we were out of the way, it wouldn't matter if Pa dislodged more rock or took a fall to where we'd been hanging.

'What shall we do?' This was Fergus, still sounding surprisingly calm.

'Get out of his way.'

I hope I sounded as calm as he did because I didn't feel it. I could climb out of the way myself, no problem. But how was I going to get Fergus and Vince to safety? Neither of them could climb. One of them didn't know how and the other was unconscious. Plus Vince had put a temporary anchor into a crack in the solid rock between them and Pa. To keep the ropes clear. And it was holding them in place beneath him.

Voices called down from above. The driver and camera assistant had recovered from their shock. Not that they'd be any use.

The boats were below, though. And Fergus's rope went all the way down. He could lower himself to safety. That solved half the problem.

'Right,' I said to Fergus. 'You know how to lower yourself?'

He nodded.

'That's what you're going to do. All the way down to the water. The boats will pick you up.'

His hands went to the rope and the Grigri, ready to pull the lever that would let the rope slip through the device.

'Will you lower Vince?'

'Yes,' I lied. 'But I need you out of the way. And fast.'

He set off, camera slung over one shoulder. One of the boats moved in to collect him. Good.

Now for Vince. I couldn't lower him. Both of us were on shorter ropes that stopped too far above the water. But if I could release the anchor he'd put in above, his rope should swing him out of the way.

More grit tumbled down the cliff between us. At the same time, Fergus reached the water and the waiting boat. Hands reached up and grabbed him, unclipped his harness and the boat sped away.

I looked up. My eyes met Pa's staring down over his shoulder at me. He clung to the rock. His fingers crimped into two small pockets while his arms shook with strain. He wouldn't be able to keep still much longer.

No time to think.

I swarmed up the rock, smearing my feet against its smoothness and trusting my fingers to find pockets and edges to crimp into. Momentum carried me up. I thought of nothing except reaching the crack above and releasing Vince's rope. Small rocks tumbled past me but I hardly noticed. I got to the anchor and reached up a hand to fumble with the carabiner holding the rope in place while the other gripped the side of the crack. It was impossible to unclip with one hand.

I twisted a foot deep into the crack to hold me in position while I stretched up the other hand. Felt the thin flesh covering my ankle bruise and graze with the pressure but I didn't care. Unclipped the carabiner and released Vince's rope. His body swung loose and away.

Another wave of grit rolled down the cliff. Pa yelled something.

I released my foot, wincing as the blood rushed back into the bruised flesh and kicked off to the side, scrambling across the rock until I was clear.

'Now, Pa,' I shouted.

I heard him rather than saw him. I was too fixed on getting as far to the side as possible. He climbed. Which was the right decision. The top was closer. And as he cleared the patch of chossy rock, his feet sent a farewell avalanche down into the water below. It bounced against the face where the three of us had been, then hurtled down and hit the water with a thwacking splash, sending great circular waves rushing out.

I thought what might have happened.

Someone, Pa probably, started to haul Vince up. I vaguely wondered if he'd rigged a belay up top but I didn't think about it much. It was time to get off the cliff myself.

There was an easy way out, too. A perfect way out. One that meant I wouldn't have to climb with my foot starting to throb and face Pa at the top. Pa whose stupidity had nearly killed us all. The others might not realise what he'd done but Vince and I did.

Besides I wanted to fly.

I unfastened my harness and gripped the rope as I turned to face out, then pushed off the rock in a great arcing dive into the water, aware only of Fergus standing in the boat with his camera trained on me and of Vince suddenly waking, lifting his head and reaching out his arms.

It was summer but the water was icy. It shocked the pleasure of the dive out of my blood and once I'd kicked my way back to the surface, my sodden clothes weighed me down. It was a relief when a boat arrived and arms hauled me aboard.

Twelve

They took me to dry land as fast as the boat's puny engine would let them. Water ran from my clothes and pooled in the hull. Someone wrapped a blanket around me. It made no difference. The chill was inside. Even after stripping off, changing into some spare and warm clothes one of the production assistants conjured up and sitting in a car with the heater on full blast, I felt frozen.

Another boat brought Fergus back. He came over and asked me if I was OK. I nodded.

'If you'd told me you fancied a swim,' he said, 'I'd have recommended the swimming baths at North Woodside. Beautiful, they are. Victorian.'

'I wanted to wash the grit out of my hair. Seemed like the easiest way.'

'Lassies. You're all the same.' He brushed some of the dust off his own face. 'Not supposed to say that nowadays, am I?'

'No.'

'I'm on my way,' he said curtly to an assistant hovering at his elbow. 'Well, I best go and let them see what we've shot this afternoon. Lucky I brought the camera down with me. Will I see you before you go?'

'Yes.'

He let the assistant escort him to one of the Winnebagos. The car park burst into life as the crew packed up and prepared to leave. The van bringing Vince and Pa and all the climbing gear drove in. Pa went straight into the same Winnebago. Vince and a first aider came over. They leaned through the window.

'I'm fine,' I said quickly. 'Just got a bit wet.'

I glared at the first aider; no way was I going to let her examine me. She gave up and left.

'Get in,' I said to Vince.

'She's not happy. She wanted me to go to hospital.'

'You should. You were out of it for a while.'

'Not totally. I knew what was going on. Just didn't feel like moving.'

'Thought you'd let me sort it out. Typical.'

But underneath the banter, I knew we were both thinking the same.

It was all Pa's fault. He should never have abseiled down right above us. Never, ever, ever. He could have killed us all.

'He knows,' Vince said quietly. 'Charlie knows what he's done.'

'Has he told you that?'

'No. But he didn't need to.'

But he did, I thought. He did. Except the great Charlie Shaw, one of the most renowned climbers of his generation, couldn't bring himself to say it out loud. The horror I'd seen in his eyes. How much of it had been for us? And how much had been because he could see the headlines? *Charlie Shaw kills three people during film shoot.* How had his future looked to him then with his reputation in ruins?

'I hooked up with him in Yosemite, you know?'

'No, I didn't. I knew you were there.'

'Charlie was climbing. In between overseeing their super, luxurious lodge. Then he got too busy. Issy needed him all the time. He was mad keen to do this film and, to be honest, I was running out of cash. So when he asked me to work on it – me doing the climbing and him advising – I jumped at the chance. Always wanted to do some film work.'

He pulled at a piece of grit that had lodged itself in the cuff of his jacket.

'It was only when we got away from Yosemite that I realised things were tense. Issy came along too. And I don't think Charlie expected that. I think he saw the film as a chance to get away from the build. He's told me a bit about it and the money side is horrendous. Plus he's being asked to make decisions all the time. And the one thing working with him has shown me is that Charlie isn't a man for details.'

'No. Doug used to do all that.'

Doug was Pa's number two. Doug had dealt with all the tiresome logistics while Pa had been the front man.

'Where is Doug?'

'He's retired.'

Vince pulled at his cuff again.

'What are you trying to say, Vince?'

'Charlie's not happy. His mind is elsewhere. He's got into this project with Issy and I think he's having second thoughts about it.'

'Well, it's a bit late for that.'

Vince said nothing.

'Shit. He's going to walk away, isn't he? Once again. He's going to walk away and leave Issy to deal with the aftermath.'

I didn't like Issy particularly but I felt sorry for her. Maybe she'd guessed Pa's heart wasn't in the lodge project anymore and that was why she'd come with him on the film.

'I didn't say he was going to walk away,' Vince said.

'You wouldn't be surprised, though, would you?'

Vince was quiet.

'Selfish bastard. Never thinking about the consequences.'

'And you're just like him.'

98

I was too startled to speak.

'How could you have been so stupid as to dive into the loch?'

'I know how to dive from height. I was brought up climbing sea cliffs in Cornwall.'

'Diving into seas you knew, I bet. Not into murky waters where people dump abandoned wheelbarrows and shopping trolleys. I've been told there's a couple of cars in there. Charlie's not the only one who does stupid things.'

There was no breeze so no ripples disturbed the loch surface, grey with reflected sky. On the far side, the water mirrored the vertical walls of the crag so they appeared to dive down below the surface as well as stretch up high.

All an illusion.

Pa came out of the Winnebago, chatting and laughing with a small group of people. Fergus followed a few seconds later but waited in the doorway for them to move away. Vince called and waved. A final, few high-fives and Pa joined us.

'We've got some magnificent shots,' Pa said. 'I mean breathtaking. You did brilliantly, Jen.' His eyes slid away from me after the first glance and he turned to Vince. 'Hate to admit it but that cameraman knows what he's doing. Everyone's ecstatic.'

I looked over to where Fergus had last been, standing on the steps, but he'd gone.

'We're going to The Crow,' Pa went on. 'Harry, the director, wants to buy us all a drink. I'll see you there.'

He strode off.

'Are you going to say anything to him?' I asked.

'No point. He's not stupid.'

'He can't even say sorry.'

Vince and I watched him and a gang of production assistants head towards a waiting car.

'You coming?' he said.

Part of me wanted to. It had been a shit day. The pub would be warm and bright. It would be fun. I could catch up with Vince. I didn't need to talk to Pa. He'd be surrounded by hangers-on. I didn't need to have a drink. Or maybe just one to drive the greyness filling my thoughts away. I needed something…

'No,' I said quickly. 'I won't.'

Fergus appeared.

'The crew are packing your gear away,' he said. 'If you'd like to use it again, you might want to go and supervise.'

'Thanks,' Vince said.

'I'm all done. I'll be off now.'

'I'll see you at the pub.'

'You won't. I'm heading home.'

'Back to town?'

'Aye.'

'Would you give Jen a lift?'

Fergus nodded. 'I'll be in my car. It's the Discovery over there.' He walked away.

'You sure about not coming? You might get a chance to talk to Charlie about Morwenna at the pub? Without Issy,' Vince said.

'It'll be noisy and Pa will be busy.'

'What about tomorrow then? The crew are shooting interiors and Charlie and I are doing some venue research in Glasgow. I'll text you where we're going and you can meet us. We'll be on our own.'

'OK.'

A production assistant brought my rucksack and coat and a bin bag full of my dripping clothes over. I pulled my phone out of the rucksack, thanking the gods I hadn't kept it while climbing. Checked it. Duncan had called. No message. I called him back.

'Duncan.'

'Hello, Jen.' He sounded distant.

'I need to talk to you.'

'OK. Go on.'

'I mean face to face. I'm here. In Glasgow.'

'I thought you went home.'

'Yes. But I've come back. Can we meet?'

'Where are you staying?'

'Not sure yet, but I can come to you.'

'OK. I'm in the West End. Meet me in Waterstones in Byres Road. They've got a café. In half an hour.'

'I'm not sure I can get there that quickly. Can you give me a couple of hours?'

'Tomorrow then. Eleven o'clock. Same place.'

'OK.'

Shit. Duncan hadn't sounded at all keen to see me. I trudged over to Fergus's Land Rover and got in.

He drove well. Sensibly but with confidence. And tolerance, only pulling his thick brows together in a slight frown when an idiot in a BMW overtook us at speed on a blind corner and forced him to break as it pulled in sharply when faced by an oncoming car. Fergus's face in repose was pretty grim, so the frowning eyebrows didn't make it noticeably more forbidding. How old was he? Mid-forties? It was hard to tell. His reddish face was lined and weatherbeaten but that meant nothing. Neither did his rusty hair.

'You didn't fancy the pub then?' I asked, wondering if we were going to drive all the way to Glasgow in silence.

'No.'

More silence. I looked round the inside of the car. It was battered but not that old. Clean too, although it bore traces of heavy use.

'Too noisy.' I ventured another shot at a conversation.

'Aye. I'm not a great one for gab. Especially the sort of blether this lot do. We've done our jobs. Done them fine. I don't need to talk about it for hours as well.'

'Ah. OK.'

'Besides, I'm an alcoholic.'

He shot me a look and emitted an explosive bark which I realised was a laugh.

'Did I shock you? I'm not one for minding my mouth. I go to the pub with the lads from time to time. Drink pints of water. But not tonight. I'm tired and I've had a few scary moments today. The demons are always waiting.'

He didn't ask me why I hadn't wanted to go to the pub.

'I might have a few problems like that myself,' I said.

He thought about what I'd said before he replied.

'Aye. Many people do.'

There was a kindness in his voice that softened its harsh tones.

So I told him. Told him about the itches in my blood that I'd thought I'd conquered. But had turned out to be merely dormant. Like the unseen woodworm eating Ma's table in Tregonna and leaving holes in its fabric. The urge to climb, to risk, to feel the thrill ripple ice-cold through my blood had woken. And the only way I could keep a lid on it was to exhaust myself. It would be far worse to deny it. Because the only thing that came close to it was cocaine. And I'd been there, done that and managed to struggle out of the other side. I wasn't going back in.

'Not alcohol, then,' he asked.

'Not so much. It loosens me, though. And I'm afraid of what I might do when I'm not on my guard.'

Fergus dropped me at a climbing gym and once I'd filled out the registration forms and convinced them I was safe to climb unsupervised, I spent a couple of hours pushing my body to its limits, despite a few twinges from my bruised foot. It was the only way. The only way to avoid lying awake for hours at night with thoughts I couldn't bear running through my head until I was ready to do anything – anything – to silence them.

Fergus had understood although he'd been shocked the afternoon on the crag at Auchinstarry hadn't tired me out. But it hadn't. I'd spent the last two nights on the rock since I got home from France. Hours and hours climbing the cliffs of my childhood until my muscles trembled with fatigue and sweat coated my body despite the night air's chill. And then home. Home to creep into bed and lose myself in a few hours' oblivion.

Finally, I headed back to reception to collect my bag from a locker. Two police officers were there while a member of staff dabbed at a cut on the head of the guy who'd checked me in. Some young thug had done it, one of the police officers told me, when he'd been caught cutting through the locker padlocks. Skinny lad. He'd got away on a scooter. A small group of other climbers stood by the swinging locker doors.

My locker was one of the ones he'd forced, but my bag was still there. Opened, though. I checked it. My phone was missing.

Shit.

I told the police and asked if I could use the gym phone to report it stolen. A walkie-talkie crackled into life and one of the officers put up his hand.

'Hang on. I think the wee bastard has dumped everything. Aye, he has.'

I resigned myself to a few hours of form-filling at a police station to get my phone back but for once I was lucky. Another officer arrived with a rucksack containing the phones. We each picked ours, proved to the police they belonged to us by putting in passwords or using fingerprint recognition and were free to go. I suspected they didn't fancy the form-filling either and, as the youngster had got away, there wasn't much point.

Fergus was still outside.

'I thought I'd give you a lift to your hotel,' he said.

'Actually, I haven't found one yet.'

'Aye. Thought so. I've spoken to my daughter. She's living with me at the moment. We've a wee spare room and if you want to stay with us tonight, it's fine. And, of course, she'll be there. If you were worried I...'

I had no worries about Fergus and I was ready to sleep.

'Thank you. I'd like that.'

Thirteen

I woke early. And lay for a few minutes, listening to Fergus and his daughter, Tam, chatting in the kitchen. His marriage, I'd gathered, had failed because of his drinking. But since he'd become sober he'd rebuilt a few bridges, he told me, and was on friendly terms with his wife. He was clearly close to Tam, given that she was living with him while she saved for a flat of her own. A short woman of my own age with glasses and pale, red hair caught untidily back in a large clasp, she and I had said *Hi* briefly last night before I went straight to bed and let my tiredness drag me down into glorious sleep. Fergus had said they were both heading off early to a film shoot – Tam worked as a make-up artist – so I stayed in bed, dealing with the returning memories as I did every morning.

Nick was dead.

It was probably my fault.

My life was shit.

I wanted something to help me forget.

In a nutshell.

I told myself to get a grip. There were people in far worse situations than me. Got out of bed and went to the kitchen, put the kettle on, found the tea and a mug. Once I'd made it, I sat at the small table by the window. It looked out over the back gardens of the row of tenements that contained Fergus's flat. His was on the top floor, with high ceilings and large rooms. Things he told me were typical of tenement flats when I'd commented last night.

A woman in a dressing gown appeared with a dog in one of the gardens below. She pulled at the petals of an overblown rose as she waited for it to pee. Day was starting. Time to think positively. Today I was going to make Duncan stop Basset.

I googled Pierre Basset. I'd done it a lot since Calais. That and climb the cliffs without ropes at night. Neither were good things to be doing. But I couldn't help myself. Nothing new in my search except a brief newspaper article.

Des gendarmes en mode pédagogie was the headline. *Police officers in educational mode*, according to Google translate. The article explained how the gendarmes had visited a local school to discuss road safety. The photo showed Basset and another officer standing by a young boy who was holding a certificate. The other officer was shaking the boy's hand but Basset's eyes were staring into the camera. If you looked hard enough you could see he had his hand on the boy's shoulder.

It made my skin crawl.

I took a screenshot of the article and the photo. And then a close-up of Basset's face. I'd show them to Duncan.

Then called Angel again. His mobile went straight to voicemail. As I was thinking of trying the bar, a text from Vince arrived.

Glasgow Botanic Gardens. 9.30 am. Queen Margaret Drive entrance. Just me and Charlie. Issy not coming.

According to my phone, the Botanic Gardens wasn't far from Fergus's flat, nor from Byres Road where I was meeting Duncan. Perfect.

I arrived early and hung about between a couple of redbrick lodge buildings by the gates, wondering why Pa and Vince were doing location research in this ever so middle-class-looking park. Pa was startled to see me. Clearly Vince hadn't mentioned I might be coming along. Also a bit shifty. As well he might.

'Great to see you,' he said, avoiding my eyes and reaching out his arms to hug me.

I dodged the embrace. Easy enough as he was so much taller than me.

'Look, Pa,' I started. 'About Tregonna.'

There was no point trying to sweet talk him. I was going to give it to him with both barrels. He owed Ma this. He'd waltzed off to do his own thing all those years ago and left her to bring Kit and me up. And after yesterday, he owed me too. I'd got him out of the shit, big time. And I was quite prepared to spell it out if I had to.

'Wait,' he said. There was an unusual lack of confidence in his voice. 'Give us a minute, Vince.'

'Sure, I'll be over by the station.'

Pa looked tired. Like I said, he was tall, almost lanky, with long limbs. Not the best physique for a climber. But he was super fit. You could see it in the way he moved. Easy, supple and in full control of his legs and arms. Not at the moment, though. He shifted his weight from foot to foot as though he couldn't find his balance.

'We're all over social media, you know? Or you are, anyway.'

'What?'

'There's a lot of interest locally because the cast includes some starry names. Some idiot shot you diving into the loch and plastered it everywhere, hinting that something went wrong. The production company have had to issue a statement, saying the dive was all part of a thoroughly planned and rehearsed stunt.'

I laughed. I couldn't help myself.

'And I've had journalists calling me to find out what happened. They might call you.'

He looked doubtful.

'I'm not going to say anything,' I said. 'But, Pa —'

He cut me off. 'Morwenna can take as much time as she needs.'

'Really?'

'Well, a reasonable amount of time. How long do you think is reasonable?'

I reassessed at speed.

'A couple of years...'

Thoughts chased themselves across his face. 'OK.'

I hadn't expected it to be this easy. Guilt? Or something else?

'You'll tell your solicitors? Get them to write to Ma's?' I didn't ask if he'd told Issy.

'Yes. I'm going to London in a couple of days. I'll see my solicitors then. I've resigned from the film, you see. Vince will do a perfectly good job without me. Too many other things on my plate. I'm not thinking clearly. If I was, yesterday would never have happened.'

I realised this was the closest he was going to get to apologising.

'Anyway, I've had an interesting offer.' His eyes lit up. 'And if it's as good as it sounds, I'm going to do it. I'm heading for London to discuss leading an expedition to Greenland. East Greenland. The chance to tackle a few virgin climbs. Explore some new routes.'

He started talking about fjords and granite towers and peaks, all with long and strange names.

East Greenland. I'd never been. I'd have liked to go. What climber wouldn't? Beautiful and wild. And full of spectacular walls and cliffs. Many of them dwarfing the ones in Yosemite. Some of them still unclimbed. They call it the world's last great climbing frontier. It was a fantastic opportunity. And probably Pa's last chance for something so important.

'You could come with me, Jen. I'm sure I could wangle it.'

His words scattered my thoughts. I'd love to. Oh gods above, how I'd love to. Pictures raced through my head. Craggy outcrops of granite poking through green-grey lichen and snow. Slopes swooping down to meet the milky blue waters of the fjords broken only by the white of small icebergs. Days spent on the rock. Thinking of nothing but the next climb. Walking on land few people had walked on before me. Waking in the morning and seeing nothing but mountains for miles. No people. No buildings. No noise.

Nothing to remind me of what I'd lost.

Except I couldn't. I knew I couldn't. Of course, I couldn't.

'Maybe,' I said. 'Let me know when plans are more advanced.'

I told myself it was a good idea to keep in with Pa and that was why I hadn't refused.

'I will but keep it quiet for the moment. I don't want anyone to know.'

It crossed my mind this might include Issy. Pa disappearing to East Greenland wouldn't fit in with their plans for the lodge. Then because I wanted this discussion to end before I gave in completely. 'What are you and Vince doing here? There's not much opportunity for climbing. Except for a few trees.'

'That's where you're wrong. Come and see.'

I checked my phone. I had time before my meeting with Duncan so I followed him down a side path until we reached a metal-fenced walkway running over a passage cut deep into the ground. Vince was there, looking over the railings and chatting to an elderly woman who tugged at the lead of her shaggy-haired terrier to stop him nipping Vince in between sentences.

A sign fixed to the railings explained that we were looking down into the ventilation shafts to the old Botanic Gardens Station, once part of the Glasgow Central Line but long since closed down.

'It's below us,' Vince said unnecessarily. 'An abandoned railway line runs under the park. You can see the old station platform.'

I looked over the railings and down into a deep cutting. It was amazingly green. Plants had forced their way through the fence and trailed over the stone walls and moss-lined concrete beams that kept the roof of the old station open to the air. Below, shrubs and flowers had taken advantage of the sunlight and colonised what must have been the railway track, although the lines and sleepers were long gone.

The terrier lunged at Vince's ankles and the woman left, dragging the dog after her.

'She told me Glasgow's riddled with old tunnels. But then most cities are,' Vince said. 'Railways and, of course, old rivers gradually gone underground.'

I knew this. I'd gone exploring with the Urbex madmen who make it a point of honour to break in and visit otherwise abandoned buildings and sites. With their *'leave no traces behind, take only photos'* philosophy. Many of them went underground too, exploring railway and sewage tunnels, and forgotten rivers that had been culverted so roads and buildings could pass easily over them. But there I'd drawn the line. I hate dark, enclosed places. I'm always frightened the bricks and concrete above will crumble and engulf me.

'The plot has our hero captured,' Vince went on. 'Then tied up and left to die in an old, abandoned tunnel under Glasgow. This one looks too pleasant. We need somewhere grim and claustrophobic but we'll take a quick look now we're here.'

I shuddered.

'It's grim enough for me.'

'Luckily our hero is made of stronger stuff. He manages to untie himself and wanders round before climbing up a ventilation shaft and shocking everyone when he emerges.'

I laughed. 'Why didn't the baddies just shoot him rather than leave him to escape?'

'There wouldn't be a film if they had because that's the beginning,' Vince said. 'Anyway the intricacies of the plot are above our pay grade, aren't they, Charlie?'

But Pa kicked at the gravel on the path and didn't reply. His phone rang.

'I'm going to have to answer this.' He walked away.

'We're just looking for somewhere the hero might feasibly be able to climb out of.'

'It would be easy enough here.' I pointed to the convenient concrete beams. The bracelet Rania had made for me, always a little big, slipped off my wrist and dropped onto the old track below.

'Shit.'

'Something important?'

'Yes. But never mind.'

'I'll have a look for it when we go down.'

'Are you climbing in?'

'Someone from the council is coming to let us in. There's access at the other side of the park,' He glanced at his watch. 'We should head over there soon.'

Pa was still on the phone.

'Charlie. We need to make a move.' Vince tapped his watch. Pa finished and we joined him.

'I'm heading off, Pa.' I'd got what I'd come for, so I didn't want to stay. Especially if it meant poking around in dark tunnels.

'OK.'

We stood there. One of those moments when the weight of all the things between you makes you dumb.

'Bye,' I said.

'I'll let you know. About what we discussed. You'd be very useful, you know.'

And, just like that, the years fell away and I was back climbing the coastal cliffs near Tregonna with Pa. I felt the sun-warmed granite and heard the waves slosh against the rock beneath us. Seagulls quarrelled above. *Not bad*. He'd said when we reached the top. *Not bad, at all. You're becoming quite a useful climber*. I'd been twelve or thereabouts and full of pleasure. Even then I'd known this was the highest praise Pa ever dished out.

I walked back towards the glass domes of some greenhouses and found a bench. Called Ma and told her the good news. The thought of everything we'd have to do to make Ma's plan work was a bit daunting, though.

'We've got a year to get ourselves sorted, so you need to get moving.' I lied a bit. I didn't want her to hang about.

'Has Charlie actually told his solicitors? That will be the first thing Mr Penrose asks.'

'No, but he will. He's off to London soon. He said he'd see them then.'

'He can be tricky, you know. He needs the money for some grand project he's got.'

'Maybe not.' And I told her about the East Greenland expedition and how I suspected Pa was going to use it to walk away from Issy and everything else. Her reaction surprised me.

'Poor woman,' she said. 'Charlie wasn't meant to be in a relationship. The gods gave him great gifts. He was meant to inspire others by his deeds but not to let them close. Still that's her voyage of discovery.'

And then we chatted for a while. Or rather she did. Telling me little details of their day. Rania kept on talking about learning to climb. I told Ma to ring a friend of mine who did classes at the local gym and organise it.

'How is she?'

'Unhappier. Crying at night. She's sleeping in my room.'

'I'm sorry.'

112

'The sadness and the weeping are not bad things.'

'I'll be back soon,' I said. 'I've got to see someone first. How's Yasmiin?'

Ma was slow to reply. 'Yasmiin'll be fine.'

But she didn't sound sure. Yasmiin had opened up a little about everything that had happened. Ma didn't go into too much detail but I gathered the shelter she'd gone to in London was fine in every respect except one. It was a magnet for predators. And Yasmiin had been taken in by one of them.

In the background I heard Rania call her name.

'One minute,' she called back to Rania and then to me, 'I've just thought of something. Yasmiin said to tell you she'd remembered Leila's surname. Leila paid by card in the shop where they bought their clothes and Yasmiin saw the name on it then. Samaan. Leila Samaan.' She spelled it out.

I stared at a rose bed after Ma had gone and thought about Leila. Someone came and sat next to me. A youngster. Skinny, pale and scabby round his nose, where it was punctured with jewellery. It wasn't a great look but then neither were his bitten nails and their black varnish.

He stared at me. I stared back, then got up and left. I couldn't concentrate with his eyes sliding all over me. I mean, I'd rather have smacked him in the face than walked away but some inner caution told me it might be a bad idea.

I found another bench in a little sunken garden away from the main path and started exploring on my phone.

There were surprisingly few Leila Samaans in the UK, at least Leila Samaans whose name was written the same way as Ma had spelled out. If I was right and she was working undercover, I was surprised they hadn't chosen a more common name. Maybe they'd used a real person. Wasn't that what they did? Looked for babies who'd died and used their names?

Maybe I was wrong. Maybe she wasn't undercover. I started clicking through the pictures of all the different Leila Samaans, looking for one who might be young enough, but realised my battery was very low. I hadn't charged it last night. Plus I'd left my charge pack at Fergus's. It was time to meet Duncan anyway. I'd sort the phone later.

I stood and looked for someone to ask the way to Byres Road. The skinny youngster with the piercings from earlier was still hanging around. He walked towards me and as he approached his eyes flicked to my phone. Some sixth sense warned me. He was quick. I'll give him that. I whirled round as he grabbed at my phone and punched him before he could seize it, then ran. Ran back to the entrance. When I turned to look behind me, he wasn't there.

Just a nasty little thief. Well, he'd picked the wrong person to mess with.

I asked a kind-looking woman in a headscarf the way to Byres Road.

Fourteen

Waterstones café, where Duncan had told me to meet him, occupied a small area at the front of the shop with a counter between it and the bookshelves. I tried to remember the last book I'd actually had time to read from beginning to end. Duncan was waiting. Not in uniform but wearing jeans and a white polo shirt that emphasised his broad neck and shoulders. His squareness made me think of Nick again. I focused on why I was there.

Stop Basset.

'I didn't know if you'd want tea or coffee,' Duncan said as I slipped into the bench facing him. 'So I got both. I don't have a lot of time.'

His face was shuttered and I had no idea what he was thinking. The café was full but the buzz of chatter made it easy to speak without being overheard. I swallowed a big mouthful of tea, felt its warmth soak into me and started. I told him how Nick and I had met up on his last assignment. I didn't give him any details. I thought I probably shouldn't and, anyway, they weren't important. But I said enough for him to know that Nick and I had been close. Friends, at least.

'Jamie and I,' I went on and then, because I couldn't bear it any longer, 'Look, I can't call him Jamie. I knew him as Nick.'

He nodded.

'So Nick and I, we ended up together in Calais. Things got chaotic and we went our separate ways. I didn't know what had happened to him.'

He started to interrupt me but I spoke over him.

'No, let me finish. Then Angel told me he was dead. I suspected the worst. I thought it might be my fault.'

And because I needed Duncan to know about the child-trafficking, I told him a little about Rania and the danger she'd been in and how Nick had helped rescue her. How he'd come back for us both. And how I was very afraid it had led to his death.

'So I needed to know how his life had finished. How he'd died. You understand that?'

He nodded.

'You couldn't tell us much so Angel and I, we went to Calais, to the gendarmerie to find out some more.'

'And did you?' His face was utterly blank.

'No. Or at least nothing you hadn't told us.'

'I see.'

'But here's the thing. I recognised the gendarme – the one in charge, the one you must have met too.'

And I told him the whole saga about the money changing hands at the lighthouse and how I'd known straightaway Basset was the same man. That he was a child-trafficker.

Nothing on Duncan's face showed if he believed me or not. On the contrary, he looked sometimes as though he was barely listening but conducting an internal dialogue about something else.

'You can't be sure,' he said when I finally ground to a halt.

'I am. His face is burnt into my brain.'

But Duncan shook his head.

'Basset was keen to see us, you know. He asked lots of questions about Nick. Why would he do that if he wasn't involved with something illegal?'

'Lots of reasons. It means nothing.'

I was losing him.

'But he called me Jenifry. I'd only used Jen. I think he worked out I was the woman Nick's boss interviewed. I think he suspected Nick was working undercover and he knew I was trying to find out how he'd died. I think he killed Nick. Or his men did. On his orders.'

'You can't be sure. You can't be sure of any of this.'

'Not about killing Nick. No. Except Basset is a gendarme and a gendarme would have been the first to learn someone was working undercover in Calais. Especially a gendarme involved in child-trafficking. He'd have been alert for the slightest sign of anything suspicious. He needs to be dealt with. Or at the very least looked into.'

'It's not always that simple.'

'What's not that simple?' Anger flared inside me. 'You have to stop him. I want him stopped. I want him in prison. Before he takes any more children.'

I remembered the screenshots I'd made of the article with Basset's face so clear.

'Look.' I seized my phone. But it was dead. I should have charged it up as soon as I got here.

'OK, I'll think about –'

Fury overwhelmed me.

'Don't bother, I'll do it myself. I thought, as Nick's cousin, you'd be as desperate as I am to see Basset brought to justice, especially as there's every possibility he was involved in Nick's death. My mistake. Never mind. I'll find a way.' A thought came to me. 'I'll go back to Calais and I'll report him myself. I'll make his life hell.'

'No. You mustn't do that.'

'Why not?'

He stood up.

'Not here. Come on.' And he strode out without another word, turning at the café entrance and beckoning me forcibly.

What was going on?

I followed him into the street. He walked fast, staring at the ground, oblivious to the people weaving round him. I wasn't even sure he knew I was there until he dived down into Hillhead subway station, stopped at the ticket machine and bought two tickets, one of which he handed to me.

We went down to the platform, to its far end, where he sat on a bench. I sat next to him.

'What is it?' I said. 'What's going on?'

'Let me think.'

A train arrived, disgorged a stream of passengers and swept up the ones waiting. Latecomers clattered down the steps and squeezed in through the closing doors. The train heaved itself into motion and rattled away into the tunnel. Then the platform was empty.

'Jamie and I used to come here,' Duncan said. 'On Saturdays when we were teenagers and his dad was working. If the weather was good, we'd go to Pollok Park or the Botanic Gardens or up to the canal. And if it rained – which it often did – we'd go to Kelvingrove Museum and look at the stuffed elephant, or we'd come down into the Subway and go round and round, reading or talking or playing at being spies. You know following people and the like. Typical boy stuff.'

He gave a sharp laugh then fell silent.

'Duncan,' I said after a while. 'What are we doing here?'

'Jamie…' He hesitated. 'I don't know what to do. I really don't know what's for the best. The thing is…'

The thing is. The thing is what? What was Duncan having such trouble trying to say?

'Jamie is alive.'

It made no sense. What did *alive* mean. My brain came up with *not dead*. That made more sense. Not dead. Nick wasn't dead. Nick was alive.

'Alive?'

'Aye.'

A train came in on the opposite side.

Alive…

I hugged the word and its meaning. Let it sink into my blood. Somewhere out there Nick was alive. Maybe he too was sitting in some quietish corner of a busy place staring at a row of posters advertising a music festival in a park nearby.

'But why –?'

'Your turn to listen.'

Duncan had been heading back from seeing his mother in Helensburgh one Sunday several weeks ago – he always went on a Sunday unless he was working – when Nick had flagged him down on a quiet stretch of road, a shortcut only known to locals. Nick had been waiting for him.

'I didn't know he was supposed to be dead when he stopped me. I was so used to him disappearing off the radar for months at a time. He told me the job he'd been on had ended in chaos and confusion. And he'd been caught.'

'Did he say who caught him?'

'No. But it was in Calais. You were right about that. He told me he'd been very lucky. A one in a million chance had saved him. That and the fact the smugglers wanted his death to look like an accident. They wanted him drowned. No bullets. No knife wounds. So they dumped him in the Channel but he was picked up.'

A peace settled through me. Those awful images of Nick desperately trying to keep his head above a dark and raging sea would no longer keep me awake. Someone had found him.

'It was vital the smugglers thought he was dead,' Duncan went on. 'That's why he was waiting for me in secret. He needed me to help him. He said that when a convenient body washed up, it would be identified as his. As Jamie Kincaid's. And he needed someone from his family to collect it from Calais and, if necessary, to confirm it was his.' He swallowed. 'I was glad I didn't actually have to look at the body, though. Jamie told me I wasn't to reveal the truth to anyone. Not a word. Not a gesture.'

'I understand.'

And I did. Honestly I did. Although my fists clenched with the urge to punch Nick. How could he have done this to me?

'Even you,' Duncan said.

'He spoke about me?'

'He said I'd find it real hard not to tell anyone. Particularly not to tell my mam, nor Angel from Spain, nor you. But I had to. Someone might be watching us. And believing he was dead was the best way to make sure none of you gave the truth away.'

He stared past me and I wondered if he was remembering the conversation with Nick. Probably. I thought his face had looked then like it did now. Blank and with clusters of sweat gathering in the hollows at his temples and below his hairline.

I felt quite sorry for him.

'It's fine,' I lied.

'I've only told you now because... Well, Jamie said you and Angel would come to the funeral in Glasgow and give me the third degree about his death. And he thought you might go to Calais to find out more. It would be normal for you. And that was fine because they wanted everyone to think Jamie had been undercover but was dead. But you mustn't go stirring things up in Calais now. Especially not with the French police. You could jeopardise the assignment and put Jamie in great danger. I don't think you should have come to Glasgow again.'

'What assignment? Is he after Basset? And why do I need to keep away from Glasgow?'

Duncan tightened his mouth and I knew he was going to be stupid and stubborn about telling me.

'Listen. I've been through hell for the last week or so. You've told me he's alive now. Well, that's great but it's not enough. Not after all this. And certainly not enough to make me crawl home and wait patiently for him to get in touch. No, you can tell me what he's up to. Or as much as you know. What does it matter now?'

He laughed. A bit croaky but definitely a laugh and for a brief moment I saw the grinning boy in the photo with Nick.

'Ach, I'd love to tell you everything. It'd be a relief. I feel like I've been living in a dark bubble. And I can't bear to be with Mam. She's...' He shook his head. 'You're right there. It's not fair on you all.'

'So tell me.'

A few people had come down onto the platform for the next train. A tired-looking man, carrying supermarket bags of food, put his shopping on the seat next to Duncan. He wasn't close enough to hear us but Duncan shuffled to the end of the bench.

'Jamie said there were three people he trusted enough to ask them to identify the body as him. Angel, me and you. He chose me because he needed me to do something else as well but he trusted you, so I will too. He needed to meet with someone. Someone in the Glasgow Police force. I could arrange it for him.'

A train came in. The man collected his shopping and got on. Duncan waited a few seconds for the departing passengers to clear the platform.

'He wanted to meet with Sandy. He's a DCI in Glasgow. He was a pal of Jamie's dad and he looked out for us both. Mentored us when we were at Police College. You saw him at the wake. Mam had a go at him.'

I remembered the angry and grieving man storming out of Duncan's mother's flat, followed by his wife and son, Xander. No wonder he'd looked angry if he knew Nick was alive and Duncan's mother was blaming him for something that wasn't true.

'You mean Xander's father? Xander who I spoke to at the wake?'

'Aye. Sandy knows everything about who's up to what in Glasgow. He's worked for the Glasgow Police for thirty years. Jamie wanted information about the local drugs business and there's not much Sandy doesn't know about the families running it. Jamie was going undercover here. Sandy could give him all sorts of insights into where he could start to infiltrate and the characters of the main players – the sort of person who would appeal to them, where they operate, their little foibles and who is pally with whom. He knows them all you see. Probably knew their parents.'

Another train arrived, filling the platform with noise. We both fell silent. The picture Duncan's words had painted was troubling. Duncan could have been talking about Sandy's friends rather than the criminals he was employed to put away.

The train left. Once again the platform was empty.

'In Glasgow?' I said. 'Is Nick in Glasgow?'

Duncan nodded. 'So I don't think it's a good idea for you to be here.'

Nick was in Glasgow. He was walking these streets. Probably using these very trains to get around.

'Isn't Nick the last person who should be doing this? With his connections to Glasgow? Someone might recognise him.'

'I thought that. But he said he could change how he looked. That not even I would recognise him if I met him.'

It still seemed unspeakably dangerous to me.

'He said he was the only person who could do the assignment.'

'Why?'

'He didn't say. The only thing he told me was that someone is using the migrant boats to bring drugs into the country. At Calais.'

I remembered Yasmiin telling me about the men who'd slipped down the beach after the boat had landed in England and after the police had picked up the refugees. How they'd removed packages taped to its hull. Why bring in one paying cargo when you could bring in two?

'And Jamie knew a large number of the consignments were ending up here. He uncovered a link when he was in Calais. A link in a chain that led from Calais all the way to Glasgow.'

'Basset?'

'Ach, I don't think so. The chain Jamie wanted to uncover followed drug shipments to the local organised crime groups. The OCGs. Nothing to do with child-trafficking. Although the OCGs will do anything profitable.'

Drugs. Drugs and terrorism. It was all Nick's department cared about. What about the people-traffickers? The child-traffickers? The children with no one to stop them being abused?

'All this for a few drugs,' I said.

'You have no idea what you're talking about. None whatsoever. Drugs are behind most of the crime we deal with.'

'Maybe'

'There's no maybe about it. And it's not just petty stuff like users stealing to fund their habit. It's a big business and it's run exactly like a business. They're into selling guns and money laundering. Anything to make money and keep it. Maybe child-trafficking. They're certainly involved in trafficking adults. They've got their dirty fingers everywhere.'

A train sped into the station and opened its doors. People surged past us. I watched them, scanning each face in turn. In case one of them was Nick. Because they could be. One of them could be him. It was possible now. A group of schoolchildren got off the train, all with backpacks and chattering excitedly. Off on a school trip.

'How old do you think these bairns are?' Duncan's voice penetrated my thoughts.

'Nine?' I said. I'd got better at guessing since living with Rania and Aya.

'I guarantee some of them are already being drawn into the drug business – delivery boys or lookouts. And there's nothing we can do about it. We try. We take down one OCG and another one takes over. That's if the first one doesn't continue operating their business from inside prison.'

He carried on talking about the corruption that was endemic in the prison system and elsewhere. Local councillors, the CPS and, of course, the police themselves. I sort of knew this but it was depressing to have it confirmed so vehemently by a serving police officer.

'How long have you been in Glasgow?' he asked suddenly.

'Barely twenty-four hours.' It seemed longer.

'Well, if you leave straightaway, they probably won't even know you've been here.'

'OK.'

'I need to get the next train. I'm late already. Look –'

I jumped in. 'Don't tell me I need to keep this quiet. Believe me, I know. I won't breathe a word to anyone.'

He looked as though he'd have liked to tell me anyway but the rumbling of a train approaching stopped him.

'You've got to do something about Basset, though.'

He looked doubtful.

'If you won't, I will.'

'Ach, I'll do my best but I need to be careful.' He stood. 'My phone might be hacked. Call me if you want, but remember that.'

'Can they listen in to us talking?'

'It's possible. But there's no connectivity in the Subway. That's why I came here. Give me twenty minutes before you leave. I'm fairly sure we weren't followed but you can never be too careful.'

Fifteen

I watched the train depart. And the next one and a couple after that. I didn't want to leave the station. Wanted to stay in this warm, bright cocoon, and glory in the knowledge that Nick was alive.

But eventually I knew I had to go back into the world. What then?

Back to Fergus's to pack, then go home to Cornwall, of course. As quickly as possible. In the hope no one had noticed I was in Glasgow.

I remembered Pa telling me how I'd been splashed all over social media, diving into the loch at Auchinstarry. Shit. That hadn't been one of my better decisions. I thought he'd said they'd mentioned me by name. Double shit. I needed to check.

Except my phone had died.

I went back to Waterstones, found a seat with a socket. My phone buzzed into life. It wasn't difficult to find. **Daring rock climber dives into Loch Auchinstarry**, someone had written, with a video that was a bit clearer than Pa had led me to believe. It was a beautiful dive.

You really wouldn't have known who it was, if they hadn't mentioned my name.

Jen Shaw shows she's a chip off the old block with this stunning dive up at Loch Auchinstarry. Word is she and her dad, the great Charlie Shaw, are working together on the latest Jason Statham blockbuster filming in the UK at the moment. So expect some excitement when it comes out!

I wasn't working on the film but it was no bad thing they'd said that. It gave me a reason for being here. A reason that had nothing to do with Nick. So probably no harm done, provided I went home now and kept away from Glasgow. And Calais...

Except Calais rankled. Basset was still free. And able to continue his vile trade. I wasn't sure Duncan was going to succeed in stopping him.

I should call Angel. What was I going to say? I didn't have it in me to keep pretending Nick was dead with him. Sod the lot of them with their mistrust and secrecy, I was going to tell Angel. Not on the phone, though. I'd have to go and see him. Nothing suspicious about that. Grieving friends spending time together etc. And we could also discuss Basset.

There was no answer from his mobile so I tried the number for the bar. It rang out for ages but neither Angel nor any of his staff ever picked up when they were busy. Just as I was about to give up someone did answer. An elderly voice, thick with accent, jabbered a few words in Spanish at me.

'Is Angel there? Could I speak to Angel? Angel?'

Silence while the owner of the voice took in what I'd said. Finally he spoke.

'Away. Gone away.'

'When will he be back?'

Another silence.

'Long time. *No lo sé.*'

No lo sé meant I don't know. One of the few Spanish phrases I did know.

And then he hung up.

Had Angel really gone away? Or was he avoiding me?

I drank my tea and wondered. I didn't think he'd refuse to

speak to me. He was too kind. I was worried he'd decided not to wait until I could get hold of Duncan and gone to Calais to take matters into his own hands.

Shit.

I called his mobile again and left a short message saying I needed to come and see him. Nothing more.

My battery was still low but it would last me back to Fergus's if I closed everything unnecessary. I swiped away the video of me diving into the lock and stopped.

A photo of a girl looked up at me from the screen. In sports kit and clutching a tennis racket and a shield. She looked very like Leila. Much younger than when I'd met her but very similar. And when I clicked on the picture, I was taken to Glenbrae Tennis Club's website and the announcement that L. Samaan had won the club's annual junior league.

Why was the picture on my phone? Of course. I'd been scrolling through pictures of people called Leila Samaan before I'd gone to meet Duncan.

L. Samaan? Leila? Was she the same person? I dug deeper. Luckily for me, Leila Samaan had been an outstanding tennis player. Good enough to win Glasgow competitions and finally, seven years ago, to come second in the Junior Scotland Open in the under-fourteen age group.

A photo of her, grinning as she stood next to the winner who'd narrowly beaten her in the final, confirmed what I thought. The Leila on the beach and the Leila who was an ace tennis player were one and the same person.

I could find nothing more recent.

What had happened? How had the Leila of seven years ago with the slightly goofy grin revealing teeth covered by braces become the quick-witted woman on a Calais beach with a gun and the confidence to use it several weeks ago.

127

I bought another tea and thought. Maybe the pictures weren't real. Maybe they were faked and planted to back up Leila's cover story. Maybe I was right and she'd been working undercover too. But maybe not. And if Leila was a real person, she had information that would help us. She'd definitely been in with the smugglers. She might know something about Basset. Something that would help to take him out of the game.

And I was curious.

I discovered a Rami Samaan living in Bearsden, not far from the Glenbrae Tennis Club. In a modern villa set well back from the road and surrounded by high hedges and trees according to Google Earth. Whoever he was, Rami Samaan had done well for himself.

I'd go to Bearsden to the tennis club and then have a look at his house and see what I could find out about the mysterious Leila. It would only take me a couple of hours. Afterwards, I'd do exactly as Duncan had said and get out of Glasgow.

The tennis club had closed down. It had never been more than a couple of courts and a hut. Now weeds had pushed through the ground and a sign on the padlocked and chained gate informed anyone who was interested that the nearest tennis courts were in Jubilee Gardens.

Perhaps I was right about the cover story. It would be easy enough to fake a website for a defunct local tennis club.

Nevertheless I headed over to Rami Samaan's house. It wasn't far, in a quiet road of huge houses, all hiding behind walls or hedges and trees. Not the sort of place where you'd come across a chatty neighbour in a garden. In fact, there wasn't anybody much about. A loitering pedestrian like me stuck out like a sore thumb.

I walked back to some shops I'd seen and bought a bouquet of flowers, traipsed back to Rami's road and buzzed on next door's gate. No answer. A woman was in the house on the other side but she was an au pair recently arrived from somewhere in Eastern Europe I guessed from her accent. I gave up on her quickly.

I struck gold opposite.

An elderly woman wearing a floral overall – who knew people still did? – opened the door. Her face lit up when she saw the flowers.

'How lovely,' she exclaimed.

'Samaan?' I said.

'No. They live opposite.' She looked disappointed.

'No number on the label,' I said by way of explanation.

'I suppose they're for Jalila. I doubt there'll be anyone in, though. They all work.'

I stored the name away. Jalila. Probably Rami's wife.

'No, they're for Leila. Leila Samaan.'

'Must be the daughter. I didn't catch her name.'

I risked a question that no delivery person would ever ask but nothing ventured, nothing gained.

'Do you know them?'

'Not really. I don't live here, you see. I'm housesitting for my son and his wife while they're on holiday. Feeding the cat, you know. They don't like to leave the house empty. There are a lot of burglaries in this neck of the woods. Hardly surprising when you know how expensive the houses are.'

'They look very pricey.'

She seemed keen to chat and I guessed that she was a little bored all alone in the house with only the cat for company.

'Oh heavens, yes. My daughter-in-law's parents are very well-to-do. They helped them buy this.'

'I suppose the Samaans are well-off then.'

'Quite the success story, they are. Richard, that's my son, says. He took me over and introduced me. They're neighbourly and

Richard said to go to them if I had any worries. Nice family. Rami and Jalila and a son and daughter. Mr Samaan runs a company. IT. Something to do with building management but Richard says he's working on other... applications. My son, he works for IBM, so he's very up on that kind of thing. My other son is a doctor.'

And then she started to chat about her family. I couldn't see any way of getting her back to the Samaans so I waited until an appropriate moment and said goodbye.

I pressed the buzzer by the Samaans' gate. I was sure I could get over their wall but it would be as well to check the house was empty first. Someone answered, though.

'Delivery,' I said. Why not? I had flowers.

Whoever was on the other end opened the gates for me and I walked up the gravelled drive. The house was even bigger than I'd realised from the road. Big enough to warrant cleaners at the very least. Maybe I'd be lucky again and get a chance to talk to a bored and chatty cleaner.

But the young woman waiting at the front door wasn't a cleaner. She wore a hijab along with jeans and a short tunic and clutched a tissue to her nose. The daughter? But not Leila.

I held out the flowers. And had another brainwave.

'Samaan. Leila Samaan.'

The hand she'd reached out to take the flowers dropped like a stone.

'No,' she said. 'No. I mean, no one of that name here.' And then, after a pause, 'Who are they from?'

I pulled out my phone and pretended to look at it.

'Sorry. I meant Jalila. Jalila Samaan. That's who they're for. No information who they're from. There'll be a card inside.'

I thrust the flowers into her hands and left. The epitome of the busy and uncaring delivery person. Back at the gates, I pressed the button to open them but peeled off into the shrubbery and waited. After a few minutes they closed with me still inside. Something about the emotion that had flared in the young woman's eyes when I'd said the name Leila stopped me from walking away.

I spent an exciting afternoon (not) exploring the Samaans' garden. I learned little except that, if they were employing gardeners, they were wasting their money. All the shrubs and trees needed pruning.

No one came in or went out of the house until early evening when, from my vantage point behind a leggy rhododendron, I saw a motorbike and two cars arrive shortly after each other. Clearly the family. Jalila in one car, and a middle-aged man I guessed was Rami in the other. The younger man on the motorbike must be the son.

All was quiet for a couple of hours and I began to think I should leave. I was fairly sure I could get back in whenever I wanted. Then the parents and the daughter I'd given the flowers to came out of the house and got into Rami's car. They left. The son followed shortly afterwards and went to his motorbike. My phone rang.

Shit. The son looked up. Had he heard?

I rejected the call.

The son looked around for a couple of seconds, then put his helmet on and went too. I waited until the gates had shut and walked round the outside of the house peering in through the windows. All the rooms seemed empty.

My phone buzzed. A voicemail.

Jen. It's Pa. When I went down into the tunnel I found – He broke off as someone spoke to him. I guessed he'd found my bracelet. *No, No thanks,* he said and then he carried on. *Listen, I'm going to London tomorrow now. I've organised a meeting to discuss – our project. I'm sure I can get it sorted for you but it would be good to meet again before I go. I've got a couple of ideas about what you could do.*

From the background chatter, it sounded as though he was in a bar. Maybe that was why he was being so mysterious about his East Greenland expedition. I supposed he still hadn't told Issy.

He sounded really keen for me to come to East Greenland with him. The cynical part of me suspected he thought the press might like the father/daughter angle. I should try to meet him. Keep him sweet and dodge round the question of whether I could go to East Greenland or not. I'd try to get into the Samaans' house and have a quick look round, then see Pa.

I texted him. Meet me in Botanic Gardens where we met before around 8?

I didn't want to meet Pa in a bar. It would take forever to get away. I'd go back to Fergus's afterwards, pick up my stuff and, if I kept the meeting with Pa short, I'd get the sleeper train to London.

OK, he texted back.

I put the phone on silent, then stepped back into the middle of the lawn and examined the back of the house. A couple of upstairs sash windows were still open at the top. Bathroom ones judging by their frosted glass. But as I traced the route to the window in my head, someone unseen pushed one of the windows up and closed it.

I stood open-mouthed for a few seconds as the meaning of what I'd witnessed sunk in. Someone was still in there.

And for absolutely no reason I was sure it was Leila.

I stomped round to the front of the house, suddenly sick of all the subterfuge, held my hand on the buzzer and, when no one answered, hammered on the door.

Still no one.

I'd had enough; I was going in. The other bathroom window was still open. It wouldn't be tricky. A walk along a branch that was maybe thinner than I'd have liked and a leap to grab the top of the window while ramming my feet onto its ledge.

Easy, really.

My phone buzzed again. I turned it off and shoved it deep into a pocket. I didn't want anything breaking my concentration. Took a deep breath and ran at a tree whose branches hung enticingly close to the house, used the momentum to carry me far enough up the trunk to grab the lowest branch and hoist myself onto it. From there it was a simple climb until I was level with the upstairs windows.

I ran along a branch, jumped and landed perfectly on the windowsill. Absolutely perfectly. Then forced the window down and clambered inside.

I was in a shower room. Opulent with white marble and waterfall taps. A door led through a dressing room into what I supposed was the master bedroom. Very white again and painfully tidy. The only colour from the photos on the walls. Photos of three children growing up in Glasgow. Two girls and a boy. And the younger girl was definitely Leila.

Gotcha!

I walked swiftly through the rest of the upper level. Four more bedrooms, each with their own en suite bathroom, three of which had signs of occupation, which meant someone else apart from the parents, son and daughter I'd seen leave was living here. They were all empty at the moment.

So was downstairs.

The lounge was formal and elegant, shades of taupe with angular light fittings. The kitchen was equally tasteful. Black granite and sleek grey cupboards surrounded an expanse of matching slate tiles. Except the people who used the kitchen didn't care about style. They'd plonked a large and much-used wooden table in the middle of the room, and filled every available surface with things. A row of battered recipe books occupied the gap between the jars of wooden spoons and spatulas, whisks and knives. The fridge was barely visible beneath the notes of appointments, postcards, photos and drawings held to its doors by colourful fridge magnets. Bottles of oil, jars of spices, jams and cereals jostled for space on the counters. This was the room the family used although it too was empty now.

There was nowhere to hide downstairs apart from the cupboard under the stairs. A quick glance showed Leila wasn't skulking behind the array of coats and shoes. She wasn't in any of the upstairs wardrobes either nor under a bed.

'Leila,' I stood on the landing at the top of the stairs and called. Loudly enough to be heard but not yelling. 'It's Jen. Leila, please come out. I'm not leaving until I talk to you.'

Utter silence. I thought of threatening her with the police or with the press. She clearly had something to hide.

But I didn't want to.

'Please, Leila. Yasmiin helped me track you down. You remember her? She came ashore with you and you looked after her. She's staying with us now. With me and Morwenna and, of course, Aya and Rania. Rania told me how you saved her.'

There was a rustle and a cracking noise. I held my breath. A minute later Leila appeared at the bottom of the stairs. She was dressed, like her sister, in jeans, tunic and hijab. Her hands plucked at the tunic but, other than that slight movement, she held herself rigid.

Sixteen

'Hello, Jen.' The trace of a Scottish accent in her voice startled me. 'I'm so glad Rania is safe. I've thought about her a lot.'

It was such a contrast to the last time I'd seen her, in the dark and the rain, striding along the beach with Nick, a gun in one hand. Hard to reconcile that memory with the edgy young woman standing before me, biting the loose skin on her lips.

Suddenly I wasn't sure. Was the whole household a deep fake? An elaborate cover for a nest of agents?

'Are you really Leila Samaan?'

'Yes.'

'Then... then what is this all about?'

I started to walk down to meet her.

'Stay upstairs,' she said. 'My family should be gone for a couple of hours but sometimes my mother comes back. She says she's forgotten something but it's to check on me. I'd rather no one knew you'd been here.'

I followed her to one of the bedrooms I'd looked in before. She sat on the bed and gestured to a pink beanbag and a white wicker chair. I chose the chair. It was a strange room. The bedding and cushions were pink and frilly. Ariana Grande posters covered the walls and a pile of soft toys filled one corner. But the rest of it was as austere as a monk's cell. The surfaces were empty – no ornaments, no clutter of make-up and jewellery, nothing apart from a thin portable computer on a desk in the corner.

135

'How old are you, Leila?'

'Twenty.'

Far younger than the grim and determined Leila I'd watched on the beach had seemed, yet older than she looked now in this bedroom more suited to a fifteen-year old. I still wasn't sure what she really was. My mind seethed with questions but before I could pick one to ask, she asked one herself.

'Why are you here?'

'Because I don't understand, I don't understand how you came to be travelling with the migrants. Pretending to be the daughter of one of the smugglers.'

Her gaze shifted away. She swung her legs onto the bed and moved up to lean against the frilly pillow.

'I was coming home,' she said, her eyes now fixed on the wall.

'From Malta?'

She shook her head.

'Libya?'

'I came through Libya.'

'You're not answering my question.'

She sighed. 'I don't think I can.'

'Why not?'

'Because you won't understand.'

'Try me.'

I watched the battle play out on her face.

'Please tell me, Leila. I have reasons why I need to know. To do with Rania. I think you knew what was going to happen to her. I think that's why you tried to help her. It's all tied up with that.'

She picked up one of her pillows and hugged it.

'OK,' she said. 'I was coming home from Syria. I went there when I was sixteen.'

Her words unleashed a horde of thoughts. Of Syria and the civil war. Of Isis and the Caliphate which the radical Islamist movement had set up there. Of floods of refugees fleeing the country. But also of an army of foreign jihadists pouring into Syria to fight.

And of the girls and women who'd gone there too.

She was motionless on the bed. She didn't even glance at me to see how I'd reacted.

'I see.' It was all I could think to say.

'What do you see?'

'I suppose you were a... a –'

'A jihadi bride?'

'Yes.'

Her eyes dared me to ask all the questions running through my head. And part of me did want to ask why she'd gone and what she'd done there, but most of all I wanted to know how she'd come to be travelling with the people smugglers and what she could tell me about their operation.

'You got out, though,' I said.

'Yes. I was lucky. My husband – I was married as soon as I arrived in Syria. You understand that? You've read enough reports to know what happens to girls there?'

I nodded, although I didn't know. Not really.

'But as I said, I got lucky. My husband was kind and when I begged him to get me out, he helped. He arranged for someone going south to take me to the Lebanese border and I crossed it with a crowd of other people fleeing the fighting.'

'How did you get from Lebanon to Malta?'

She gave a half-laugh. 'I did what every youngster in trouble does. I phoned my parents. Once I got to Lebanon, I ended up in one of the refugee camps. I used the last of the money my husband had given me to pay someone to let me use their phone to send my parents a text and receive a call.' Her eyes flicked into the past. 'Waiting for them to call back was probably the worst moment of all. I was so frightened they'd think it was a hoax or the text wouldn't go through. Or they'd be too angry with me to reply.'

She stood up suddenly and walked to the window. Her hands traced the outline of a tree through the glass.

'That was the worst moment. The camp was... terrible, you know what I mean?'

I didn't have a clue. Not really.

'But your parents did call you back.'

'Yes. And again I am lucky because my father has money. And contacts. I don't know how much he paid to get me home but there were no new cars this year and no holidays.'

She sat down on the bed again and told me her father organised for her to fly from Lebanon to Benghazi in eastern Libya. She travelled with a family and thought her identity documents belonged to their dead daughter. There was no shortage of dead relatives among the people fleeing the fighting. In Benghazi, she'd been met by the first in a chain of smugglers. She was hazy about the journey from Benghazi to western Libya.

'It all looked the same. Flat and dusty and dry. Desert and rocks. We were transported in trucks mainly but rarely on roads. Sometimes we took big detours to avoid towns or fighting. There were other people travelling. People who'd paid to be transported. And there were packages. Packages as valuable, if not more so, than us. To the smugglers, we were all just packages to be delivered. Preferably in as reasonable a condition as possible.'

At some point she'd been taken off the truck and put in a car along with some of the boxes and driven to a big city. She'd waited there for a while, shut up in a room in a flat and then she'd gone to Malta by boat.

'One of the refugee boats?' I asked, thinking of the horrors I'd seen on the news and the story that Rania had told us of her voyage to Malta.

'No. I was far too valuable. As were the boxes we took with us. We came at night on a fishing boat and transferred to a smaller boat when the lights of Malta came into view.'

On Malta she'd stayed in with one of the smugglers. And his sister. Or a woman who claimed to be his sister. She'd been kind to her.

'I was almost happy,' she said. 'After everything that had gone before, Malta felt... wonderful. There was no noise of fighting. No one carried guns. There was music on radios and in the supermarkets. And happy voices. Voices speaking English. Chatting about nothing much: the weather and which bus to catch and whether to have a barbecue this weekend. Water came out of the taps and there were towels and shampoo. And shops. I was allowed to go out with the sister provided I didn't speak to anyone. The shops were full of things to buy. People could pick and choose. In the cafés, people left food on their plates. I can't explain how amazing it felt.'

I thought I understood.

'How long were you on Malta?'

'I don't really remember. I slept a lot at first and then the days blended into one another. We were waiting, you see, for the right person to take me on the next part of the journey. But then something happened and the smuggler said he was leaving and he'd take me himself. And I met you on the boat. The rest you know.'

'No, I don't. Why did you save Rania? I'm guessing it was because you knew what was going to happen to her. You travelled with the smugglers and stayed with them. You knew what they were doing, didn't you? With Rania? With other children too, I think?'

She was silent.

'I know there must have been other children, Leila. Otherwise why did you try to save Rania?'

'I knew what was going on,' she said.

'How?'

'Lots of people visited the house in Malta. Some during the day but most at night. They met in the front room and I overheard more than I wanted to. It was impossible not to and they didn't care if I did. I was just one more package to them.'

I gathered the house was a centre for all sorts of activities. Some almost legal, such as putting refugees looking for work in touch with companies who'd employ them. The rest not so much: migrants looking for clandestine passages to continental Europe and the people with boats prepared to take them; men looking for women to 'work' for them on Malta and on the mainland; goods needing to be transported to Europe secretly. The smugglers weren't fussy. They made up consignments, often a mixture of goods and people on the same boat.

'And, occasionally,' Leila said, 'the night before a boat was due to leave, children would be brought to the flat and we'd feed them before they left. They were always excited. They talked of getting to mainland Europe. Of going to school.' She paused. 'I'm not stupid. I knew what was going to happen to them. I got a gun then. The smugglers bought and sold them. Just another sideline. I stole one I knew how to use and the right ammunition.'

'How did you know?' I asked.

'I spent months in Syria. I didn't learn much but I did learn how to use a gun.'

Her face was sombre in the dim glow of her bedside light. The things that had happened to her in Syria had left some steel beneath the nervous exterior. Who was Leila Samaan?

'I knew what was planned for Rania,' she went on. 'I heard them at Calais arranging to hand her over. And, on the beach, when they went to grab her, something snapped inside me. I don't suppose you understand.'

'I think I do.'

'She ran. They'd have got her, though. So I ran after her and fired my gun. I think I had some idea of warning the men off. But Rania fell over. For a moment I thought I'd hit her. But when I caught up, I realised she'd just tripped. So I shot over her head at short range and screamed that she was dead.'

She stood up suddenly, went into her bathroom and came out with a glass of water.

'If they'd checked to see if she was dead I might have killed her.' She gulped at the water and her teeth clinked on the glass. 'It would have been better for her. But they didn't.'

I didn't know what to say. Could I have gunned Rania down in cold blood to save her from the child-traffickers?

'I'm glad I didn't have to, though,' she added.

She drank some more and once again I thought how little I understood her. How I could probably never understand her.

'But only Brahim came after me.'

Nick, she meant Nick. I breathed in sharply.

She looked at me curiously.

'He was coming to rescue her, too. But that's no surprise to you, is it?'

'No.'

'You know him, don't you.' It wasn't a question. 'He went back to the shore – from the boat – to find you.'

'Yes. I know him.'

Careful.

'Or rather I knew him. He's dead.'

'I'm sorry. He knew who I was. I don't know how.'

There was a question in her voice. I couldn't answer it. I suspected Nick had known she wasn't the smuggler's daughter and worked the rest out. Or asked his department to identify her.

'The child-traffickers killed Brahim,' I said.

The memory of believing Nick was dead was strong enough for me to speak as though it was still the truth.

'They need to be stopped, Leila. That's why I'm here. You said the smugglers sent children to France regularly. Who were they going to?'

'I have no idea.'

'None at all?'

She pulled off her hijab and ran her fingers through her hair, massaging her scalp and stretching her neck to unlock the knotted muscles.

'No. The men on the beach, they were nothing. Just hired hands. Some of them were migrants themselves, probably from the camps at Calais. They'd been told to keep Rania and hand her on once the boat had left. Someone was waiting, but I don't know who.'

I did. I knew more than she did. I knew the children were handed over to Basset. What about the other end, though? They needed to be stopped too. What about Malta?

'Who brought the children to the smugglers?' I asked. 'On Malta?'

'I didn't see them,' she said.

But quickly. Too quickly.

'No,' she repeated. 'I never saw them.'

I thought she was lying.

A car crawling up the gravel broke the silence. Leila was off the bed and at the window in one fluid movement.

'My family,' she said. 'They're back already.'

Car doors slammed outside and voices rang out.

Seventeen

'Please, Jen. They mustn't know you're here. Please get inside.'
She slid her wardrobe door open and moved the clothes to one side. Someone called her name.

'I'm in my bedroom,' she called back.

Her eyes begged me.

'You're lying to me,' I said. You know who brought the children to the smugglers.'

'Not really,' she said again. 'But I… It's complicated.'

I waited.

'I'll tell you. But later. Please.'

I got inside the wardrobe. She slid the door shut but I pulled it open a fraction. I can't bear confined spaces. I caught brief glimpses of her mother who came in and hugged Leila as though they'd been gone for days rather than a couple of hours. She went downstairs but Leila hung back a few seconds.

'Please stay there,' she muttered by the wardrobe door.

I didn't. I couldn't. I waited until I heard her footsteps on the stairs and stepped out. I'd have enough time to hide again if I heard anyone come back up.

It was a long wait. Judging from the sounds below, the family were having some kind of supper together and it went on for ages, giving me plenty of time to think. I realised after a long while I wasn't going to make my meeting with Pa. Couldn't text him, though. Or call. My phone was once again out of battery. The charge I'd got in Waterstones hadn't lasted long. I found a socket and plugged it in, then heard someone coming upstairs. Back in the wardrobe again. And this time I stayed put as people came upstairs and went down. Bedroom doors opened and closed. Everybody except Leila.

I watched her bedroom clock through a narrow crack in the door as it ticked over the minutes. The time for my meeting with Pa came and went. It was close to eleven when Leila finally appeared. She put a finger to her lips before I could speak and jerked her head towards the en suite bathroom. I followed her in as she turned on the water in the shower.

'They won't hear us now,' she said. 'They're going to bed.'

I sat on the bath but she levered herself into a corner on the floor. She'd been crying. A lot judging from the state of her eyes.

'What took you so long?'

'I've been talking to my father,' she said. 'About what it cost to get me home. I hadn't dared ask before.'

'Did you tell him about me?'

'No!'

'If you want we can meet somewhere else. Tomorrow. Just say when and where.'

'I can't. I can't leave the house.'

'What?'

'Because I'm not here. Leila Samaan never came home.'

'I don't understand.'

'My parents are terrified someone will find out I'm back. They managed to keep my disappearance quiet. They didn't make a fuss. It wasn't in the papers. I left during the school holidays when I was due to move schools anyway. So they told my new school that I'd changed my mind and was going elsewhere. But they did report me missing to the police. And if I reappear they'll have questions for me. I could be charged with terror offences.' She paused. 'I don't want to go to prison. Or worse.'

She meant that they might deport her.

'So I'd rather my family don't know you're here. It will terrify my mother and I can't put her through anything else. We don't speak about it much. It's too difficult. My mother just gets upset. She doesn't understand why I went and she blames herself. She keeps on saying she's sorry and my sister gets angry and says she has nothing to be sorry for. And it's true she doesn't.'

Tears started to roll down her cheeks.

'I didn't think I had any left,' she said.

'Why *did* you go?' I asked.

She sat absolutely still and I wondered if she'd even heard my question or if she didn't want to answer.

'That's what everybody wants to know,' she said eventually. 'I was barely sixteen, you know, and a young sixteen at that. I realise that now. And as confused as any teenager is. About who I was and who I was going to be.'

She stopped and retreated into her thoughts. I wondered what else she was going to say. Most of us felt like that at her age but we didn't charge off to join a murderous regime. And then some of the things I'd done thrust their way into my mind. I'd played with danger for the love of it. I'd nearly lost myself in drugs. I'd been stupid, so stupid. And I'd been much older than Leila had been.

'School didn't help,' she went on. 'I see that now. My father sent me to a private secondary school. I was bright and he had the money. It was OK except there weren't many kids who looked like me. I wasn't bullied or anything but I never fitted in. My friends were the girls at our mosque. One in particular. We shared everything. And we had great plans. We were going to change the world. We spent hours discussing it. She went to Syria first. My parents didn't know because her family had moved the year before but we'd kept in touch on Snapchat. I think her moving away was part of it. We were very close. Her family is Bangladeshi but we were both Muslim girls. And I missed her. Going seemed like a great adventure. A chance to be part of something different. We were in touch with other women who'd gone and they all spoke about being a sisterhood building something new. They said we'd have to fight. That it would be hard. Not to expect a soft Western life with constant electricity and water, with shops full of food and clothes. There'd be times we'd be cold and hungry. But if we held together we'd win through.'

She'd stopped crying as she spoke and some echo of the ardent pilgrim she'd been lit up her face.

'But I couldn't,' she said quietly. 'I wasn't strong enough.' She stood and found a flannel, wet it in the shower and washed her face.

'No more,' she said. 'I can't talk about it anymore.'

She dried her face in a pristine white and fluffy towel, her hands burying themselves in its thickness.

I understood the yearning for adventure. How strong it could be. And how much Leila had wanted to be part of something. Rania came into my thoughts. Would she have the same difficulty fitting in? Ma and I had walked into things we weren't equipped to deal with. We'd never be able to fully understand the conflicts she'd feel. Like I couldn't really understand Leila's.

'No more,' Leila said again. 'Please, Jen.'

'OK…' I said. 'Tell me about Malta. And the children.'

'Yes. Malta. I'll tell you what I know, but you mustn't tell anyone how you found out. Promise me, Jen.'

'Sure… but why?'

'It would be very difficult for me. Very difficult for my family.'

'I promise.'

'It was always the same person who brought the children. They never came in while I was there. They talked outside, though. And I did hear them, one night. It was hot and my bedroom window was open. I recognised the voice. Or at least I thought I did. And when she walked away, she turned for an instant and I caught sight of her face. I recognised her straightaway.' Her eyes gazed at the tiles on the wall and I guessed her mind was back in Malta.

'Her?'

'I asked the sister about her but all she knew was that the woman worked for one of the associations helping refugees on Malta.'

The hairs on my arms and neck began to prickle.

'Here's the thing. The person who delivered the children, she is also the person who got me out of Lebanon and through Libya to Malta and I suppose she organised my trip to France. She's the daughter of a family my parents are friends with here. When I went missing, my parents spoke to them, asked them for advice and, after I called from Lebanon, they told my father they could get me home. And they did. My father doesn't know how. He only knows he mustn't talk about it and that it cost a frightening amount of money.' She blinked her eyes rapidly. 'It's going to make a difference to our future. He and Maama have nothing left. They took all the spare cash out of the business and sold part of it, remortgaged the house and used every penny they'd saved.'

She ground to a halt, her expression as fixed as the face of a ship's figurehead staring at the sea but not serene. Whatever she saw in the future, it was a burden.

Her mother's voice called from the bedroom. She snatched a towel, wrapped it round her hair and stuck her head round the door.

'Just having a shower, Maama.'

Her mother said something I couldn't make out.

'Love you too,' Leila replied. 'Sleep well.'

She waited a few minutes then turned the shower off. 'They've gone to bed. No one will hear us in here and no one will come in now. It must have been the daughter who organised my trip home. She had all the right contacts.'

'And the daughter's name?'

'Shona. Shona Cameron.'

As soon as Leila had mentioned a woman working for an association helping refugees, I'd thought it might be Ma's friend, Shona. I knew she'd worked with unaccompanied minors. I suspected her of betraying me to the people smugglers. And I'd never liked her. Now Leila's revelation meant I was sure she was my betrayer as well as being the person who lured the children into the child-traffickers' traps.

It meant Peter hadn't betrayed us. It meant I was probably responsible for his death. But I couldn't think about that now. I'd have to deal with it later.

'You know her?' Leila was staring at me.

'I met someone called Shona when I was on Malta. She was Scottish and, like you say, working for an association helping refugees. She worked a lot with unaccompanied minors.'

'Yes,' Leila said. 'It's not a coincidence, is it?'

'I don't think so. It must be the same Shona.'

'There's a photo downstairs of her. I'll get it for you so you can check.'

She tiptoed out.

A few minutes later, an alarm shattered the silence. I slipped back into the bedroom, ready to hide in the wardrobe again. Through the noise I heard someone come out onto the landing. I peered through the door as a slim man in pyjamas, spectacles rammed over his unruly hair, ran downstairs.

A few seconds later the noise stopped.

'I forgot about the alarm.' Leila's voice was clear. 'I came down for a drink. I couldn't sleep.'

I couldn't hear her father's reply but Leila came back into the bedroom clutching a glass of milk. She put her finger to her lips, sat down at her desk and scribbled on a piece of paper then handed it to me.

Can't talk. He'll be awake for ages now. There are alarms by all the doors and windows downstairs. Forgot.

I tried to speak but she shook her head wildly and thrust the pencil and notebook at me to reply.

I'll come back. Tomorrow? Will they be out during the day?

I wasn't leaving Glasgow yet. Not until I was sure about Shona.

Yes. They'll be at work.

How can I get out?

She thought for a moment.

I don't know. You came in through my parents' bathroom, I think?

Yes.

You can't do that now.

I didn't think I wanted to. I didn't fancy jumping from a tiny window ledge onto a branch in the dark.

She wrote some more.

You'll have to stay here and I'll let you out once they've all gone to work in the morning.

There was no other option. Unless I climbed down from her window. I cast a cursory glance outside. There were no useful pipes or ledges at this side of the house and no nearby trees.

OK. I wrote. *I'll stay.*

What will you do about Shona?

I thought for a few moments.

Not sure but I will do something.

She wrote for a while and then passed the notebook back to me.

Please try to keep me out of it. It will be awful for her parents and Mrs

Cameron has been a very good friend to my mother. It would be terrible if she knows I'm involved.

I nodded.

Don't worry, I already had reason to suspect Shona.

She offered me her bed but I refused, taking her beanbag and cushions and making myself a nest in the bathroom. I thought both of us would sleep better if we knew a quick glance into her room wouldn't reveal me. I suspected her mother might well look in to check she was still home during the night. I didn't sleep immediately. At first, my brain spent time whirring through everything that had happened today. Mainly good things. Some wonderful. Nick was alive. I'd told Duncan about Basset and now I had another lead. Shona. I'd tell Duncan about her. He would know what to do. The problem of Ma and Tregonna was sorted too.

Shit.

I'd have to tell Ma that Peter was innocent. That helping us had probably got him killed. Nick and his colleagues played a very dirty game. Although I'd played my part in his death. I'd played the game to get what I wanted. I wished I'd never got involved – except Rania wouldn't be safe if I hadn't. As soon as I'd spoken to Duncan, I was going back home. And then I'd leave everything alone.

I'd missed my meeting with Pa too. I hoped I hadn't blown it. For Ma's sake. It was too late to call him. And my phone was in the bedroom. I'd just have to be very apologetic in the morning. After all, he'd let me down often enough.

And strangely my last thought as I drifted off into a doze was of Pa and Vince. I wondered what it was like down in the tunnels under the Botanic Gardens. I remembered the platforms I'd seen below, deserted apart from the myriad of green bushes and weeds that human absence had allowed to flourish. Probably animals and insects too. A sort of natural paradise untouched by humanity.

Hunger woke me. Not surprising really. I couldn't remember when I'd last eaten anything. Hunger and grief. Until I remembered that Nick was alive. I lay and felt happy for quite a while. And afterwards I just felt hungry. I couldn't get the thought of food out of my mind. I remembered the glass of milk Leila had brought upstairs and left untouched, crept into her dark bedroom, drank it and then retreated back to the bathroom to curl up once more in my nest.

Eighteen

I came to all of a sudden. Leila was shaking my arm.

'They'll be gone in a minute,' she said.

I sat bolt upright.

'What time is it?'

'Seven thirty.'

She handed me a cup of tea and a new toothbrush.

'Thanks,' I said and, after she'd left me, I tried to make myself look as though I hadn't slept on a bathroom floor in my clothes.

She was waiting for me in the bedroom, her face serious.

'Have they left?'

'Not yet,' she said.

'Can you get the photo?'

'Let's wait until they've gone. It won't be long.'

We sat in silence, listening to the sound of the family preparing to leave below. The front door slammed and a motor bike started up outside.

'That's my brother,' Leila said.

'What are you going to do? Long term, I mean. You can't stay in hiding for ever.'

'Oh, I think I can. This is so much better than Syria.' She waved her arm towards her surroundings. 'There are no planes flying overhead and dropping bombs, no going out in the morning and seeing a friend's house obliterated – a pile of rubble where it once stood. No stepping over bits of bodies left in the

152

street. I have food and water. I can wash when I want to and my clothes are clean. And I'm warm. Warm all the time. It was cold sometimes in Syria. I didn't expect that.' She hugged herself. 'It was too much. I thought I'd be able to deal with it but I couldn't.'

Once again, she sounded as though she thought she'd failed. As though she'd been wrong to want to get out of Syria. I wondered if she still held true in some way to the beliefs that had motivated her to go there in the first place.

'Do you –'

The front door slammed again cutting me off. Leila stood up and crossed to the window. Both cars drove off. The house was quiet.

'Do I what?' she said.

'Nothing. Let's get going.'

In the kitchen, Leila went straight to the fridge and pulled one of the photos off the door. It showed a family of four standing on some wide marble steps. The Eiffel Tower rose through the clouds behind them.

'It was their Christmas card last year,' Leila said. 'A photo from a trip where they all met up in Paris. That's Shona, their daughter on the right.'

Shona stood on the lowest step. It was the same Shona I'd met in Malta. With her hair long and blowing in the breeze and still wearing the hippyish flowing dresses and silver bangles that reminded me of Ma.

So Shona was the person picking out children, promising them a better life and sending them on to be assaulted and raped.

I looked harder at the photo and sat on the nearest chair with a thump.

'Are you OK?'

'Can I have a glass of water?'

Shona's brother stood on the step above her, then her mother and, finally, her father on the top step.

I'd met them all.

Shona's brother was Xander. The Xander with the red hair and beard I'd spoken to at Nick's wake. A police officer. Working in cybercrime. Her mother was the woman with the dark, polished bob and the beautiful clothes who'd been speaking to Nick's aunt, Fiona, and who'd swept past me when Shona's father had stormed out of the wake, enraged by Fiona's accusations.

Shona's father was a police officer too. And unless I'd totally misunderstood Duncan, he was Sandy. Sandy the DCI who had advised Nick before he went undercover in Glasgow. Sandy who was the only other person who knew Nick was alive.

Sandy Cameron.

What did it mean?

Leila put the glass of water on the table in front of me.

'Is everything OK?'

'So what do Shona's family do?'

I couldn't think what else to ask.

'Her mother teaches business studies. Her father and brother are in the police. Which makes it really difficult about Shona.'

She carried on talking about what a lovely family they were and how hard it was going to be for them to deal with Shona's crimes. Especially Mr Cameron who adored her. They had always been close. But I only half-listened. I was starting to panic.

The smugglers who ran the routes the children passed along weren't fussy. They'd transport anything and anyone that made them money.

And that terrified me.

Because, according to Duncan, Nick had uncovered a link at Calais that led to the drugs trade in Glasgow. A route for drugs to be brought into the country and up to Scotland? A smugglers' route.

I was beginning to wonder if Shona was involved in more than child-trafficking. And if somebody else in Shona's family was involved too. Someone with huge experience of how the drug trade worked here and who knew the families who ran it.

DCI Sandy Cameron. Who was so close to his daughter Shona.

Duncan hadn't held back when talking about the power of the organised crime groups. How they had contacts and informers in all walks of life: the prisons, the prosecutors and, of course, the police.

I didn't like what I was thinking. I didn't like it at all. I was probably being paranoid. It was guesswork. But if there was the slightest chance DCI Sandy Cameron was corrupt, Nick was in great danger.

Leila's words interrupted my thoughts. 'I haven't breathed a word to the Camerons about seeing Shona in Malta.'

I thought her caution might have been misplaced. It was so much more likely that Shona's father knew exactly what she was up to. That her father was the person with contacts among the vast and disorganised network of drug-smugglers and people-smugglers, traffickers and criminals that he could use to get Leila home safely. That he had used. At a price. At a huge price. But everything in this world seemed to have a price and I was beginning to wonder if DCI Sandy Cameron had been bought. Maybe years ago.

What did it mean? I wasn't sure. But nothing good for Nick. I needed to call Duncan and as soon as possible.

'Do the Camerons know you're home?' I asked.

'Yes, of course. They were the ones who told my parents to keep it quiet. The press are after anyone who went to Syria at the moment.'

I bet Cameron wanted it kept quiet. He wouldn't want anyone investigating how Leila had got home.

I looked inside the card.

Happy Christmas, it said. *With all best wishes from the Cameron family.*
Should I tell Leila what I thought?

'Is Shona still in Malta?'

'Yes.'

And probably still sending children up the chain.

'Is everything OK?'

The skin round her eyes was creased with worry. Was there anything else I could ask her? I didn't think so. And I wouldn't tell her about Sandy Cameron. Because I wasn't sure. I had a sense of wheels turning within wheels. No, not wheels. Of cogs driving hidden cogs inside some elaborate but secret mechanism. There were things going on I didn't understand.

'Just a bit tired,' I said to Leila. 'Your bathroom floor isn't that comfortable. I think I'll head off but can I come back and see you? If I think of anything. I'll make sure everybody's out first.'

'OK.'

We headed to the front door.

'One last thing, Leila. You said you didn't want your family to know I'd been here. Well, don't tell anyone.' I couldn't think of a reason why she shouldn't so I muttered something about it being dangerous. I didn't need to worry. She was clearly as keen as I was to keep my visit quiet.

Nineteen

I didn't leave by the gate. Some caution held me back. And scaling a few fences and walls and climbing trees hanging over the boundaries between houses let me stretch out the niggling stiffness left over from sleeping curled up on Leila's bathroom floor.

Once I'd got back on the road and hung about for a while to check no one was following me, I turned my phone on and called Duncan.

He answered straightaway.

'Hello.'

'It's Jen.'

Silence.

'Duncan?'

'Jen. Aye. What's up?'

He didn't sound at all pleased to hear my voice. In fact, he sounded shocked.

'I need to see you. Urgently.' I remembered his warning that his phone might be compromised so I didn't mention Nick. 'Something important has come up.'

'I see. Are you still here?'

'Yes.'

'OK. Let me think.' He told me the address of a café near Glasgow Central. 'Give me… four hours. I'm stuck at work for the moment.'

'Duncan, it's really urgent.'

'I'll call you if I get away sooner.'

He rang off.

Something felt wrong. And once again I had the sense of hidden cogs spinning in the shadows. I began to wonder about Duncan's story. I was sure he'd met Nick. Sure Nick had been alive. Sure Duncan had gone to France to identify a strange corpse, bring it home and bury it.

But were there things he hadn't told me?

And things Nick hadn't told him?

Had I been too trusting? Truth was a commodity in Nick's line of work. A commodity to be shaped into a reality that suited the moment.

I tried Pa but it went straight to voicemail. I didn't leave a message. It would be easier to talk to him.

Fergus had texted. He wasn't sure what had happened to me last night but he hoped I was OK. He'd be in all day so I was to come round whenever I wanted to. Rania had sent me a photo of a kitten asleep on Aya's bed. He was called Scooby, which made me smile despite my fear for Nick. Scooby was Aya's favourite programme so I hoped she'd chosen the name herself. Ma must have relaxed her 'animals aren't pets but wild creatures' philosophy. I texted Rania back *Good Choice* and a heart emoji.

I caught a bus to Fergus's and texted him I was on my way. Then looked up the train times to Cornwall. There was nothing I could do for Nick here. Duncan would have to contact Nick's department and let them deal with what I'd learned. They were the only people who could get Nick out. Fear needled its way through my blood. I might be too late. Nick might be… But I couldn't even bring myself to think the word.

Fergus answered his buzzer immediately and I ran up the stairs to his top-floor flat.

'I'm heading home,' I said. 'Got a quick meeting first in a few hours but, if it doesn't go on too long, I should make the train that gets in at midnight.'

'Tea?'

'Please.'

I called Ma while he made it. She answered immediately.

'Jen. Thank the gods.'

'What's up?'

'I was just going to call you.'

My phone bleeped. I pulled it away from my ear. Maybe Duncan was trying to call me but it was a message arriving from an unrecognised number. I ignored it and caught up with Ma mid-sentence.

'—dead.'

Dead? No, please no.

'Ma, who's dead? You cut out.'

'Charlie. Your father's dead.'

Dead. Pa's dead. What did she mean?

'You do mean dead? Really dead?'

Sometimes Ma used *dead* to describe people who weren't as aware as she felt they should be to the mystical forces around us.

'Of course I do.'

'But I only saw him… yesterday. I saw him yesterday and he was fine.'

I stared out of the window, held frozen in the unreality of the moment. Outside cars still drove down the hill. A bin lorry arrived and dropped off half a dozen men who disappeared into different tenements, then emerged pushing bins out onto the road.

How was it possible life was still going on? Surely the shockwave that had ripped through me and left me numb should have stopped everything as it shot out to engulf the world.

159

Ma told me what she knew. Not much. Her source of information was a phone call from an incoherent Issy. Someone had pushed Pa under a train. Last night.

I tried to take it in but the words were slippery and wouldn't stick to my brain.

'A train.' It was all I could get out. 'Someone pushed him?'

'That's what Issy said. Last night. The police came and told her very early this morning.'

These things happened. Someone with mental health problems had a crisis and... Or an awful gang initiation rite. You read about it in the papers but you never thought it could happen to someone you knew.

Or at least not to Pa.

He'd been so alive. The last time I'd seen him, so full of life and excitement about the East Greenland project.

'I'll go and see Issy. Find out what happened.'

Pa is dead. How can that be?

'I don't think you should.'

'What?'

'Don't go and see Issy.'

I started to protest but Ma spoke over me. 'She thinks you're responsible for his death.'

I couldn't speak. How could it be my fault? Issy was mad. That was all. Lashing out in her grief. I wouldn't go and see her though. I felt weird enough already.

I thought of Kit. He'd understand how odd I felt. In a way Ma couldn't. His relationship with Pa had been as strange and strained as mine.

'Have you told Kit?'

'Yes.'

'I need to speak to him. I'm going to call him now. I'll call you later. Bye.'

More than anything I needed to speak to my brother.

Fergus and Tam stared at me from the kitchen area of the big living space.

I blurted the news out.

It shook Fergus. He muttered a few words about how alive Charlie had been. How it seemed impossible he was dead.

'How did it happen?' Tam asked.

'Ma said someone pushed him. Under a train.'

'Ach. We live in a terrible world.'

Tam glanced at her father, reaching out a hand adorned with iridescent nails and gothic rings to touch his shoulder.

'I need to call my brother,' I said.

'We'll give you some space.'

'No, I won't drive you out. I'll go into the bedroom.'

But as I looked at my phone, I saw someone had sent me a picture. Taken from above it showed a man asleep on what looked like a gravel path full of weeds and wild flowers. It looked vaguely familiar. I zoomed in. The man was Pa. And the ground around his head was stained red.

What was this?

And then my brain made sense of it.

It was the abandoned railway line in the Botanic Gardens, site of the old station. Taken by someone standing on the walkway. The same walkway the three of us – me, Vince and Pa – had stood on yesterday as we stared down into its overgrown and deserted depths.

A text message followed.

This is just the start, it said.

For a few seconds I could do nothing but gape. Who had sent me this? And why? Why did this picture show Pa's body at the Botanic Gardens?

'Jen? What is it?' Tam had seen me falter.

'I think my mother might have made a mistake. Maybe Pa

161

didn't die under a train.' My voice sounded as though it came from someone else. Someone speaking a long way away.

Another message arrived. From the same anonymous source.

It was a video or rather a sequence of photos. All black and white. All showing naked men, their faces out of shot. With children. Huge hands holding small children. Naked children. The details were hard to make out but I understood straightaway. And the faces of the children were clear. Some were blank. Some were terrified. Most had bruises and a couple of them cried.

The sequence ended with a shot of Rania and Aya on the beach near Tregonna. The photo I'd taken myself just a few days ago. How had they got hold of it? I hadn't sent it to anyone.

There was some text superimposed.

Easy meat, it said. **Keep your mouth shut about Calais or they'll be starring in the next photos we send you.**

And my brain, which had been jarred by the news of Pa's death, settled into pin-sharp focus.

'Fergus, can I use your phone? I can't use mine.'

'Aye.'

'Ma,' I said as soon as she answered. 'It's Jen. You have to leave. You and the girls. And Yasmiin,' I added.

I was leaving no hostages behind.

'Leave?'

'Leave Tregonna. Now. Go into hiding.'

'But Jenifry –'

'Ma, I've rattled someone's cage. And they're threatening Rania and Aya.' My voice broke into splinters. 'Ma, please. Go. As soon as you can.'

Silence.

'Ma, I know how bad this will be for the girls. I wouldn't tell you to go if I wasn't scared. Shit-scared. Shona's involved. And she knows exactly where you all are.'

There was a moment of silence. Then Ma spoke.

'Does that mean Peter –'

'Was innocent? Yes. It does. But there's no time to discuss that now. I don't want any more deaths on my conscience… or worse. You've all got to get out now.'

'OK. We'll go to –'

'Don't tell me,' I said quickly. 'And don't call me. I don't trust my phone… I'll find a way to be in touch. Make sure you take your phone with you.'

Fergus and Tam had understood most of the conversation. That much was clear from their horrified faces.

'Pa,' I said to them. 'I think he must have died at the Botanic Gardens. Could you check?'

But Tam was ahead of me. 'I looked on the news,' she said. 'As soon as you said. Read the report.'

She passed her phone to me.

Glasgow Police have asked for witnesses to an incident in the Botanic Gardens yesterday evening at around 20:23 when a man fell onto the old railway track from the walkway over the disused Botanic Gardens Station. His name has not been released until all next of kin have been informed. Anyone who passed through the Botanic Gardens from 20:00 onwards is asked to contact the police.

I couldn't speak.

'Could that be Charlie?' Fergus asked.

I nodded and from somewhere found some words. 'I was supposed to meet him there. Last night. At 8.'

'Your mother misunderstood, then.'

'Yes.' And from somewhere I managed to find the words. 'I think he was killed because of me. To warn me off. Because of something I know.'

Neither of them asked me what the information was.

'Call Vince,' Fergus said. 'See what he knows.'

Why hadn't I thought of that?

He answered immediately.

'Jen.'

'What happened, Vince? What happened to Pa?'

'I was going to ask you the same thing.'

'I don't know. Did it happen at the Botanic Gardens?'

There was a sudden silence at the other end.

'What is it, Vince?'

'Charlie went to meet you there last night.'

'I know but I didn't make it. Something came up.'

More silence. This time it went on for an age. All I could think was, *Vince doesn't believe me.*

'Vince, you can't think I had anything to do with it.'

'Of course I don't.' But his voice told me he had doubts. 'I thought you might have climbed down together. And had an accident. It's the sort of thing you'd do.'

'I didn't.'

He sighed. 'Well, the police want to talk to you. You need to contact them. Where are you?'

Alarm bells rang in my head.

'I'm just warning you,' Vince carried on. 'Issy has told them that you were very angry with Charlie because he wouldn't let Morwenna stay in Tregonna.'

I opened my mouth to tell him that Pa had changed his mind and shut it. Pa and I had been alone during the conversation. He'd told me he'd tell his solicitors when he saw them in London. I doubted he'd had a sudden change of heart and let them know immediately. So it would be Issy's word against mine. And I had no way of proving she was lying. She probably wasn't lying anyway. I suspected Pa had never told her. Much easier for him to let her find out after he'd left.

The entrance buzzer interrupted my shocked silence. Fergus looked out of the window.

'It's the police.'

I cut the call.

'I wonder what they want?' Tam said.

I had an awful feeling I knew.

'I think they might be after me.'

Fergus and Tam looked round.

'I was supposed to meet Pa at the Botanic Gardens. Last night. At 8. Something came up and I didn't show. But the police want to talk to me. Issy told them I was angry with Pa.'

'Hello,' Fergus answered the intercom, his voice soft and slow, almost slurred. 'Who is this?'

'Glasgow Police. Could we come up?'

'Ach. If it's about the party over the weekend, that was the flat below us.'

'Just let us in please, sir.'

'OK. I'll put some clothes on. I'm just out of the shower.'

Tam crossed to the window. 'Another police car's arrived.'

'They want me,' I said. 'I'm sure of it.'

'Only natural if Issy has been making accusations about you. I'm sure it will be sorted out quickly.'

But I couldn't risk it. I'd been told to keep my mouth shut. Rania and Aya had been threatened if I didn't. Whoever was behind this would freak if I went with the police. Anyway, I needed to be free. I needed to meet Duncan in a few hours.

'I can't be seen talking to the police. Give me a few seconds start before you let them in. I'll go out the back and leave through the garden.'

Tam disappeared into the back bedroom and came back a few seconds later.

'There are police in the road out the back too. You could get into the garden but they'll grab you as soon as you go over the back wall.'

The buzzer sounded again.

'They must know you're here,' Tam said. 'They're very insistent.'

'But how? I haven't told anyone I've been staying here. Never mind, no time to deal with it now. Is there anywhere I can hide?'

'The attic,' Tam said. 'You can get up into it from the landing.'

She grabbed a set of steps from the kitchen and I charged out after her while Fergus watched us anxiously from the front door. The buzzer sounding continuously behind him in the flat. It all felt wildly over the top. I wasn't dangerous.

Tam shot up the steps and undid a padlock holding a trapdoor in the ceiling shut, then leaped down. She grabbed my leg as I shoved the hatch aside.

'Give me your phone,' she said.

'My phone?'

'You said you didn't trust it. Could the police be tracking you with it? How else would they know you're here?'

I flung the phone down and hoisted myself into the attic.

'Keep as still as you can,' Fergus called as I pulled the hatch closed after me. 'You can hear every noise from above in the flat.'

It wasn't pitch dark. A skylight with two small panes let some daylight into the space, which was low and lined with wooden rafters. Boarding beneath my feet meant I was in no danger of plunging through to Fergus's flat. A grey metallic water tank stood in one corner but otherwise it was empty apart from the webs of a few hopeful spiders. I smelled dust and saw it dance in the light coming through the skylight.

A couple of minutes later, I heard the police pound up the stairs, a few muffled words as Fergus answered the door to them and then nothing. I sat down very slowly, careful not to make a noise. And then I waited.

And waited. In silence and in the gloom. My body was utterly still, every muscle held tight although a whirlwind of fear gusted into the furthest corners of my mind and sent up showers of questions.

What had just happened?

Someone was threatening me and I wasn't sure why. No, I knew why. They'd mentioned Calais. It must be because I'd recognised Basset. And they'd found out.

But how?

My thoughts shot back to my phone.

Maybe Tam was right. Someone had been tracking me via my phone. But not the police. No, not the police.

I remembered the night at the climbing gym. My phone had been stolen and then swiftly returned. I'd thought I was lucky. But what if someone, who wanted an easy way to keep tabs on me, had spotted an opportunity and seized it. Put something in it or programmed it so they could follow my movements and listen in to my calls. Probably read my messages. And, of course, see my photos. Then arranged for it to be found so conveniently.

It meant they'd been able to monitor me from that moment onwards. Back to Fergus's flat last night. To the Botanic Gardens with Pa and Vince. And then...

Shit, shit, shit.

To my meeting with Duncan. Where I'd told him about Basset. About recognising him at Calais as a child-trafficker and how I would do anything to bring him to justice. Could they listen in to people talking? It would have panicked them. Then they'd have picked up my message to Pa about meeting in the Botanic Gardens. Had they gone there to take me out and when I hadn't turned up, killed Pa to frighten me into keeping my mouth shut?

Panic fluttered in my ribs. Duncan had told me about Nick. The panic calmed. He'd told me nothing until we were in the Subway.

Where there was no signal. So even if they could listen in to my conversations — and I still wasn't sure that was possible — they wouldn't have overheard us.

My phone had run out of battery anyway before we'd gone down to the station. I wished I knew when. Not that it mattered. Clearly they'd heard enough. But it meant they'd lost track of me.

And after that my phone had only been on from time to time.

I had to get to my meeting with Duncan. And untraced. If they'd listened to our conversation in Waterstones, he was in as much danger as I was. Much as I loathed them, Nick's department were the only people who could sort this mess out. For Nick as well as me and Duncan.

The minutes ticked by. Glued themselves into fractions of an hour. And then into an hour. How long was I going to be up here?

And after I'd met Duncan, I thought, I'd lie low. What was the phrase Pa had always used? *Get out of Dodge.* Yes that summed it up.

Pa...

A scratching from the floor to my right. Rats? No, the hatch was opening. The police? Shit. I should have hidden in a corner. Over by the tank maybe, where a casual glance wouldn't have revealed my presence.

'Jen?' Fergus's voice came from below. 'It's OK. They've gone. I waited a wee while to be sure.'

I scrambled out and followed him back into the flat.

'What did they say?'

'Well, they *were* looking for you. I told them you'd been here but left and hadn't come back. They searched the flat, though.'

Fergus kept his home very tidy. I'd noticed he put things away as soon as he'd finished using them and that everything had its place. Not now. Drawers were half-open and the neat rows of books had been piled on the table along with a couple of dirty glasses and a half-drunk bottle of cheap vodka. I realised what the smell that had been bothering me was. Fergus saw the look on my face.

'I'm not drunk. I've no drunk a drop but it was easier to let the police think I had. I've a record, you see, Jen. Nothing very serious. The police have better things to do than charge drunks in Glasgow. Mainly they just shut us up for the night. But I'm known. So once they saw the alcohol on the table, they didn't expect much sense from me.'

He went into the kitchen, pulled a grey packet out from one of the drawers and put it on the table.

'And it meant they didn't bother to keep their mouths shut. I learned a few things. They'd had a tip-off you were here. An anonymous call. Then, not long after they arrived, they got a message you'd been seen somewhere else and went haring off. Two of them stayed to search the flat. And they weren't happy. They had a good moan about it.'

An anonymous tip-off. But who? No one knew where I was except the people tracking my phone. They'd told me to keep my mouth shut. The last thing they'd want was for the police to pick me up.

The sound of a key unlocking the front door and Tam came in. Her normally smoothed-back hair had escaped from its clasp. She pulled a tissue from her pocket and wiped her glasses as she gazed around the room. 'Wheesht, they had a good look round, didn't they?'

'What did you do with my phone, Tam?'

'I turned it off as soon as you gave it to me and went out the back, shimmied over the wall to next door. I've got a friend with a flat there. She let me in and out of their front door. Then I went down the road and threw your phone into one of the bins just before the lorry picked it up.'

169

That sounded OK. OKish. Although they might come back and look for me here once they realised they'd lost me. I'd bought myself some time anyway.

Tam's gaze fell on the table with its books and bottle. Her body tightened.

'Dad?' she said.

'Not a drop,' he said. 'Look.'

He opened the packet he'd taken from the kitchen, and pulled out a self-breathalyser kit, ripped open the packaging and blew a deep breath into the tube.

'It's OK, Dad. I believe you.'

'Well, you shouldn't,' Fergus said. 'Alcoholics lie. To everybody. To themselves. All the time.'

'I don't want you to do this.' She was trying not to cry.

'I do.' He put the tube on the table. 'Two minutes. Jen, will you tell us when two minutes are up?' He took the bottle into the kitchen and poured it down the sink. 'It was water. I filled an old bottle and chucked some ancient aftershave that had lost its scent around the place. That's the alcohol you can smell.'

'Two minutes,' I said.

'Check it, Tam,' he said.

She hesitated.

'Tam.'

She crossed to the table and picked up the tube. 'It's clear,' she said.

They met in the middle of the room and hugged tightly.

'I'll do another in fifteen minutes, so you can be sure,' he said.

The last traces of the strain that had stiffened Tam's body slipped away. She sat down on the sofa with a thump.

I understood how hard won and fragile the trust between her and her father was. Fergus knew it too.

Tam's phone buzzed.

'No,' she said and passed it to me. It was a news alert.

Glasgow Police are urgently looking for 32-year-old Jenifry (Jen) Shaw, last seen in the Botanic Gardens at around 20:40 last night. She is described as medium height with brown curly hair and last seen wearing jeans, a white T-shirt and green jacket. Anyone knowing her whereabouts should call 101 immediately.

'At least they're not telling members of the public to keep their distance from me,' I said.

'There's a photo of you.'

It was the one Polly, the assistant, had taken of me for my security badge. It was a reasonable likeness too.

'I'll see if it's made the local TV news.' She turned the TV on.

'Maybe you should talk to the police,' Fergus said. 'Explain about your father's death. I know a good solicitor.'

'I can't risk it. People are threatening my family. Evil people. They'll freak if they know I've gone to the police. You understood that's what's happened, didn't you? From my conversation with Ma?'

'Some of it. We could be very discreet.'

I shook my head. 'No,' I said shortly.

The police weren't a safe haven for me. Not with Sandy Cameron around. Once they had me in their clutches, it might be very easy for him to arrange a convenient death. A suicide. Jen Shaw, full of remorse at her part in her father's death…

Far too easy and believable.

But maybe I could buy myself some breathing time. Enough to get to my meeting with Duncan. If I called the police. From a new and untracked phone.

I needed to think it through carefully first.

'Could you buy me a prepaid sim and a cheap phone?' I said. 'I'll call the police from that.'

But Fergus already had an old phone and sim provided by the production team on a shoot. He went to look for it while Tam flicked through the TV until she found a local bulletin. The alert for me was sandwiched in between a story that more than 17,000 potholes had been reported to Glasgow City Council and one about a house fire in Bearsden.

'What are you going to tell the police?' Tam asked.

She pointed the remote at the television and cut off a reporter talking over pictures of a burnt out house mid-sentence. I stared at the blank screen for a couple of seconds, forcing my brain to think.

'That I wasn't there. That I know nothing about it. And then I don't know. Try and get them off my back.'

I was sure it wasn't going to work.

Fergus came back with the phone.

'Don't stay on too long,' Tam said. 'They might trace it.'

'I don't think it's as easy as that with a prepaid sim.'

I hoped it wasn't.

Twenty

I made the call from the bedroom. A woman answered. Her voice changed when I told her I was Jen Shaw and she asked me to wait while she put me through to the officer in charge of the investigation. I had a vision of hands beckoning and excitement in a crowded room like you see on television.

It took a few seconds to connect and the officer talked banalities about how pleased they were I'd called and suchlike. I thought about what I was going to say and gazed into the open toolbox on Tam's desk. They both used the spare bedroom as an office. The box was full of brushes and bottles and tubes. Fergus had said she was a make-up artist on films and TV, and she certainly had all the equipment. A row of wigs on blank heads eyed me from her top shelf and beneath them were boxes with intriguing labels: Cheek Implants; Teeth; Misc Hair; and best of all one containing Scars and Minor Wounds.

'Putting you through now.'

The line went silent. No music or anything to indicate I wasn't in a labyrinth of lost calls.

'Hello, Jen. We're so pleased you've called us.' The voice was older and the Scottish accent was soft and pleasant. A male voice this time. 'We've been trying hard to locate you. Your family are very concerned. They'll be happy to know you've got in touch.'

Liar, I thought. Ma would have told me not to call. Since her

173

radical days when she protested against almost anything, she'd hated the police.

'Who am I talking to?' I asked.

'I'm DCI Cameron. Sandy Cameron.'

The shiver started at the base of my neck and travelled up to the top of my scalp before sliding down my arms and into my fingers leaving a hair-prickling trail behind.

'Hi,' I said.

He doesn't know you know, I told myself.

'Where are you, Jen?' His voice still reassuring.

Oh, but he might, my brain said.

'At– near the station. Glasgow Central. I'm heading home.'

I went to Leila's after seeing Duncan. Does he know? I turned my phone on while I was there.

'I see. We really want to talk to you. I'll send a car to collect you.'

'No. I'll come to you. Where are you?'

But I couldn't do this any more. Not with him. Not if he knew I'd been with Leila. Not if he thought I knew about him. Besides he wouldn't believe anything I said. I swallowed and cut the call.

Leila.

The news report Tam had switched off earlier swam through my mind. I shot back into the living room.

Fergus looked up from the phone he and Tam were poring over. 'What did the police say?'

'It's complicated. That news report. About the house fire. I want to see it.'

'You're all over the local news groups,' Tam said as she looked for it. 'Someone'll recognise you as soon as you leave the flat. Here it is.'

She held her phone out. A picture of firemen and engines clustered round a house whose walls were charred around the windows and front door. The same one I'd seen on the news earlier. Something about it had struck me then and now I realised why.

It was very like Leila's house.

I looked more closely. The house *was* Leila's. I recognised the trees at the front and the curly shape of the gates. I read the article.

25 firefighters called to a house fire in Bearsden.

Fire crews were alerted to a fire in the detached property, home of the Samaan family, shortly after 08:00 this morning. Two fire engines were quickly on the scene and the fire has now been declared extinguished by Glasgow Fire and Rescue Service.

All occupants are accounted for and an investigation will be carried out to establish the cause.

Group Manager John MacGregor, said: "We believe the fire started in the sitting room on the ground floor of the two-storey property. Arson can never be ruled out at this stage but we've found little evidence of accelerants. The family were all at work."

I thrust the phone back to Tam then paced up and down the room.

It couldn't be a coincidence. They'd tracked me to Leila's house. And Cameron knew Leila was living there. They must have been terrified when they'd realised the two of us had got together. Each of us knowing a separate piece of the puzzle. So they'd got rid of her, too. More than anything it pointed to Cameron's involvement.

I felt sick now as well as terrified. I'd been running around Glasgow contaminating the safety of everyone I met. Like some sort of disease carrier, spreading death and damage.

'This is my fault, too,' I said.

Confusion and concern chased each other across Fergus and Tam's faces as they watched me. I realised I'd told them very little.

'The people who are threatening me,' I said. 'They've been tracking me for the last couple of days. I told you my phone was stolen at the climbing gym but I got it back very quickly. I thought it was luck but it wasn't. It must have been tampered with then. Something was put in it or some information taken off it, which meant I could be traced. And my texts and calls intercepted. Like the ones between me and Pa.'

I told them everything. I had to. I couldn't stay in their flat without letting them know how dangerous the world had become for me and everyone I met.

It took a while. Partly because I couldn't seem to think coherently and I kept on having to go backwards and forwards in time to explain who someone was or why something had happened. Partly because they interrupted me with questions. Partly because the shakes took my voice away when I spoke about Pa and Leila. I was responsible for Pa's death and I was terrified I might also have caused Leila's.

It was time to leave to meet Duncan once I'd finished telling them.

'Can you lend me something to hide my hair or change it, Tam? And a jacket?'

'I could make you look unrecognisable, given a bit of time.'

'Wait,' Fergus said as she stood. 'I don't think you should go.'

'She can go out the back and through next door like I did, Dad, if you think anyone's watching.'

'Maybe they are but that's not what I mean. She shouldn't go. She shouldn't meet this Duncan at all.'

'I have to. He's my only hope at sorting this mess out.'

'Think about it, lass. Duncan's a police officer. He must know about your father's death and how you're implicated. Are you sure this isn't a trap?'

'But he wouldn't –'

'He doesn't know about the Chief Inspector, does he? He doesn't know how dangerous it would be for you to end up in his hands. Unless you told him when you called.'

'No.' I thought back to the call. Duncan had seemed shocked to hear from me. I'd thought it was because I hadn't left Glasgow already but maybe it wasn't. Maybe he knew about Pa's death.

'Dad's right. You can't risk it.' Tam shook her head violently, dislodging her glasses. She straightened them, then took them off and started polishing them with her T-shirt. 'Or at least call him first and see if you can work out what's going on.'

'Maybe I can hint at the danger.'

I didn't call immediately because his number was in my phone and I couldn't remember it. I got his mother's landline number in the end and she gave it to me. Clearly she hadn't heard I was wanted by the police but I guessed she was the sort of person who watched the news at six o'clock rather than receiving constant updates on her phone.

If only everybody was like that.

I asked Duncan as soon as he answered if he'd heard about Pa's death. The silence following my question gave me the answer.

'Is that why you needed four hours before you could meet me? So you could organise the best way to grab me with your buddies?'

'Jen. You must come and talk to us. I'm sure it was a heat of the moment thing. I'm sure you didn't mean for him to fall.'

'I wasn't even there.' I was yelling now.

'We have a witness who saw you.'

My thoughts reeled.

'A witness?'

'He gave a very clear description of you and of the argument you had with your father. An argument about your mother and money.'

177

Tam shoved her face in front of mine and made cut the call gestures. She was right. This was a set-up. They were probably trying to trace the call as we spoke and I was sure half the Glasgow Police Force were listening in to us. I couldn't go without trying to warn Duncan, though. And maybe, help myself. But how?

Duncan's voice changed. He spoke softly. 'Please come in, Jen.'

'I can't. I can't talk to you. I can't talk to the police. It wouldn't be good for me. Nor for others.' I tried to stress the word *others* hoping he'd think I meant Nick and, maybe, him and, if Cameron was listening, he'd think I meant Rania and Aya.

'I promise you it will be all right. Trust me.'

You're so wrong, I thought, as I cut the call.

Anger and fear forced me to keep moving and I paced up and down Fergus's sitting room again as I told him and Tam the gist of the call.

'I'm stuffed. Completely stuffed. Cameron and his friends have stitched me up. As soon as Issy told them about the issue of Ma and Tregonna, they magicked up a witness who'd conveniently overheard me and Pa arguing about it. There's nothing I can do. My only alibi is Leila. And she can't talk to the police – if she's even alive.'

I couldn't stop the shakes now. The dreadful images I'd been sent of children being abused ricocheted through my head.

'Did you manage to warn Duncan?'

'That Nick was in danger? I tried. Duncan probably is, too.'

The picture of Rania and Aya on the beach with the threat written over it floated back into my mind and something else. Something I needed to remember. Jarred awake by the thought of Rania and Aya's photo. Photos. What other photos were on my phone? And I remembered downloading the French newspaper article about Basset. Just before I went to see Duncan. Was there a chance that was what had made them realise I knew about Basset? Rather than my conversation with Duncan?

'Maybe Duncan's safe,' I said.

'What are you going to do?' Fergus held out a cup of tea. I gulped it.

'What am I going to do?' I repeated, and before either of them could speak, I added, 'My question was... whatever it's called when you don't expect an answer.'

'Rhetorical,' Tam said. 'But you should do as they say. Lie low.'

'Get away from Glasgow first.' Fergus overrode her. 'Life is very cheap to the kind of people you've described here.'

This was true. Leaving was definitely the most sensible thing to do. Any half-intelligent person in my situation would do exactly that.

'Fergus,' I said. 'Would you call Tregonna?'

I gave him the number and waited. There was no answer.

'Should I call your mother's mobile?'

'No.'

Ma's mobile was probably safe but I wasn't prepared to take the risk. Normally she'd have been home now. Quiet time for Aya after lunch.

'Try the house number again. Please.'

Still no answer.

Please, gods, let this mean she'd taken me seriously and fled Tregonna already. If she had... there was a chance she and the girls and Yasmiin were safe. For now.

Because I clearly wasn't even semi-intelligent. And I wasn't sensible. And I was also ringing with anger. It buzzed through my veins and heated my blood. Maybe I wouldn't feel like this if I hadn't spoken to DCI Sandy Cameron myself. If his soft, pleasant voice hadn't licked my ears, promising safety and kindness. Like a snake's forked tongue, testing the air, before it bit its venom into your body.

'We can smuggle you out of Glasgow,' Fergus said.

'No,' I said. 'I can't do any of this. I can't run away.'

'But you can't *do* anything.' Fergus's reply was swift and I guessed he had also been thinking through my options.

'I know.' I nodded and swallowed more tea. 'But I have to try. Otherwise I'll always be frightened. If not for me, for Rania and Aya. I can't live with the threat they'll be snatched hanging over me. And I won't let these monsters get away with it. I won't spend the rest of my life knowing they're out there somewhere... torturing children. I'll try Tregonna later. To be sure that Ma's left.'

'What can you possibly do?' The words burst out of Tam.

'I'm going to find out what Sandy Cameron is up to.'

'But how?'

'You said you could make me unrecognisable?'

She nodded.

'Good because I need to disappear. I need them to think I'm doing what they've told me to. But I'm going to spy on Cameron.' My plan took a clearer shape. 'And I'm going to try to find Nick. But it all depends on how different you can make me look.'

Her eyes ran over my face. 'Very. If you don't mind some of it being permanent.'

'Anything. I don't care.'

'So you're going undercover.'

I thought for a moment.

'Yes, I guess I am.'

How strange.

Twenty-one

There's nothing out of the ordinary about Janelle Bridges — not that anyone's called her by that name for years. You'll see women like her in every big city. She's known as Nell or, in the past, Snowie. Nell, because she always hated Janelle. And Snowie — partly because of her extreme pallor and white blonde hair but mainly due to her predilection for stuffing cocaine up her nose. Those days are long gone, though. She's moved on to an improved product. One that gets her to where she needs to be quicker and sharper. The feeling doesn't last as long but there's always a trade-off.

Scotland is famous for many things – haggis, bagpipes, the Loch Ness Monster… and cocaine. Glasgow is the reigning cocaine capital of the world. Perhaps that's why Nell stayed after following a boyfriend here on holiday. The boyfriend has long gone home. It was only ever something casual for him and he'd seen that Nell's drugging was moving into territories he didn't want to visit.

But her wee job as a call-service agent barely covers the rent of her room with shared bathroom in Castlemilk (all bills included mainly because the landlord knows he can't trust the bunch of no-hopers living there to pay them) and running her battered little car.

So that's why she's been hanging around for hours in this car park in the middle of blocks of flats whose height makes it a place of permanent shade, and whose inhabitants have long since given up putting their rubbish inside the bins scattered across its cracking concrete surface. No one who lives here actually wants to. It's home to people who are too ill, or too beaten down, to fight to get out. They're the weakest of the weak and natural victims for the predators who dominate the place just as the towers dominate the car park.

The flats belonging to the most vulnerable are taken over regularly. 'Cuckooing' they call it. Using someone's home as a base for distribution – a pop-up shop, if you like – until someone complains and social services or the police drive the 'cuckoos' out. Not a problem, though, as there's a plentiful supply of easily commandeered nests.

Nell's bought there on and off over the last few days and spent a lot of time hanging around because she knows her money's running out and she needs more work to fund her habit. So she's going to apply for a job. The thought of it almost makes her laugh. But why not? Selling drugs is a business. And, judging by the youngsters she's bought from in the flats, the entry-level requirements are low.

A car pulls up and sounds its horn. It's black and brash. If Nell knew anything about cars, she'd recognise it as a BMW 3 series. No one gets out. It waits until one of the no-hopers Nell has just bought from strolls out of the building. The driver flicks a switch and the car boot opens. The youngster shoves a rucksack inside, shuts it and goes round to the window. It rolls down. They exchange a few words. A similar rucksack is handed through the window which slides up as the youngster goes back into the tower block.

It's the delivery Nell has been waiting for. And the car makes her think it's been done by the management of this outlet and many other outlets rather than a delivery service.

It's now or never. Nell knows that. But still it requires every bit of grit she has to make herself walk the few steps round to the front of the car and look in at the driver. She can just about see him through the tinted glass. She lets him have a good look at her, knowing what he'll see. Jeans and a hoodie, both a faded grey-blue, with a patina of greasy dirt that no wash no matter how hot will ever remove. Baggy enough to disguise her skinny frame. The blurred outlines of a tattoo snaking up her neck and onto her cheek give its age away. Her skin is dirty white although there is still some plumpness round her cheeks that show she's not quite given up eating. Her hair, blonde and razor-short, is beginning to show the ravages of her habit with naked patches peering through the stubble.

He sounds the horn but she doesn't move. She makes herself wait until she hears the swish of the window opening. Round she walks. She's been told this dealer's OK. Not mad. Not bad. Just another person trying to make a living. He's got a family in a reasonable part of the Southside. Niceish house. Kids in a niceish school but he has a record. A stupid teenage thing that follows him round like a bad smell so he was always last in the queue for any decent work.

'You want something?' He's rolled the window down a short way. Not enough to see his face but enough to hear. His voice is rough and impatient.

'A job,' she says. 'I know you need people. I've got a car. And I'm not fussed what I do. Deliveries. Selling. Whatever.'

He waits.

'I need the money.' She lets a note of desperation colour her words. 'I've got a kid. Not here. She's with my mother in England. But I send money. They're expensive, kids. But maybe you don't know that.'

She sees him nod and she can almost persuade herself his lips curve in a smile of recognition.

'I'm useful. I'm not stupid. Not like...' She jerks her head in the direction of the recently departed youngster.

'You use?'

183

She doesn't know why he asks. They all do.

'Not much. Just need a dunt now and again. To take the edge off everything.'

He winds the window all the way down and she realises with a sudden chill he's not alone.

'There's other ways you could make money,' he says.

But his companion turns and stares at her through black sunglasses, lowering and raising his head as he looks her up and down. 'Not much money, though,' he says once he's finished surveying her body.

Something tells her not to rise. Nothing matters except getting a job. She drops her gaze, realising she's staring too hard, and watches her foot in its tattered trainer nudge a crushed Irn-Bru can around.

'Got a phone number?' This is the dealer and when she looks back up he's wound the window almost to the top.

She nods and gives it to him.

'I might be in touch. If I need someone.'

She nods again. It's something. Maybe not as much as she'd hoped.

Silence.

They're waiting for her to leave, so she turns and walks away. She feels rather than hears the car roll silently after her and this more than anything unnerves her. At the exit she turns sharp right and right again and walks half a mile until she reaches the car she's left parked on a main road. No one would leave a car in the part of town she's just come from. Not even one like hers. As she gets in, the BMW that has been following her picks up speed and disappears.

I've done it, she tells herself. *My first breakthrough. I made a plan. I carried it out. I achieved my goal.*

She tries to feel something. Something like pleasure. Or satisfaction. But she can't. The sweat bursts out of her body as though it too has been holding itself in until she was alone. Her hands are shaking too much to drive. Instead she digs into her jeans pocket and thrusts the small package of dirty white lumps into the back of the glove compartment. It doesn't have a door but at least now her skin can't feel the packet's imprint. And she can no longer see it.

I can't do this. I just can't do this.

I have to do it.

I forced my hands to stop shaking, gripped the wheel and shut my eyes. For a few seconds I let myself be Jenifry Shaw instead of Janelle Bridges. I knew I shouldn't. I'd never have got through the meeting with the dealer if I hadn't been so deep inside the Nell personality I'd constructed with Tam and Fergus's help. But right at this moment I needed to be Jenifry Shaw.

Because the little packet of rocks in my glove compartment called to me. I'd had to buy from the youngsters in the flats. Like I'd had to buy all the other times. In case anyone asked around. In case anyone scratched beneath the surface of Nell Bridges. Nell would have put some of what she'd bought into her body as soon as she could. Heating it in her pipe and sucking it deep into her lungs. And a smile would have creased her face as the high hit her. For a short while she'd have been cocooned in happiness.

So now Nell had to stop being.

But it was hard when I'd worked to absorb her into my body, to move like her, to think like her, to bury every shred of myself under her. Especially because at these moments when Nell reached for the drugs, some part of Jen Shaw reached too.

I knew all the reasons why I shouldn't take it but they didn't seem to matter. Some part of my brain thrust greedy hands through the arguments and stretched out for the crack.

Or were they Nell Bridges' hands?

Maybe they were both. Maybe this was where the two women overlapped. The awful truth at the centre of each of them.

I can't do this. I just can't do this.

I have to do it.

I'd give myself ten minutes. Ten minutes of being somewhere else. I shut my eyes and rested my head against the steering wheel. Let Nell and her fake life, her fake ex-boyfriend, her fake job and her fake daughter slip away. Shut out the stale smell oozing from my clothes and body and searched my brain for a memory.

And funnily enough it wasn't a climb that came to the front of my thoughts. It wasn't even a single memory. It was a host of everyday childhood ones. Of me and Kit and Ma. A jumble of times and places. Playing I Spy while squashed in the back of a friend's car. Wincing while Ma slathered some hideous green salve on a grazed knee. Arguing with her about having a television. And giggling with her and Kit as we hid upstairs from the man who'd come to cut the electricity off because Ma had forgotten to pay the bill. Or so she claimed. And the warmth of those moments reached out from the past and held me steady as they mutated into more recent memories. Watching Rania and Aya playing on the beach. Ma and her mad ideas of making money from pressing wildflowers. I felt the past and present twine into a thick rope that stopped me from falling.

A knock on my windscreen brought me back to the present.

A police officer.

Not the first I'd met in the last two weeks. So far my disguise had been good. I hoped it still was.

I wound down the window – the car was old enough to have a handle.

'Yes, officer.'

Any faith I had left in the police was gone. The cuckoos in the flats were always tipped off when there was a raid. And everyone I'd met while drugging dismissed them with contempt.

'You can't sleep here.'

'Just going,' I said and, to my relief, he waved me off.

I stopped round the corner, checked Sandy Cameron's car was still in the police car park and drove back to my room.

A patchwork of different linoleums lined the hall floor outside my room, barely visible beneath pizza boxes, empty beer cans and flyers. One of the tenants had cleaned out their room by sweeping all the rubbish into the hall. A ratty old broom leaned against Number 3's doorframe so it was probably the woman who lived there. Not that I was sure it was a woman. I hadn't seen them but when they started shouting at night they sounded like one.

I went to unlock the padlock I'd added to reinforce the lock on my door, bolting it into the frame, and froze. It was open.

Shit.

Police?

I hoped not because they wouldn't have to look far to find the stash of crack and other stuff I'd bought over the last two weeks in a desperate attempt to cover as many dealers as I could. That was before I realised there were too many. Far, far too many.

No, not the police. They'd have nabbed me already.

Who then?

The door opened.

Tam stood there. A wary-looking Tam whose face relaxed when she saw me.

'What are you doing here?'

'Come to redo your hair. I used the spare keys. I didn't want to hang around outside.'

'No need. I can do my hair.'

'And Dad wanted me to check you were all right. He's feeling very responsible.'

'He shouldn't.'

187

I pushed past her into the room, unlocked the padlock I'd installed on the window and thrust it wide open.

'It does stink a wee bit,' Tam said.

'If you think the room's bad, wait till you get near me.'

I knew I sounded curt but I was struggling to deal with Tam's presence. I wasn't sure why. I owed her a lot. Her and Fergus. They'd helped me bring Janelle Bridges to life. Maybe because I was Jen Shaw to her. And I so wanted to go back to being myself. None of that was her fault, though.

I made a big effort to sound less like I might be building up to slapping her.

'People like me aren't too fussed about personal hygiene.' I managed a smile. 'You'd know that if you visited the bathroom here.' I pulled the only chair in the room over to the window and sat down. 'It won't be so bad here.'

She pulled a face, though, when she stood over me and started running her fingers over my head.

'The colour's fine. A bit of root showing but not much. Your hair's quite dark with grease anyway. But the bald patches are growing back. You're going to have to watch that. I'll sort it now and I'll leave you some depilatory cream although it's not easy to do your own head.'

The sharp smell of the cream fought against the stale odours that not even the open window could disperse.

'Five minutes and I'll check it.' She sat on the floor by the open window. 'How did it go today?'

'Fine. Your dad's friend was right. This dealer is… OK.'

It had only taken a few days of trawling through Glasgow, trying to meet as many dealers as possible and buying a lot of crack, to realise how impossible it was going to be to find Nick this way. Fergus had asked a friend from his addiction self-help group, a currently clean crack addict, for help in identifying a dealer one rung up from the youngsters on the streets. And one who was low on the scale of criminality where mid-range was someone who'd kill you without thinking twice. And I'd spent the week since Fergus told me where he hung out waiting around to meet him. The days, anyway. The nights were for my other project.

'I made contact and now I have to wait for him to call me. If he calls me. And even if he does it feels pretty hopeless. I can't just ask him to give me a rundown on who's who in the drugs business in Glasgow. I doubt he'll even want to chat to me.' I sighed. 'No wonder Nick wanted the information Sandy could give him.'

Tam looked beyond me at the walls adorned with mould, the sticky floor and filthy sheets that barely hid the brown stains on the mattress. 'Maybe you should give up. Try something else.'

'I can't. Is this stuff ready to come off yet?'

She scraped a patch of cream off my head. 'Another minute or so.'

'And then you have to go.' I took a deep and wobbly breath and tried to sound less harsh. 'I mean it, Tam. I can't explain but you being here... so normal and clean and... it makes everything worse. I can cope better if –'

'OK.'

She removed the cream and packed her stuff away.

'You sure there's nothing else I can do?'

'There is one thing...'

'Go on.'

I pulled a rubbish sack from under the bed, opened it and tossed the crack I'd bought at the flats into it. 'I've had to buy a lot of shit to get this far. Could you get rid of it for me? I hate asking you but...'

She took it. I didn't need to say anything else but some part of me wanted to confide in her. She deserved it.

'Maybe your Dad told you but I had — that is *have* a problem with cocaine. I thought I could handle it. This is crack, anyway. But...'

'It's fine. And Dad didn't tell me by the way.' She hesitated by the door. 'I'll come back any time to remove it. If you want.'

'You won't need to. I'm going to stop hanging out with the low levels. I might as well stand in Glasgow Central all day on the off-chance Nick will walk through. I'll wait for this dealer to call and...'

'And what?'

'I don't know. Stop badgering me. I'll work it out. I need more time for Cameron anyway.'

She was quiet. Both she and Fergus had tried to persuade me not to follow Sandy Cameron. They thought it was more dangerous than hanging out with drug dealers. Maybe they were right, but both my missions seemed so unlikely to succeed I couldn't give up on either of them.

'Don't come back, Tam.'

'You'll check in, though. Like we agreed.'

I nodded. I'd set up several gmail addresses and used one of them to communicate with Fergus and Tam.

'Dad rings Tregonna. Like you asked. There's never any answer. No one's there.'

'Thanks.'

And she left.

And as soon as she'd gone, I wanted to run after her and beg her to come back.

'Why did you tell her to go?'

I'd spoken out loud but the sound was reassuring. It was my voice. Not Nell's. Not even the sullen version of myself I'd been with Tam. Sometimes I needed to hear my own voice. To remind myself I had one.

'I can't spend time with Tam. Being someone else – it's all or nothing.'

And now I was talking to myself. Well, why not? I wasn't the only person in this building who did that. The sound of voices throwing words into the emptiness filled the space during the nights I'd spent here. It was why I preferred sleeping elsewhere. I wasn't that different to the other inhabitants after all. I wondered if they too had long imaginary conversations in their heads as well. I spoke to Ma and sometimes to Nick. It made me feel better.

'Get some sleep,' I told myself.

I checked Sandy Cameron's car again then lay on the bed and let myself drift for a while. With the bag gone, the room felt better. I could let go and be nothing now. Not Jen. Not Nell. Just a body lying on a bed. Unwatched. Untouched. As anonymous as the pebbles on a beach washed over by the incoming tide. I heard the water's murmur and I slept.

The afternoon was over when I woke. I felt better. No more buying shit. It was the right decision. Its presence in the room had been a battle I'd had to fight over and over again.

'I'm an addict.'

I'd never said it out loud before. Not the actual words. Something clarified inside me. I didn't have time to explore it but I would. Later. For now I had a pressing appointment with a certain police officer. Time to make myself look nondescript.

I treated myself to a quick wash with a flannel and a bottle of water, avoiding the faded tattoo Tam had painted onto my neck. My Nell clothes smelled so bad after two weeks of no washing that a clean body beneath them would make no difference when I put them back on. I used the chemical camping toilet I kept under the bed. Nothing would make me use the loo in the house. Then put clean clothes on – black sweat pants and a black t-shirt.

Bliss.

I pulled a beanie down over my head to complete the change and went out, my thoughts full of Nick. I had some idea now of what it must have cost him to deal with Ma and me turning up in Malta when he was consumed by another identity. To step out of it enough to come up with a plan to rescue Rania and ensure we got back to the UK safely.

I'd have liked to talk to him about it. In reality. Rather than in my head.

In the couple of weeks since I'd started following DCI Sandy Cameron, I'd been surprised to discover how regular his hours were. He arrived at divisional headquarters at eight o'clock every morning, put his car in the car park and left between five and six. Either he was a shirker or police work was more routine than I'd thought from watching television.

He never seemed to leave the office, either. I'd watched the entrances and the car park for the first couple of days, until the woman serving behind the counter at the nearest café had started to give me a suspicious look when I went in. Then I hung around on the street but watching someone isn't as easy as you'd think. People start to notice you and I was worried someone would eventually report me to the police. If I'd been able to park anywhere near, it would have helped but the roads around were all delivery only. Plus I needed time to visit dealers and buy crack.

So I took a leaf out of Cameron's book and bought a GPS tracking device, which I stuck to his wheel arch one night and tracked on a smartphone I used only for that. It wasn't ideal. He could still leave on foot or in another car but I figured he was less likely to engage in criminal activities with another police officer present, which was probably naive. It was the best I could do, though. It was all I could do. I'd quickly learned a sole operator, like me, couldn't manage twenty-four-hour surveillance. I still followed him in and out every day, figuring those were the moments when he was most likely to peel off and see someone.

Before I went to follow him home, I drove to a pub in the West End whose Wi-Fi signal reached the narrow road behind it, parked up, logged on with another phone – this one without a sim – and explored the local news. It was probably paranoid but the fear of being found because of my internet searches felt very real. There seemed to be no end to what the experts could do to track me if they wanted. No news about Leila's house. Still no bodies found in it, either. Which gave me hope she was alive. I didn't see how a body could have been hushed up. I prayed she hadn't fled the fire into something worse. Had she been snatched as she escaped and killed elsewhere?

I enlarged the search to cover the whole country. No unidentified female bodies. Nothing. And no news about Ma. No reports of missing children. I didn't think it meant anything but it made me feel better. I wanted to call Ma. Desperately wanted to. I wanted to know they were all safe. I wanted to know they were all well. But I was frightened I'd betray them if I did.

There were no reports of unidentified male bodies, either. Not in Glasgow nor anywhere else. I breathed a sigh of relief. I knew it didn't mean anything. I knew if Nick was dead there was every chance his body would never be found. But I couldn't help checking and feeling better when there was nothing reported.

'Where are you, Nick?' I'd spoken the words aloud but I didn't care. 'There's so much I need to tell you. So much you need to know. Why did you go and disappear like that?'

I smacked the dashboard.

'I had to.'

I could hear his voice saying the words. I knew that's what he'd say. Just like he always did.

'You know that, Jen. It's my job.'

And he'd say that too.

'Your job. Your shitty job.' The words burst out of me. 'How can you do it? It's driving me mad, you know. This being undercover stuff. Look at me. I'm pretending to have a conversation with you.'

'It's OK. Anything that keeps you sane is fine.'

His voice in my head was soft and kind. I wanted it to be real so badly.

'I'm not sure I am sane,' I said. 'Not anymore.'

'Then stop. I mean it, Jen. You should stop.'

'So easy for you to say. But I can't. Basset and Cameron. They're threatening Rania and Aya. You don't know that, do you? Because you're not here. You're never here. You're always off doing something else.'

I was shouting now but I didn't care.

'And they killed my father.'

The force and volume of the last words shocked even me. Shit, I was losing it big time. I didn't care. Ranting made me feel better. Even if it was only to people in my head.

The alarm on my phone bleeped. It was time for me to go after DCI Sandy Cameron.

I drove to Glasgow Police Divisional Headquarters and waited until DCI Sandy Cameron's now familiar metallic grey Volvo estate came out of the car park. I followed him home, then parked my car up the street, took my rucksack out of the boot and walked to his house – modern and very cream apart from the rows of brown brick that framed the windows and front porch. It was detached although the high shrubs and bushes in the garden disguised the fact that the neighbours were close. A quick glance into the drive showed me his car was still there alongside his wife's Sandero, so I strolled down the road to the nearby park and waited, sitting on a bench against a tree that hid me from the entrance.

Sure enough Sandy appeared shortly afterwards with a tubby Jack Russell trotting along beside him, came into the park and walked around its perimeter path. I didn't follow him. I'd done it the first few times and there wasn't enough cover to be discreet. There was no point, anyway. In twenty minutes time, he and the dog – now slightly out of breath – would emerge from the other side of the park and walk slowly back to his house. And they would probably stay there all evening, only emerging for a quick walk in the garden with the dog later on. A couple of times, he and his wife had gone out. Once to what was clearly a dinner party at a friend's and once to the cinema where they'd seen *Ford vs Ferrari* but left before the end, which was a pity because it was one of my favourite films. But normally they stayed in. Somewhere between 11 and 12, the lights upstairs would come on for half an hour and then nothing until morning. Except the cat. They had a cat too. A black and white one with ragged ears. A fighter. He was in and out of the cat flap all night long, checking the garden for trespassers and doing a macabre, teetering sideways dance when he saw them, hair raised and spitting. Until they scuttled off. The cat lived life on the edge but Cameron's was screamingly dull. And I was screamingly bored. And screamingly stressed. A strange combination. I knew it was starting to play games with my head. Only the thought I might miss the one night Sandy gave himself away, the one night he gave me a lead I could follow to find out exactly what he was up to, kept me grimly sticking to my routine.

Back at Sandy's house, I waited, as usual, until he'd gone inside and until the elderly man who lived in the house opposite and spent his life in the garden had watered his pots which he did as regularly as clockwork just before *Eastenders* started. As soon as the opening music wailed out through his open windows, I checked the street was clear – it always was – and climbed the stately lime tree at the far corner of Sandy's garden until its canopy surrounded and hid me. I found my spot, wedged between three branches stretching outwards and upwards towards the sky, pulled out a thin rope from my rucksack and tied myself in. One evening I'd grown so tired, I'd dozed off and nearly fallen.

I loved this tree. Sitting in it, bathed in the light filtering through its leafy branches was the only time I felt at all calm.

It was old. Far older than the houses and the road. It had first thrust its roots into the earth before Bonnie Prince Charlie had fled overseas. It had witnessed the Highland Clearances bringing people to the big cities, which had prospered thanks to the linen, cotton, sugar and tobacco trades and, in Glasgow, the growth of the Clyde as a shipbuilding centre. And as a centre for the transport of slaves. I wondered if the lime tree would think anything much had changed over the years it had been alive.

Money was still the big imperative.

It drove trade whether it was in sugar, or cars, or people, or drugs. People wanted money. The desire for it ran beneath everything and as I stroked the lime's gnarled and knobbly trunk, twisted and intertwined over the years, a sudden image came to me. A memory of the times I'd climbed cranes and watched the day deepen into night beneath me. Watched as the lights came on and showed the city's arteries, a vast network of major and minor roads, of streets and avenues, and drives and paths, all lit up in the dark. I'd thought them beautiful. They'd given me a sense of connectedness. But now the image seemed ugly. Money was the only thing that connected people. Linking traders to buyers. Forcing the have-nots to work for the haves. And if you were one of the many who didn't have money, you were somehow seen as second-rate. A failure. An also-ran in the great race of life.

I shook the thought off. It was too depressing. Not everybody was like that. Somehow, though, it was hard to believe. I tried to think of something else. Shut my eyes and leaned my face against the lime's warm bark. Thought of the woods behind Tregonna. Waited for a memory to come.

'Green or black?'

It was Nick's voice.

'Green or black?' he said again.

And I was back in Alajar. In the weekly market in the square outside the bar, staring at the plane trees that shaded it in summer but were now stark and bare. The day was full of noise and colour, though. Everybody came to the market. To buy from local farmers and artisans but also to catch up with the local news.

'Green or black?'

'I don't mind. You choose. You know I'm not that keen on them anyway.'

He shook his head at me in mock disgust.

'Come and taste them. There must be one sort you like. Maybe the big black ones cured in oil and garlic? Or these little green ones soaked in salt and lemon? They're all so different. You can't dislike them all.'

But I did. All olives tasted the same to me. Bitter and harsh. I couldn't make out the differences Nick talked about.

The memory of their taste was sharp in my mouth, though, as I waited out the hours until the lights in the house went out and memories of the other sights and smells in the market crowded out the bad thoughts. Once all was quiet, I climbed down, unrolled my sleeping bag and slept in a gap between the shed and a cluster of bushes, near enough to the drive to be woken if Sandy took his car out. I could have slept in the tree. I'd have loved to sleep in the tree but I didn't have the gear and I suspected any specialist climbing shops where I could buy it might have been told to watch out for me.

In the morning, as usual, Cameron repeated his walk to the park with the dog and, as soon as he headed back to the house, I went to my car, waited for him and followed him to work. I risked a coffee at the café where the woman had started to recognise me but, today, there was a man serving. He barely looked at me as I took the cup.

'Nice morning,' I said.

He just grunted.

'Coffee smells good,' I added, desperate for him to reply.

'Uh-uh.'

I gave up and sat down.

'Don't draw attention to yourself like that.'

Nick was in my head again. Only saying what I knew, though. Because he wasn't real. Not real. Not really real.

'Sometimes I have to talk.' I couldn't help muttering a reply. 'Speak to a real person. To check I still exist. I'd like to speak to you but you've sloped off and left everybody thinking you're dead. How could you do that?'

I realised I was behaving like a nutter and shut up.

There was Wi-Fi here. I went through my normal routine of checking the news. No dead bodies. No missing children. Nothing about Ma.

What should I do today? Now that I'd decided to abandon checking out drug dealers.

Go back and sleep? I wasn't tired. The nights weren't cold and my nest amongst the Camerons' shrubbery was more comfortable than the bed in my room. It smelled a lot better too. I couldn't, I absolutely couldn't, do nothing. I'd go mad. I ran through the possibilities – frighteningly few. In fact, just one.

Break in to the Camerons' house and search it. It was all I could think of. I was fairly sure I could get in, but not without it being obvious someone had. There was no easy way to do it discreetly. The dog worried me, too. Plus there was no pattern to Mrs Cameron's absences. I'd watched her for a few days and she was at home most of the time and, when she did go out, it was a quick walk to the shops.

I sipped at my coffee. I'd go back to the Camerons' house and watch. If Mrs Cameron went out, I'd scout round and see if I could work out how to break in without leaving a trace. Then I had a brainwave. A neat way of getting in and out unseen. I went to a pet shop and bought an array of dog treats and to a car accessories shop for a few bits and pieces.

I took a quick detour via Leila's house on the way back. I'd gone in to the garden one night soon after going into hiding and had a good look round the outside. All the doors and windows had been boarded and it was clear no one was living there.

I passed by most days. It wasn't far from the Camerons. There was never a sign of life, which struck me as odd. I'd have expected the site to be crawling with insurance assessors and surveyors. I was tempted to call in on the friendly lady whose son lived opposite and see what she knew. I thought she might invite me in and talk to me. I'd have liked that. But caution won the day. Besides, I looked pretty rough.

I drove past slowly and parked a hundred metres or so up the road, then walked back and past without stopping or changing pace. The house stood quiet among the bushes. The grass had grown and already the garden had an abandoned look. Dark shadows left by the smoke flared out from the boarded-up windows.

Glasgow had turned out to be as dangerous for Leila as Syria.

As I turned to walk back up the road, a car drew up at the gate. A young woman I recognised as Leila's sister got out. She knelt down and fiddled with the gate mechanism, then stood and pushed it open, got back in the car and drove through. The power must be cut. She didn't bother to get out to shut it again, so I counted to fifty, slipped in after her and crawled through the shrubbery until I could see the front of the house. Her car was parked there and the padlock chaining the temporary door shut hung open. Maybe she'd come to fetch something. Or maybe, just maybe, Leila was still there.

Sure enough, when she came out half an hour later, she was empty-handed. She locked the padlock but instead of pocketing the key, she walked round to the water butt at the side of the house, lifted its lid and hung the key inside.

I waited till she'd gone and retrieved it.

Twenty-two

The stink inside was overpowering. The fire had started in the sitting room, now a charred ruin with blackened walls and the ceiling burnt through to reveal singed rafters. It had reached the kitchen and dining room but the fire service hoses had done more damage there than the flames.

Upstairs was largely untouched although it reeked of smoke and damp ash. Most of the easily moveable items – clothes, bedding, ornaments and so on – had been taken, and only the furniture remained. Leila's bedroom had been emptied as well.

I was sure now the fire hadn't killed Leila. It hadn't penetrated upstairs. Maybe the smoke would have been a danger but with no dead bodies reported, I thought it unlikely. She'd escaped the flames but what had she escaped into?

She wasn't here, though. No one could have stayed in this damp and stinking ruin. Nevertheless I searched, hoping at the very least to find some indication she'd survived. Upstairs didn't take long. No bedding on the beds and the wardrobes were empty.

Downstairs I peered into the empty kitchen cabinets and checked the cupboard under the stairs, crammed full of coats and shoes before, but also bare now. I even looked under the blackened ruin of the sofa. Nothing. Or was I missing something? I'd hunted high and low for Leila in this house before and not found her. She'd appeared in the hall last time, when I'd been upstairs. I went back to the cupboard under the stairs.

Something about the floor caught my attention. Before it had been hidden under the mass of discarded boots the shoe rack couldn't accommodate. Narrow wooden boards covered it except on the far left where a larger slab of wood had been inset. It looked exactly like the topmost of a set of stairs. Were there steps in here leading down to a cellar? A cellar that had been blocked off?

There was a narrow gap round the outside of what I'd thought was a wall to my left. Maybe it wasn't a wall. Maybe someone had fixed a board there and painted it to match the walls of the rest of the cupboard. To hide the steps down to a cellar? I gave it a gentle push and then a harder shove. It didn't budge but it felt more insubstantial than a wall should. I tried to lever it out with the blade of a multi-tool I'd carried ever since running into trouble a few months ago, but with no success. Then I ran the knife down the side and met an obstacle. A bolt, I thought. A small one, though. It wouldn't take much to break it.

I gripped the frame of the door between the cupboard and the hall and lifted myself off the ground, swung backwards and forwards a bit, then kicked out at the door. It was an awkward move round to my left but it was enough. The board swung open. The far side must have had hinges holding it to the wall.

Behind it, steps ran down into a dark space. Not an empty space. At the bottom Leila stood, both hands raised and pointing a gun at me. Every muscle in her body was poised with deadly intent.

'It's me. Jen,' I said quickly. 'I'm alone.'

She lowered the gun and a slight shudder shook her frame.

'Push the board shut behind you,' she said. 'And come down.'

The house must be older than I'd thought and extended and modernised out of recognition because the cellar was a small space with walls of unpainted brick, made smaller by the low ceiling. Someone had tried to make it as comfortable as possible. An old piece of carpet with rugs piled over it covered the floor and there were two armchairs and a bed. A set of shelves contained books and food and bottles of water. There was light too. Powered by a portable battery over in one corner. A petrol stove radiated enough heat to fight the damp. It wasn't bad. And it definitely smelled better than my room. The fire hadn't reached here.

'It's not for long, we hope.' Leila had followed my eyes as they looked around. 'My father is finding me somewhere else but we need to be careful, very careful.'

She looked thinner than when I'd last seen her and tougher. More like the Leila I remembered from the beach at Calais. The Leila who'd learned her way round a gun in Syria. Her arms were nothing but bone and muscle leaping as she flexed and stretched her hands continually.

'You were hiding down here the first time I came, weren't you?'

'Yes. When I first got back, I couldn't sleep for fear the police would come and grab me. And send me back. My father made this for me and put the alarm in. And cameras so I could see who was outside. I slept down here for the first couple of weeks.'

She poured some water into a glass. 'Do you want some? I can't make you tea because the kettle uses up too much battery and the light is the most important thing. And the 5G.'

I nodded and she gestured for me to sit in one of the chairs for all the world as though we'd met for a coffee and a chat.

'What happened?' I asked.

'After you went, almost as soon as you'd gone, two men broke in. I'd barely shut the front door when they broke the back window in the kitchen. Very quietly. If I'd been upstairs, I don't think I'd have heard. I just had time to hide down here.'

'It was my fault. I'm sorry, Leila. They'd hacked my phone and used it to follow me. And I turned it on while I was here.'

'They? Who are they?'

'Shona's father. DCI Cameron.'

'Ah.'

'I should have told you more about what was going on.'

I told Leila the bare bones of what had happened. Enough for her to know that Sandy Cameron was as involved as Shona and that they were after me because they knew I knew. She didn't seem surprised and I wondered if she'd had her own suspicions.

I didn't mention Nick.

It was warm down here. I pulled off my beanie. Leila's eyes flickered.

'What happened to your hair?'

'Sacrificed. To stop men like the ones who broke in here from catching up with me.'

'They were after you too, you know.'

'How do you know?'

'They called your name. Then mine. Then searched for us. I watched them. I told you my father had set up cameras. Some outside and a couple inside. He set up a 5G access down here so I could monitor them on my phone. '

'Was Cameron with them?'

'No. It was two men I'd never seen before.'

'What did they look like?'

'One of them was skinny and pale. He had, I think, a lot of piercings but it was difficult to tell. The quality of the camera image isn't tops. I saw the other one more clearly.' She shuddered. 'He was horrible. Bald and covered with tattoos. His head, I mean, as well as his arms and neck. And squat, like a toad.'

In my brief career undercover, I'd seen no one who fitted her description of the second man but the skinny and pale man with piercings rang a bell.

'I heard them search the cupboard under the stairs,' she went on. 'They pulled all the coats off the walls. But they didn't find the way down.'

'I expect they dumped them on the floor and covered it.'

'They stopped hunting after that and I could see them in the hall, looking at the skinny one's phone, so I crept up to the top of the stairs to listen. He said you'd just appeared down the road.'

That must have been when I'd turned my phone on. Thank the gods I'd left the house via the neighbours' gardens. I had a feeling I'd have run straight into the two of them if I'd gone out through the gate. They must have been hanging around, waiting for the family to leave before breaking in.

'Then they said, there was no one here so they might as well burn the place down, like Cameron said.'

'Cameron?'

'Yes.'

No wonder she hadn't been surprised when I'd told her he was involved.

'I could hear them quite well at that point. They went into the sitting room after that. There's no camera there so I couldn't see what they were doing, but my father told me that was where the fire started. When they came back, I could only hear one of them – the skinny one – because he was leaning right up against the cupboard door. The other was further down the hall looking into the sitting room. And then the power went out so I could only listen. The skinny one said, *Excellent*. And that they'd wait to be sure the fire took. Then they chatted.'

I remembered the news report about the fire Tam had shown me. The fire chief had said there was no evidence of accelerants. I guessed they'd created some kind of electric fault. It was easy enough. An electric heater with the screws in the plug loosened and some insulation scraped off the wires inside. A tug on the cable would cause a short and heat or sparks. If it was next to some curtains... They'd clearly not wanted the fire to be suspicious. I still wondered why they'd set the house on fire in the first place. If they were sure neither of us were there.

'They talked about children.' Leila's voice cut through my thoughts.

'Children?' I forgot about everything else.

'The children. The skinny one said, *the children*. Like the other would know who he was talking about.'

'You're sure?'

'Yes. It was weird. Once the power went out and the cameras stopped working, it was like I could hear better. He definitely said, *the children*, and then the other one interrupted him. His words were a mumble, though. No idea what he said.'

She leaned forward and the light caught her face. She'd shut her eyes tight and her skin was taut with concentration.

'*They've been moved.* The skinny one said that next. And I think he meant the children. *Everything's up and running again. But they've been moved. It's for the best really. The new place is much more convenient for us.* Or something along those lines. I heard the last bit clearly.'

'He said *They*? Not *It*?'

'Yes. He must have been a couple of feet away from me at this point. I heard everything very clearly.'

They meant children. People not objects. Not drugs. Where were the drugs in all this? I didn't know what to think. Except maybe Nick'd got it all wrong. Or maybe Cameron did a bit of everything. Like the other traffickers. Were some of the children ending up here in Glasgow? I thought so. It was the only thing that made sense. Cameron was running a child-trafficking ring here in Glasgow. Somewhere in one of the streets like the ones I walked or drove down every day there were children locked up. Children like the ones in the photographs he'd sent me.

'Did they say where the children were?'

'No. But they must have been nearby. He said it was more convenient. Then something about the 26th. *Everything ready for the 26th*? That was the toad man and it was a question. I didn't hear the answer. Because I crept back down the stairs. I smelled the smoke.'

'Shit.'

'I didn't dare leave.' Her voice cracked although I wasn't sure if it was the memory of fear or something more like anger. She breathed in and out a few times, then carried on. 'I was sure they were outside waiting and watching. So I called 999. If you stand at the top of the stairs, there's still signal. I called 999 and said I lived opposite and I'd seen fire and smoke. Then I called my father and told him.' She paused. 'The firemen got here very quickly.'

'And you stayed in the cellar? Even though the place was on fire.'

'There's gratings in the wall letting in air from outside so I was safer down here than...'

She was probably right but it must have taken some steel to stay put.

'My father texted me from time to time. And after everyone had gone, the firemen and the police, he came down here. I told him everything then. About the men. And Shona on Malta.'

'Ah.'

'I kept remembering your face when you saw the Christmas card. And the fact they broke in looking for you. I guessed it might all be related. So he's told the Camerons I've gone missing. Gone missing *again*, he said. As if he thought I might have absconded once more. And as if he was furious with me. Like washing his hands type furious. And suspecting I might have started the fire. He sent Maama to her sister's in Aberdeen because he wasn't sure she could keep the lie going. Told the Camerons she was beside herself with grief.'

'Sandy Cameron didn't know about your hiding place down here.'

'No.'

'I guess he thinks you left with me.'

She nodded.

'What are you going to do?' We spoke simultaneously.

'You first,' I said.

'Stay in hiding. My father's going to try to find me somewhere else.'

'I think you should move soon. I think they might work it out eventually.'

'Maybe. I got my father to get me a gun. If they do come back, they won't find it easy to get me.' She paused and her face stared into the past. 'I won't be easy meat again.'

'Easy meat?' It was the phrase Cameron had used when he'd threatened Rania and Aya.

'The men, the traffickers. They use it a lot. Like they're blaming the women and the children for what's going to happen to them.'

We sat in silence for a few seconds after that.

'I was wrong, you know.' She spoke in a low voice I could barely make out. 'I told you I was happy living a hidden life. But I started thinking about it after you'd gone. And it isn't enough. I want a real life and I can't see how I'm ever going to have one.'

Neither could I.

'If only I could go back and do things differently.' Her voice was still low but filled with some passion I couldn't identify.

'You were young. Very young. And misled, I guess?'

Leila heard the question. 'Yes. But I believed. Maybe that made me easy to exploit but I believed.' She gave me a hard look. 'My father asked me if I still believed. We've talked a lot more openly since the fire. I know you tried to ask me the same question.'

I wondered if she'd answer. And if she'd tell the truth. Or if she even knew it.

'No, I don't,' she said eventually. 'Not like I did when I went. I was blind. But yes, too. I do still believe that there are other and better ways of living. But I didn't find them in Syria. Not at all.'

There were so many diffcrent sides to her but this thoughtful one felt the closest to a fusion of them all. Not that I understood her. Not that I was sure I trusted her. I wasn't in the right frame of mind to trust anybody.

'I suppose you're in hiding too?' she said.

'No.'

'No? Why the disguise?'

'Well, I am hiding, in a way. But I'm doing it because I'm going to deal with Cameron. I'm watching him. I'm going to find out what he's up to and get him put away. And the men in Calais. And as many of the others as I can.'

'I wish I could help.' The words burst out of her.

'You can. Maybe.'

She shook her head. 'I can't leave here.'

'I don't mean physically. You know Cameron. Tell me about him. Everything.'

'I don't know much. Maama is friends with Alice his wife, really. Alice teaches Business Management at Glasgow Caledonian Uni and Maama met her at an evening event designed to get local businesses on side. For workplace training and so on. We don't often see him. So apart from knowing he's in the police...'

I waited to see if anything else came to her.

'My father never liked him,' she said suddenly. 'I've just realised that. Even before I told him everything. He didn't like him. In fact, I'm not sure he liked the family.'

'What makes you say that?'

'What makes me say that?' She disappeared into herself again as she thought.

'His expression, maybe, when Maama used to go on about how brilliant Alice was. How he should employ her to give us business advice. And stuff like that. He'd ignore her and his face would go – sort of rigid. And more recently...'

I waited.

'After I got home. When she went on about how much we owed

209

them for getting me out, he muttered something about how we'd paid them what we owed. More than what we owed. And, you know, he wasn't shocked when I told him everything after the fire. I thought he'd need a lot of convincing but he believed me straightaway. Said all Cameron was interested in was money. He's kept on asking my father for more money even after I came home.'

'Why?'

'Cameron pretends it's for additional expenses but they both know it's to keep him quiet. That's another reason why my father was happy to tell him I'd disappeared again. After the fire.'

Money. It was all about money. Leila's predicament had been a wonderful opportunity for Cameron to make money.

'It's odd, though,' Leila went on. 'They never seem to have much money. Their house is nothing special. It's in a nice area but it's small. You'd think they'd –'

'I want to get into their house.' I interrupted Leila. 'Have a good look round. But I need to do it without them knowing anyone's been there. Mrs Cameron seems to come and go randomly. I never know how long she's going to be. You said she worked at the university but she's at home most of the time.'

'A lot of her teaching will be online.'

Of course.

Her phone buzzed and she picked it up.

I automatically looked at my phone – the one tracking Cameron's car. Shit. He was on the move.

'Got to go,' I said.

I gave Leila one of the gmail addresses I'd set up. Told her to let me know what happened. Told her to get her family to stop keeping the padlock key in the water butt. And went. Once again, I slipped through the neighbours' gardens until I was several houses down before rejoining the road. I didn't think her house would be watched but it was better to be careful.

Twenty-three

I checked Cameron's car again as soon as I was clear. He'd driven home. A wave of hopelessness sloshed through me as I drove back to his house wondering if he'd stopped anywhere on the way. I couldn't follow him twenty-four hours a day. Not on my own. Especially while I was also still trying to find Nick. It was too much for one person. How had I ever thought this would work?

I needed help. I knew that. I'd told myself a thousand times already. But there was none. I wouldn't ask Tam or Fergus. It was too dangerous. And it wasn't their problem. I could have asked Angel, except I didn't dare call him. They'd be watching him. Wherever he was. Duncan too. Even if he wasn't being watched, his phone could have been hacked. He'd suspected it himself.

'I'm getting nowhere.' The words burst out of me as I slammed the car door shut and drove away. Nowhere.

'You're doing fine.' I heard Nick say.

'Stop lying.'

'I'm not.'

'You always lie. Your life is a lie. You wouldn't know the truth if it slapped you in the face.'

'That's not fair.'

Maybe he was right. But I didn't care.

I parked up, grabbed some sunglasses and another hat from the back seat. More of a baseball cap this time. A pathetic attempt to look different. I'd walk past the house and, if there was no one around, I'd nip into the space between the shrubbery and the shed to watch from there.

It took two passes before the elderly *Eastenders* fan opposite finished pruning his roses and went round the back of his house. I settled down for another long and boring wait. Ten minutes later, Sandy Cameron came out of the front door carrying a suitcase. He put it in the car as Alice, his wife, followed him, holding a small bag.

'Anything else to come?' he called.

I couldn't hear her reply but clearly there wasn't as he shut the boot.

Were they going away? Together? I thought quickly. It was Friday. Friday afternoon. Were they heading off for the weekend? Might I have a whole two days to break into their house and root around undisturbed? Although I should probably follow them and see where they were going. Maybe I could do both. I slithered a little closer.

'Can you manage your suitcase?' he was saying as she got into the passenger seat.

She nodded.

'Then I'll drop you outside the terminal.'

Just her going away then. I made a swift decision. I'd stay and try to get into the house. He'd more than likely go back to work afterwards.

Once they'd left, I circled the house a few times. Just to check they'd done nothing stupid like leaving a window open or a door unlocked. They hadn't. I'd have to use Plan B. And if it didn't work, then Plan C.

Plan C was simple – break in by forcing a door or smashing a window. But it meant Cameron would know someone had broken in as soon as he got back. If he wasn't warned by an alarm. There was no giveaway box but that proved nothing.

Plan B was better. If I could make it work. He might suspect someone had been in but he'd never be sure and it was more likely to avoid any problematic alarms.

I retrieved a small black rucksack from my car and went back to their drive, empty now except for Alice Cameron's Sandero. This was the most dangerous part. I put on gloves, took out the glass breaker I'd bought, waited until a car was coming near and pressed the tool against the front passenger's window. It punched into the window, cracking it into smithereens immediately. There was only a quiet crunch, covered by the engine noise from the passing vehicle. No one appeared. No one called out. I pushed the smashed glass into the car and swept out the last pieces clinging to the frame with a small brush. Perfect. The car was parked with the passenger side away from the path to the front door and a quick glance wouldn't reveal the window was missing.

I reached in through the empty frame, opened the glove box and rummaged around until I found what I'd hoped would be there. The remote for the garage. The Camerons didn't use their garage. The drive was wide. It was easier to park the cars in front of the house. However, at some point, Mrs Cameron had put the remote in the glove box and there it had stayed.

I opened the garage and went in, found the light and switched it on as the door shut behind me. It was a bright, white-painted space with a clean concrete floor and a sharp smell of dust and chemicals. There was no room for the cars, though, because it was full of stuff. Mainly boxes that had once held irons and kettles and other household items. All precariously piled against the back wall. An assortment of laundry racks took up one corner, empty apart from a few odd socks waiting here on the off-chance their partners might turn up. Not quite ready to give up all hope of a reconciliation. A shelf rack on the wall adjoining the house was piled with detergents, cleaning materials and plastic boxes containing tools. And beyond them, a door led into the house.

Happy days! My blood pumped faster when I saw it. I'd hoped there'd be a connecting door.

It leaped even more and started pounding round my head when I tried the handle and it opened.

I was in.

I froze for a few seconds. If an alarm went off, I'd have to run for it.

Nothing happened.

My first bit of luck. I hoped it would hold. I hoped if there were alarms, they were only on the outside doors and windows. The Camerons had a dog and a cat and that made it complicated to have sensors in the rooms. Not impossible. But expensive.

The door led into the kitchen. A smallish room. Not big enough to eat in and the units were neither new nor upmarket. A noise of hoarse breathing broke the quiet.

The pug stared at me from its basket. I muttered *good boy* several times in as calm and confident a voice as I could and felt around in the rucksack for the pigs' ears the assistant in the pet shop had assured me dogs loved and would keep them occupied for hours. I walked towards it and dropped a couple in the basket. A quick sniff and it dived in, tail wagging. Clearly the gift had established I was a friend.

The kitchen was clean and tidy. Nothing left out on the counters. A small whiteboard said they needed Earl Grey tea and beef stock cubes. A hasty look in the cupboards showed nothing unusual although they had an amazing array of implements for removing bits of shellfish from their shells. Someone in the house liked coffee as there was an expensive but elderly espresso machine on the counter. Keys hung on a board by the back door and I wondered if I dared find the ones that unlocked it and nick them.

Better not. Their absence would probably be noticed straightaway and the locks changed which would defeat the whole purpose.

Downstairs there were only two other rooms: a big sitting room with windows on both sides, dominated by a large television and squashy sofas; and a formal dining room. They ate here rather than in the kitchen. Salt, pepper and mustard were on a tray on the table along with a scattering of place mats.

Leila was right. The house was nothing special, big enough for a couple whose children had left home but nothing remarkable, and the furnishings were comfortable but neither opulent nor stylish. The dining room furniture – table, chairs and sideboard – were old-fashioned and dark, although the sage green walls and matching chair upholstery made it a pleasant room. Nondescript paintings on the walls showed somewhere Mediterranean-looking. A quick check in the sideboard revealed only china.

The sitting room was even easier to search. The corner cupboard – far and away the prettiest object in the room with its delicate carving – contained nothing but drinks and glasses. The photographs on the surfaces showed groups of family and friends. There were a couple of Sandy in full police uniform, receiving awards, which made me want to spit but nothing helpful.

Upstairs, I poked around the wardrobes in the two main bedrooms. Only clothes. I went into the last and smallest bedroom. It was tiny and no longer a bedroom. Someone used it as an office with a desk by the window and shelves and filing cabinets lining one wall. I felt a bit more hopeful.

Which was stupid.

Because a quick glance revealed this was Alice's domain rather than the nerve centre for Sandy's criminal activities. The books on the shelves were about business and commerce with titles such as *Organisational Behaviour in the Modern Corporate Environment: The Fundamentals of Human Resource Management* and *Digital Transformation:*

Survive and Thrive in an Era of Mass Extinction. Her desk was empty apart from a mouse mat and a computer which was password-protected. Of course. And Alice used something other than the word *password* or one of her children's names.

I began to wonder why I'd been so keen to break in. What had I been expecting? An organisation chart on a wall of key people in the drugs trade in Glasgow? A map with the location of the children? Or maybe a calendar or diary with dates and times of appointments that I could attend? There *was* a calendar on the wall here. But Alice only used it for work, jotting down meetings and tutorials. It didn't even show her trip away today.

I remembered the conversation Leila had overheard. They'd mentioned the 26th. Something happening on that date. The 26th was Sunday. Today was Friday. So two days' time. Assuming they'd meant this month, of course.

I wondered if Cameron had chosen the date because his wife would be away.

I'd have to keep tabs on him for the next couple of days. Somehow. I checked his whereabouts on the phone. Glasgow Airport. Good.

I turned to the box files. They were marked with years and the one I pulled down contained the syllabus Alice had been teaching for that academic period along with assessment records for students and a host of other papers bearing the university's letterhead. I rapidly lost interest. Maybe there was something useful hidden in one of the boxes but I thought it unlikely.

The wastepaper bin caught my eye as I was about to leave and, remembering that spies and undercover agents often found their most useful information there, I emptied it on the desk and started unscrewing the papers. A receipt from a builders merchant for some ready-mixed plaster; several pages of a report on a business selling handmade jewellery that she'd edited in pencil; some more

216

papers that were clearly business analysis related; and a few post-its with cryptic reminders to herself. Her writing, although neat, was tiny. *Tickets Ballet* was on the first one and the second, deciphered after much screwing up of my eyes, turned out to be a reminder to buy batteries for her calculator. I shoved the papers into my rucksack. Time was catching up with me. I'd look at them later. Not that I thought any of it would be any use. I'd got everything I could out of this trip. Which was nothing.

I headed downstairs. The hall table had a little drawer. One last look in case it held anything and then back to my car.

I struck gold.

In amongst the mass of flyers and letters and bills, the bits of string, paperclips and elastic bands, were keys. Lots of keys. I pulled them all out and tried them until I found one that unlocked the back door. I'd keep it. Then I could let myself in and out whenever I wanted. They wouldn't notice. The drawer was a dumping ground for things that were rarely used.

I stuffed the papers back in. And stopped. There were fewer flyers for pizza deliveries and so on than I'd first thought. In fact, the papers were mostly bills. The final bills companies send out when their email reminders have failed. When they're about to take you to court. Plus letters from debt collection agencies and credit card companies. All dated recently.

I stared at them, wondering what they meant. I mean it was obvious on the surface. The Camerons were in serious financial shit. But how? They both worked. I imagined Alice Cameron's job was reasonably paid. Sandy had some profitable sidelines over and above his DCI's pay. Nothing about their lifestyle screamed excess. How had they got into this mess? I pulled out my other phone and took pictures of the bills.

The sound of a car arriving sent fear sparking through my nerves. I peered out of the front door window.

Shit. Sandy had come straight back from the airport. I'd forgotten to keep an eye on the tracker.

I stuffed everything back in the drawer and retreated to the kitchen. The pug snored gently. I shut the door into the garage behind me quietly so as not to wake it and turned the light off, praying it wouldn't have shown through to the drive, then squatted in a corner out of sight.

Cameron didn't come into the garage. I heard him in the kitchen, opening cupboards, and then the familiar hiss of a kettle being boiled, the clink of a teaspoon against china and the fridge door opening and closing. Afterwards all was quiet. I didn't dare move. Any noise might wake the pug up and remind it of my presence.

'Shit. I nearly got caught then.'

If I shut my eyes tight, I could picture Nick huddled down next to me. Whispering like we had in the dunes at Calais when we'd come up with the plan to rescue Rania.

'But you didn't.' His voice was quiet.

'What do we do now?'

'Wait until he goes out.'

'But that might be ages. He might stay here all night.'

'No choice.'

'Breaking in was a waste of time, wasn't it,' I whispered. 'I didn't discover anything and I've got to find the children. Where are they?'

He didn't answer. Because neither of us knew.

In the end the dog saved me. Cameron took it for a walk at the usual time. As soon as they'd gone, I used the key I'd filched from the hall table, and left by the back door locking it behind me.

I'd have liked to leave completely. Even my room seemed attractive. Except Sandy might take advantage of his wife's absence to go out and meet some colleagues. And I was very keen to get to know his colleagues.

218

He didn't leave the house but spent a cosy evening in front of the television. An Uber Eats cyclist delivered a takeaway around nine, leaning his bike against my tree, so that the smell of food wafted up to where I was perched and brought home to me how hungry I was. When Sandy opened the door, he was wearing sweat pants and a baggy top. Not the look of a man going out. I took a calculated risk and nipped to a chippy nearby before spending the night in my normal spot in the garden.

The next day was Saturday but Sandy went to work. I followed him in, then drove around until I found a parking space. I didn't dare leave. Until the 26th I was sticking close to him. So I hung around, swapping between cafés and walking up and down the street. The hours dragged, filled with their familiar combination of fear and boredom. The ever-present anxiety that someone might notice or recognise me. That Ma and the girls had been found. The thought of what might happen to Rania and Aya ran through my body like the scream of the dentists' drill, piercing every fibre and making it impossible to think of anything else.

I wanted to distract myself by talking to Nick but I did my best not to. I was sure it was a bad idea.

Sandy headed home at the normal time, took the dog out again as normal and spent some time watching television as normal. Once again he didn't notice that the window on the far side of Alice's car was no longer there. I went through my normal routine too. Climbed up into the tree once the road and gardens were clear and roped myself into place. No takeaway tonight, though. I wondered if he'd eaten some of the quiche Alice had left. Or maybe made himself a sandwich. There'd been some nice-looking ham in the fridge. Cut wafer-thin. Yes, a ham sandwich with some of the lettuce and a smearing of mustard. I could slip in tomorrow through the back door and look. See if he'd received any more letters from debt-collection agencies. Or if he'd added anything to the whiteboard. Check if he'd bought the Earl Grey Tea and beef stock cubes. No, he hadn't. I'd know if he'd been to a shop. Unless he'd asked someone to buy them for him. An assistant. He must have an assistant. Did police officers have secretaries? He probably didn't bother with the shopping. I guessed Alice did it all and the cooking. Even though she worked. The whiteboard was just a reminder to herself. And then I wondered if I could find a moment to buy them and wipe the board clean. Leave them in the kitchen for her to find when she returned. I started to giggle at the thought of it. She'd think he'd bought them. I could imagine the conversation.

'Oh, darling,' she'd say. 'Thank you.'

I'd never heard her speak but I thought of her as having quite a posh voice. Well-enunciated words. Probably an English accent. Yes, she didn't look Scottish. Not that I was sure what that meant.

He'd look startled when she thanked him. And she'd have to explain.

'The Earl Grey tea and the beef stock cubes,' I tried to mimic the way I thought she'd speak. 'I meant to buy them before I went away but I ran out of time. And you know how much I love my Earl Grey in the morning.' I gave a little laugh like I thought she would. 'Shall I make us a beef stew for tonight?'

And he'd say—

A sudden movement down below dragged my thoughts back from fantasyland.

Shit I'm losing it big time.

It was Sandy. Getting into his car. I'd been so caught up in my thoughts I hadn't heard him come out of the front door. He was wearing a suit. Black and sharply-cut. White shirt and a tie.

As soon as he'd got into the car, I untied the rope, slithered down the far side of the tree and ran, bent double, until I was clear of his house, then raced to my car.

Where was he going? Had he been called in to work? Possibly. I checked the time. It was late. Too late for any kind of socialising.

Work? Or something else?

I felt the beginnings of excitement ripple through my blood.

It ran even stronger as Sandy parked his car in Anniesland. I drove past, found a space myself and crept back until I was close enough to watch him.

After ten minutes or so, he got out of the car, first staring at his phone and then up and down the road. He waved at a white Toyota crawling down it. It stopped. Sandy and the driver exchanged a few words and he got in.

An Uber. I was sure he'd called an Uber. Shit. The tracker was useless. I'd have to actually follow him.

What was he doing?

I tore back to my car, pulled out, narrowly missing a youngster on a bluey green scooter, and caught the Uber up. There were a couple of cars in between us and overtaking was impossible. Still, it was probably a good thing not to be right behind him. The scooter I'd nearly hit wove its way through the traffic. It would be much easier to follow Sandy in something like that. Nothing ever drove very fast in the city.

The Uber dropped Sandy in the centre of Glasgow outside a brightly lit building with a wide entrance lined by mirrors. He marched up the steps, nodded to the bouncers and disappeared inside.

A car horn sounded behind me. I couldn't wait here any longer. I drove past and dumped the car as soon as I could. It was illegally parked but I didn't care. Then ran back. I wasn't going to be able to follow him in. One look at the face of the bouncers guarding the entrance told me that. Their clientele didn't turn up dressed in black sweat pants and a baseball cap, and trailing a few leaves and twigs.

Not that it mattered. I knew exactly what the building was

because it was written in large glowing letters either side of the door. Casino, they said. 24/7. And as a further enticement, large photos showed a plush interior of padded armchairs and banquettes, dim lighting gleaming off gold strips lining bars and, of course, tables of cards, roulette wheels and the ubiquitous machines with their brightly coloured screens promising fun and riches.

I dropped back, far enough for the bouncer to stop staring at me.

Was this some police thing? A raid?

I didn't think so.

Cameron finally left the casino at around four in the morning, jacket slung over one shoulder. He hesitated at the entrance, loosened his tie, rolled his sleeves up and set off on foot. I slipped out of the alley where I'd been watching and slunk after him through the almost empty streets. He walked easily, his limbs fluid and relaxed, all the way down to the Clyde, the great river running through the centre of the city, where he stopped and gazed out over its grey waters. A glimmer of light rimmed the eastern horizon with a blurry brightness although it was still early.

Cameron wasn't alone. A few other night wanderers had stopped to look out at the dawn or shuffled past him along the road. A strange mix of early morning workers, late night revellers meandering home, and people with nowhere else to go. A man bundled up in a thick black coat sat with his back to the wall lining the bank of the river. He was trying to pack an old sleeping bag and assorted clothes into three carrier bags that were splitting under the strain. A couple of women in nylon overalls smoked and chatted to each other, glancing at watches from time to time, while a runner pounded past them.

Tiredness was grit in my eyes and tremors in my limbs but I wasn't leaving until Sandy did.

'Your friend, Cameron,' I told Nick quietly. 'He's a gambler. You didn't know that, did you?'

Of course, he didn't.

'Don't tell me he came here for work,' I continued, muttering beneath my breath. 'I've circled the casino several times and there's no sign of the police. Besides the bouncers nodded to him like they know him well. And remember all the unpaid bills and bailiff threats. He spends all his money on gambling.'

I gave Nick a few seconds to reply. Nothing. Some part of me knew I should stop this now. But I couldn't. I had to share it with someone.

'Most of the time, I guess, he'll be online. Betting on horse racing and football matches, boxing and darts. You can even game online now. Roulette, Poker, Slot Machine. It's only because Alice is away, he's come here tonight.'

Cameron stretched his arms wide. Crescents of damp made dark shadows under his arms.

And I knew. Knew beyond a shadow of a doubt how he felt. He'd sat in that casino and felt adrenalin thrill through his blood as he risked everything on a game.

I knew that feeling. I'd felt it myself and I'd heard the gambling addicts talk about it in the short time I'd spent in rehab. The rush they felt every time they placed a bet online or fed a coin into the machine or placed a token on a roulette table. The excitement of turning over a hand in a poker game. That was the best bit. The breath-stealing wait to see what lay in store. And I thought Sandy had won. He'd felt the big high, the dopamine hit, the reward moment everyone hoped for. The one that was still soaking through his body.

He felt as though he ruled the world.

Maybe Sandy's excitement was contagious. Maybe it was dispersing into the air and I was breathing it in. Maybe I was sick of hiding and waiting and pretending and... sick of being alone. Because I couldn't stop myself.

I moved forward and stood near him, also looking out over the water. I felt the same thrill at the risk I was taking tear through my blood. The same strange mixture of lightness and breathlessness. I found a coin in my pocket – ten pence – and hurled it into the water. The sudden movement caught his eye and he looked at me.

What was I doing?

'That's my last one,' I said. 'I'm hoping it will bring me luck.'

His face was beaded with sweat but he laughed.

'An offering to the gods,' I added.

He looked me up and down. I held my ground. Would he recognise me? I didn't care.

'Here you go.' He reached into his pocket and pulled out a roll of notes, peeled a few off and handed them to me.

'You won the lottery, like?'

'Not the lottery. But I won and big. That's a small part of it.'

'Nothing like the feel of cash. It's real, isn't it?' I rubbed my fingers in the notes. 'Thank you, mate. You've saved my life.'

I didn't have to fake the smile. In that moment, I liked him.

A police siren sounded somewhere in the city, faint but strident.

His face changed. The reminder of his life burst his perfect moment.

What was I thinking?

My excitement drained away. This was stupid. It was going to achieve nothing. Stupid and dangerous. But before I could mutter an excuse and slip away, he nodded a curt goodbye himself, walked a few metres along the road and pulled out his phone. A short while later an Uber pulled up and he left.

I didn't have it in me to race back to my car and check he went home. Instead I pulled off my hat and let the cool air dry sweat from the remnants of my hair.

A skinny, white-haired lad, dressed in a leather jacket and his nose full of studs and rings, cast a look in my direction, crossed the road and stood near the other watchers.

He was familiar but I couldn't think why.

He ran his eyes over me then looked away. Clearly I wasn't worth a second glance. Instead he pulled his phone out of his leather jacket pocket and made a call as he walked away. I blessed Tam because he hadn't recognised me.

I knew where I'd seen him before. He was the youngster who'd tried to steal my phone in the Botanic Gardens. Not as young as I'd thought him then. Was he part of this? I remembered Leila's description of the two men who'd come looking for me and burned her house down. A square, bald creature with a tattooed skull and another, skinny with a face pierced with chains and studs. Was he the skinny one? Maybe Cameron's colleagues weren't too keen on his gambling. Maybe they were keeping an eye on him.

I wondered if Alice knew how bad things were. Maybe not. Maybe she was one of those women who didn't open their husband's mail. Or if she did, she could be reassured by claims the bill was an oversight. Or maybe she guessed but didn't want to face up to the truth.

Night faded into day as I trudged through the streets to my car. The normal morning bustle creaked into life. I walked under the long bridge outside Glasgow Central Station and remembered my first impressions of the city. I'd liked its 'what you see is what you get' attitude. Felt invigorated by its energy.

I didn't feel that now. I felt wasted. My thoughts all over the place and lacking the energy to collect and organise them.

A red mail van burst out of a side street and shot off up Hope Street. Did people still write letters and send cards? They must. Ma did, I was sure.

Ma.

And I knew I was going to give in and call her. I'd get rid of the sim afterwards. I needed to hear Ma's voice. To speak to someone real. I had to know they were OK.

I dialled her number. She answered straightaway.

'Jen.' It wasn't a question.

'Yes.'

I heard her breathe out. A long whisper of sound.

'We're all right,' she said. 'All of us.'

It was my turn to breathe.

'We're hiding in –'

'Don't tell me. And never say it on the phone.'

'Hiding in plain sight.'

I didn't have time to puzzle this out. Not that it mattered. They were safe.

'And the girls? How are they?'

'Rania is fine. I can't explain why. Not without telling you where we are. But it's been good for her. And for Yasmiin.'

She faltered.

'And Aya? I'm sorry, Ma. I knew she'd suffer. I wouldn't have told you to go if…'

The awful photos Cameron sent me flashed up in my head again. Some of them were of children Aya's age. Some of them were younger. Tiny scraps whose bodies almost disappeared in the rough hands holding them still.

'If it hadn't been desperate.'

I was almost glad I didn't have my phone any more. I never wanted to see those pictures again.

'Aya was not great for a while. She went all the way back into herself. Wouldn't look at us. Wouldn't talk or engage in any way. But it's getting better. She's not back to where she was but she will be.'

It was the best I could have hoped for.

'Scratching a lot. But then we all are.'

'What?'

'Cat fleas.'

I put two and two together.

'You took the kitten with you? What's its name?'

'Scooby. And yes, I did. It seemed like a good thing to do. And it has been.'

'Oh, Ma.'

'We got some hideous chemical from the vet to get rid of them.'

This was what I needed. This was reality. Cat fleas. Solid and mundane and irritating. And utterly beguiling.

'I'd better go. I just wanted to know you were OK.'

But I couldn't quite bring myself to end the call.

'Is Charlie's death linked to all this?' Ma asked.

'Yes.'

'Did he know something, too?'

'No, Ma. He wasn't involved at all. He was just in the wrong place at the wrong time.'

Or at least that was what I thought. Once again I remembered his message about finding something.

'Are you all right?'

'I think so. But I can't talk. Not now. But as soon as this is over, I will.'

'Will it be over, Jenifry?'

'I hope so. And soon. One way or the other. I've just had an idea that might force things to a head.'

And I cut the call.

I checked the tracker. Cameron's car was parked in his drive. I had enough time to go back to my room and pick up another sim because I was sure he was going to sleep. And hopefully for a few hours. I needed sleep too. But I couldn't. I had something else I wanted to do and now might be the only time to do it. Today was Sunday. Sunday the 26th. I had to be around to stick close to Cameron later.

I parked the car a few streets away from the building where my room was, nipped in and picked up a spare sim, some paper and a pen, and then my phone buzzed. It was a text from the dealer I'd asked for work.

You got a car, right?

Yes.

Meet me outside the flats in 30 mins.

Shit. I wasn't sure I could do this.

Might be a bit late.

You want the job, don't be late.

Well, that was clear enough.

I sat on the bed and tried to decide what to do: Take the job and go down a road that might lead me to Nick? Or push things further with Cameron?

I knew the answer. No choice really. Nick had chosen his life. And known about all the dangers.

Rania and Aya and the other children hadn't. No brainer.

I nearly told Nick. But stopped myself. I needed to stay in touch with reality. Talking to him was doing my head in.

I extracted the old sim and with it any hope of finding Nick, bent it until it broke into two bits and left. A blue-green scooter was parked a few doors down on the opposite side of the road. Like the one I'd seen weaving in and out of the traffic when I was following Cameron in his Uber. Was it a coincidence? A few stabs of panic forced my sluggish brain to focus and I raced past and took a circuitous route to my car until I was sure no one was following me. I got in and drove off, checking the mirror from time to time. But I saw no sign of the scooter.

Twenty-four

The day was grey but muggy. The air conditioning in my car was nothing but a memory along with the radio and the rear windscreen wipers, so I drove out of Glasgow with the windows open. All the way to Helensburgh, where I crawled past Duncan's mother's flat in the great house overlooking the estuary. Duncan's car was parked outside.

Yes!

It was Sunday. Nick had stopped Duncan on a Sunday after his habitual visit to his mother when he wanted to talk to him covertly. Flagged him down on a quiet stretch of road, a shortcut only known to locals.

I wanted to speak to Duncan but I'd had no way of contacting him safely until I remembered this. I didn't know the quiet stretch of road where Nick had stopped him, but it didn't matter. It was better this way. I still wasn't sure how far I could trust Duncan.

I parked the car several streets away and took the paper and pen I'd picked up from my room.

Dear Duncan, I started. Then stopped, unsure exactly what to say and how to say it. The written word and I hadn't spent much time together since I left school apart from texts and emails and I couldn't remember the last time I'd put sentences onto paper with a pen.

I kept it simple in the end and didn't worry too much about the order, figuring that whatever I wrote he'd read to the end.

I told him it would be a shock but DCI Cameron was involved with the traffickers. At the very least he was feeding them information but I thought he was actively involved. I begged Duncan, even if he didn't believe me, to pass the information on to Nick's department. And only to Nick's department. He mustn't trust anyone in Glasgow. I had proof. But I would tell it to no one but Nick.

I gave him a gmail address. One linked to the new sim. Told him to mail me when Cameron had been put out of action. And finally I added that I'd had nothing to do with Pa's death. I'd been set up by Cameron.

The letter was a stone thrown into the water. It would make waves. And ripples. I couldn't control where they washed up but I thought Duncan, no matter how much he disbelieved me, wouldn't do anything that might endanger Nick. So he'd listen to my warning about telling only Nick's department. And I hoped beyond hope they'd start investigating Sandy Cameron. It would take them a bit of time but that was good. I hadn't quite got the proof yet. I'd got Leila and what she'd told me but I'd have liked to keep her out of it. I hoped beyond hope that Cameron would lead me to something concrete tonight. And if he did, I wasn't leaving without finding out what was going on. I was sick of doing nothing. I was going to go mad if I carried on. It was time to take a few risks. The letter to Duncan was a way of making sure the investigation into Cameron continued. Even if I wasn't around.

I added a quick PS.

Cameron threatened to snatch Rania and Aya. My family are in hiding now. Please make sure they're safe.

I approached Fiona's flat from the coast side. The tide was low and the sand and shingle beach was draped with thick brown seaweed whose pods burst satisfyingly as I trod on them. The garden of the house next door opened to the beach. I'd seen no cars parked in its drive and thought it was empty, so I walked up its side, clambered over the boundary wall, and then crouched down behind Duncan's car.

I'd been going to leave the letter under his windscreen wiper but both front windows were open a crack. To let some air in. Despite the day's greyness it was getting warmer by the hour. My skin was sticky beneath the filthy sweatpants and top I'd been wearing for longer than I could remember. So I slipped the letter through the driver's window and left the way I'd come.

No one could hack a letter, and paper and ink contained no trail anyone could follow back to me. I didn't hang around to watch him open it. I drove back to Glasgow and Cameron's. Car still in drive. Upstairs window open although the curtain was closed. I was sure he was still sleeping. I probably had another couple of hours. Just long enough to check something else out. Something else that had been bugging me since I spoke to Ma.

Even on a cloudy Sunday, the Botanic Gardens was full of runners and walkers and families playing. The path over the old railway platforms was open although wisps of police tape were still tied to the railings. I eyed them up. I'd have struggled to push Pa over. He was a tall man and fit. The man – or men – who did this must have taken him by surprise. Given him no time to react. Surely the police could see that. But then I guessed the police officer who mattered – Sandy Cameron – wasn't interested in pushing the investigation to examine other possible killers than me.

I walked slowly back and forth along the path, not sure what I was looking for. There wasn't anything to find. No convenient scraps of material snagged on a convenient branch, no lipstick-stained cigarette butts, nor ripped pieces of paper with a few cryptic words scrawled on them.

It took ages before the path was empty long enough for me to climb over the railings and drop down onto the railway tracks below. I clambered up onto the old platform and scuttled under the station roof, so I was hidden from passers-by looking down.

It was surprisingly quiet down here. The noises from above hardly penetrated at all and, even though the platform roofs curved above my head, it felt like being in a secret garden rather than underground. I wasn't alone. A couple of sparrows hopped around the track pecking for seeds in the weeds. Here and there scraps of yellow broke up the green of the leaves and the grey of the gravel. I didn't remember them from last time. I realised they were crime scene markers. I was looking at the work the police had done when Pa's body had been discovered and retrieved. I noticed a patch of flattened weeds in the middle of the markers. With a dark stain on the gravel at one end.

Pa.

My mind went blank. I couldn't think of anything. Couldn't remember why I was here. I forced myself to look away. Turned my back on the markers and the flattened patch of weeds and stared at the station walls, tracing the lines of the graffiti artists who'd used it as a blank canvas, while I fought to breathe in and out calmly. To dispel the wave of rage that shook me.

I'd like to kill them.

I took a deep breath and banished the thought. It wasn't the answer. I forced myself to think rationally.

Pa's death. It seemed so unnecessarily risky. Threatening Rania and Aya with those awful pictures would have been enough. More than enough. Sure Cameron had taken advantage of Pa's death to set the police hunting for me. To make it impossible for me to act openly. But he couldn't have known Issy would conveniently point the finger of blame in my direction.

Throwing Pa down here was a crazy thing to do. The fall might not have killed him. People survived much worse. A quiet stabbing or a silenced gunshot would have been much more effective. It smacked of the improvised. Of something done out of anger when I hadn't turned up.

Or panic because Pa had discovered something down here.

I'd begun to think he might have. The thing he said he'd found in the message he'd left me. I'd thought it was my bracelet but maybe it was something else? Something hidden down here?

A rusting stairway led up from the platforms into the site of the old Botanic Gardens Station but the stairs came to an abrupt end where they'd been blocked off. At each end of the platform the track continued into a high tunnel. Access to the westerly one was difficult. Tall iron railings, with a gate cut into them, sealed it off. I was fairly sure it only ran a short way underground before coming out at the far end of the Gardens. The tunnel at the other end was open.

Was something hidden down there?

Because the children in the pictures Cameron had sent still haunted my mind. The children who must be hidden somewhere in Glasgow. The tunnels under the Botanic Gardens were a quiet and deserted place near the city centre. A good place for hiding things? Or children?

Maybe.

Maybe not.

But the only way to be sure was to look.

I took a deep breath and walked into the dark with its smell of damp and rot. I concentrated on walking in a straight line up the centre, unable to bear the idea of brushing up against years of dirt and mould on the walls. As the light dimmed, my hearing sharpened and I became aware of little rustles all around me.

Please God, don't let me tread on a rat.

As soon as I was far enough in for no prying eyes above to see, I turned on the torch in my multi-tool, congratulating myself once again for having it with me. Its beam caught a scurry of movement. An impression of grey fur. Maybe it was my imagination giving life to my fears. All the same I wished I was wearing boots.

They're more frightened of you, I told myself as I ran the torch over the arched walls. *They're more frightened of you.* It was even quieter now. Hard to believe that traffic was thundering along Great Western Road above me. And the space was empty. No plants unlike the open-roofed station and no graffiti to break up the monotony of the bricks lining the tunnel. Something about their unbroken and regular rows that curved and skewed to form the high-arched tunnel calmed me. It didn't feel underground. There was space all around me and a whisper of light and fresh air.

After a few hundred metres, the tunnel briefly emerged into a cutting. Daylight hurt my eyes. The walls were high but the profusion of bushes would have made the climb an easy scramble. The railings at the top weren't an obstacle.

I went on down the tunnel. It soon came to a dead end, blocked by a brick wall and huge metal doors which didn't quite reach to the top of the arch so grey light filtered in. This too must have been part of another station but, whereas Botanic Gardens Station had felt like an oasis below the busy gardens, this was creepy. The short run of platform and the rusty stairs leading off it were piled high with rubbish and earth. I swung my torch round. Apart from rats there was nothing alive. Besides there was no easy way in and out. It had been a stupid idea to think Cameron might keep the children here.

The sound of a motorbike made me jump. Just a noise from the cutting. Nothing else. There was no point staying here. This awful place had no more secrets to tell me. I scrambled up the cutting walls at the beginning of the tunnel leading back to the Botanic

Gardens. I couldn't face seeing the place where Pa had died again.

Anger still shivered through my thoughts. Not hot and hasty but cold and thoughtful. The notion of killing Sandy had wormed its way into my head and wouldn't leave.

Only a little voice of sanity told me it wasn't the answer. Told me I needed to sleep and eat. When had I last eaten? I couldn't remember. And I hadn't slept at all last night. Maybe I should take a break before doing anything rash?

I checked the tracker. Sandy's car hadn't moved from the drive. Half an hour, I thought. I'd go back to my room for half an hour, sleep and change my smelly clothes.

I parked a few streets away as usual and walked the rest of the way. Back in my room, I flung myself on the bed and felt sleep start to suck me down when someone pounded on the front door. The guy in the room below me with windows that looked out into the street, shouted up the staircase. I opened my door. He was yelling, 'Police. Out the front.'

Doors opened and slammed shut. People ran past my door, downstairs and out through the back. I dashed to my window and looked. Half a dozen police officers seized them as they came out of the back door. There was no escape that way.

I wasn't going to wait around to find out if it was me they were after or one of the other no-hopers who lived here. Besides my cover story wouldn't hold up in the face of police questioning.

Had the skinny man with the piercings recognised me and followed me back from that strange meeting with Cameron by the Clyde? I hadn't stayed here long enough last time for the police to nab me but maybe they'd been waiting until I came back.

How could I get out?

Twenty-five

I grabbed my rucksack and ran up the stairs rather than down. All the way to the top landing and looked up at the ceiling.

Yes!

It had a trapdoor leading to the attic space. Like in Fergus's tenement. And this one wasn't padlocked. There was no convenient set of steps available, though. Below me, the police slammed on doors and shouted. I hauled myself onto the top rail of the landing bannisters and perched precariously for a few seconds.

If only I didn't feel so shit-tired.

The police kicked down a door below. It was now or never. I forced my wobbly legs to bend and push up, jumped towards the attic and, at the top of my leap, punched my arms up and dislodged the trapdoor. It disappeared into the attic. It was nothing more than a square of wood laid over the hole. I clambered back onto the bannisters and leaped again, this time seizing the hatch's exposed edge. I grabbed it and swung my body up and into the attic. Then slid the wood back into place.

Like Fergus's place, this attic had a boarded floor and small skylights in the roof but there the resemblance ended. Fergus's attic had been empty. This wasn't. A sleeping bag lay in one corner and clothes and books were piled by it. A couple of LED lights had been roped to a rafter. The ones that would run off batteries. Someone was living here. Someone with nowhere else to go, other than the streets.

It wouldn't have been difficult.

The people who rented these rooms didn't stay long so no one knew each other. And getting hold of a front door key wouldn't have been hard, either. I'd often seen them left in the lock.

More shouting from below.

If they were after me, they'd search the attic eventually. At Fergus's the police had turned up because of a tip-off. They'd been reasonably restrained in their search. Here, if they'd been waiting for me, they'd know I was inside and they weren't going to stop looking until they found me.

Footsteps and yelling on the landing below me. Then hammering on doors. I had a few minutes at most. The time it took them to check the rooms on this floor and then they'd know I must be up above them.

I had to find somewhere to hide where they wouldn't find me. I looked around. Forget that. There was nowhere. I'd have to get out. Except there was no way out other than back through the trapdoor. The trapdoor. The door to the trap. Unless I could get out through the skylights. Two filthy rectangles of glass held together by a rusty iron join with an old stay bar holding them shut. I thrust all my weight against it. It didn't budge. I prayed the noise the police were making would cover mine as I gripped a batten joist with both hands, hung off it and lifted my legs to smash my feet through the glass and the thin rusty bar between. The glass shattered. Fragments rattled down the roof tiles outside. The bar split. I kept on until I'd cleared every shard of glass from the frame.

Voices immediately below me. Someone shouted for steps or a broom.

Shit. They'd heard me.

I dragged myself through the hole I'd made and clung to its edges while I orientated myself. Below me the slates ran down to a metallic gutter, full of dank leaves and pine needles. It looked old and flimsy. Above me a row of brown curved tiles marked the ridge.

No time. I had no time. They'd be in the attic in a matter of seconds.

I made a decision. Or rather my body decided. It didn't trust the gutter and launched itself up over the hole, slapping my hands onto the ridge tiles and gripping their rounded edges. For a moment, I hung there, my head swimming with the sudden motion, and then I headed towards the chimneys that separated the roof of one tenement from the next, scrabbling with my feet in a crab-like scuttle while my hands pulled myself along.

No noise from behind me yet. And no one could see me from below.

I reached the chimneys, hauled myself over and crouched behind them, out of sight of the heads that would soon poke through the broken skylight. They wouldn't come after me. Or, at least, not straightaway. It had been a tight fit for me. Besides they didn't need to chase me across the roof, they'd surround the row of tenements and wait for me to come down. I needed to do something now. Before they had time to organise themselves and despatch officers to watch each part of the row.

But I couldn't think. Something was whirring my thoughts into a mush and making my fingers, gripping the bricks of the chimney pedestal, weak and shaky.

Fear. I was frightened. No, I was terrified.

Not of edging my way along this roof. Nor of climbing down. The sandstone walls were rough and pitted and punctured by large windows with wide ledges. A walk in the park for me to climb down even though I was woolly with tiredness.

No, I was terrified of being caught. Terrified of what might happen to me in police custody. Duncan had said the force was riddled with corruption. With officers on the payroll of the local criminal organisations. Even if I survived being arrested, they'd be waiting for me as soon as I got out, tipped off by informants. And then I'd be in the hands of the men who hadn't hesitated before tossing Pa over the railings in the Botanic Gardens. I had to find a way out of this trap.

Shouting from behind me followed by answering calls from the garden at the back of the flat. A pathway cleared in my brain.

The chimney pots were old and crumbling. I seized a handful of loose bits and flung them back the way I'd come so they landed on the roof of the tenement on the other side. They made a gratifyingly loud noise as they landed and tumbled onto the garden below. Yells rose and I scrabbled along the roofs of a couple more tenements in the opposite direction. Then I levered my body over the ridge, hugging the tiles so that no part of me was visible from below, and clung to the roof on the front of the building. They'd expect me to come down the back. I was sure of that. They'd reason the front was more visible to passers-by and easier for them to race up and down in their cars. At the back they had to deal with high walls separating the gardens.

But they were wrong.

If I'd judged it right, I'd swung over the roof where there was a tree planted in the road. A tree that would hide me from a casual glance up. And the windows at the fronts of these Victorian tenements were always more ornate than the backs and easier to climb. I let go of the ridge and slid down the tiles, pressing my palms into the slates to slow my progress. Sharp knobs and edges gouged furrows in my skin. My feet met the gutter.

This was the worst bit.

The guttering wouldn't take my weight. I had to lift my legs up and over it and let myself slip further down. I dug my hands and fingers into the roof to slow my fall. Ignored the pain from the tiles cutting into my skin and felt for the window below with my feet. It was lower than I thought. Far lower. My hands were running out of roof to grip.

And then my right foot touched glass. A last slide of my body over and suddenly there was no more roof to grip. I held onto the gutter, praying it would hold for a few seconds and my feet met the stone ledge at the bottom of the window.

Mission accomplished.

My face was pressed against a windowpane but no one stared back at me from inside. The room was empty. I risked a quick look around. My memory had served me well. I had come down behind the tree. The police cars were still clustered outside the tenement where my room was but, even as I watched, one of them moved off and drove slowly down the road.

Shit. The officers inside would be craning their heads out to scan the tenements' facades. The tree was enough to stop me attracting the gaze of casual passers-by – people rarely looked up anyway – but it wouldn't screen me from determined searchers.

I looked around.

The window a few feet to my left was open at the top. No time to think. I scrabbled over there, grabbed the open window, forced it down, and then hurled my head and arms through. I landed in a contorted somersault, smashing my head against a bath. But I was inside and out of view of the police.

Another empty bathroom. Thank God people left their windows open during summer. There was no noise from the flat beyond. Maybe no one was in. Or maybe the occupier was frozen with fear because of the noise I'd made. I didn't wait to find out. I slipped into the hall – still no one – grabbed a pink puffer coat and cap from a stand and went out through the front door.

I forced myself to walk downstairs calmly and opened the tenement front door a crack. A police car cruised past. I waited until it had gone, put on the cumbersome coat I'd filched, rammed the flat cap on my head and went out, crossed the road and turned down an alley.

And then ran.

I reached the street where I'd parked the car but thought better before I turned into it. This wasn't a great idea. If I'd been followed back from meeting Cameron by the Clyde, they'd know my car. I'd have to abandon it.

Shit.

I had to get to Cameron's. And now. He'd wake up soon and go out to whatever was planned for tonight. I checked the tracker yet again. Car still outside his house.

I didn't dare get an Uber. That would mean logging into my account. So in the end, I caught the bus. Paying with the coins I had at the bottom of my rucksack and sitting on the top, almost sobbing with rage and impatience as it crawled through the streets. I ran from the bus stop, only slowing to a stroll as I turned into Cameron's road. His car was still in the drive. I'd known that from the tracker but it was good to see it with my own eyes. The upstairs curtains were open, though, and the window closed. He'd got up. Had he called an Uber and left the car behind? But as I panicked, the front door opened and he appeared. With the pug on a lead.

I checked my watch. It was very early to be taking the dog out. Excitement drove away the tiredness. Maybe he had plans for later. I walked ahead of him to the park, glancing behind to check he was still there. He went in and once he'd disappeared down the path, I took off the pink puffer jacket and stuffed it in a bin.

I sneaked into the garden of a house opposite with no cars in its drive and settled down in their shrubbery. This side of the road was higher than the other so I had a good view of the park exit and all the way back to Cameron's house.

A car drove past. Nothing unusual in that, although there was very little traffic normally. I'd got to know whose car was whose during the time I'd spent watching Cameron and this one was new to me. It drove slowly. Maybe someone looking for a specific house? The numbers were randomly placed and easy to miss. It stopped a hundred metres up the road, turned and drove back, parking outside Cameron's house. Two men got out. Dark clothes. Trousers not jeans and t-shirts under casual jackets. Anonymous-looking men. They walked down Cameron's drive and knocked on his door, waited a while, then went back to their car and got in. They didn't drive away.

Were they waiting for Cameron? Had they come to take him to whatever was going on today? Shit, I'd been counting on him using his car. How could I follow them without mine? I might have to steal one. I still had the gadget for breaking windows. Starting it would be a problem. I had a vague idea how to do it but I suspected practice was necessary. Then I had a much better idea. Alice's car was in the Camerons' drive, with its window already broken. There must be a spare set of keys somewhere in the house. Probably on the keyboard by the back door. And I had keys to the back door.

A mail bleeped my phone. From Duncan.

Jen. I got your note. It's over. You're safe. Sandy's been neutralised. He's not a threat. But you must stop what you're doing. Call me. I'll come and get you wherever you are. I promise you you're safe. Duncan.

What did it mean? I looked again at the men waiting for Cameron and then I understood. The two men were police. They'd come to take Cameron. Shit. Either Duncan had ignored my plea to speak only to Nick's department or he was already in touch with them. Shit, shit, shit. I hadn't thought he'd act so quickly or that

Nick's department would pick Cameron up. I thought they'd want to investigate. To follow him. To find out what was going on. Arresting Cameron would ruin everything. I'd never find the children. Never find out who else was involved. And without knowing that, I would never, ever, ever be sure that Rania and Aya were safe. In fact, picking up Cameron before I knew what was going on might be their death sentence.

No, I wrote back. No. You've got to stop them.

A movement caught my eye.

Sandy came out of the park. I was too late to stop a disaster happening.

He'd been a long time. Much longer than usual. And he looked tired. As though the exercise had exhausted him. I watched him walk towards his house. Watched the men get out of the car. It was surprisingly quick and quiet. Sandy didn't run, didn't even argue. He simply nodded, handed over the pug and what I guessed were the house keys to one of the officers, and got into the car with the other. It drove off and the first officer let himself into the house.

The street settled back into its habitual quiet. I wanted to scream.

Someone else was watching. A man stood by the park entrance and looked down the road after them. Not the type you expected to see in this middle-class suburb of Glasgow. Shaven head, thickset and carrying himself with a slight swagger that gave him the air of a hard man. That and the tribal tattoos that snaked all over his head.

He turned in my direction and I sank down into the shrubbery. But not before I'd caught a glimpse of his face. What I saw wasn't good. A casting agent looking for an actor to play the role of a criminal inured to violence would have cast him straightaway.

Was he the reason Sandy had taken so long in the park? Had he been meeting him?

Bald with tattoos. That was how Leila had described one of the two men who'd set her family home on fire. Was this him?

I sneaked my head above the wall and took a long, hard look. My wretchedness wound down. Hope glittered through my veins. There was a chance here. Tattoo Man looked like the stuff of nightmares but coming across him meant there might be a way out of this nightmare. Finally I'd caught a break.

But before I could decide what to do, a buzzing like an angry wasp disturbed the quiet, and two seconds later the familiar blue-green moped arrived and stopped next to Tattoo Man. Its rider pulled off his helmet and the two men exchanged a few words.

It was the skinny lad with the nose jewellery. He mustn't see me. I'd have to wait until he went and then follow Tattoo Man. They exchanged a few terse words, then Tattoo Man left, strolling down the road while scooter man drank from a bottle of water. I didn't dare wait for him to go. In a minute Tattoo Man would have disappeared and with him my chance of finding out what was going on.

I sank down into the shrubbery and slithered to the far side of the garden, through the hedge into the next one, then slipped out into the road behind a few parked cars and crawled away at speed, only standing when I was far enough away not to attract his attention.

Tattoo Man turned right at the end of the road. I risked breaking into a run but when I got to the turn, he was still far ahead, nearing the point where this road opened onto the main road. I sped up and reached the junction in time to see him get into a nondescript grey Volvo and drive off.

I stared after it helplessly. Shit, shit, shit. I'd blown it. Big time. No point running back to get Alice's car. I'd never catch him up and anyway there was every chance the police officer was searching it. If only that little rat-faced weasel with the nose jewellery hadn't turned up on his scooter. Rage pumped my blood.

I turned to go back with some idea of braving the officer searching the house. Maybe if I was super quick, I could get Alice's car keys. But as I moved the blue-green scooter appeared round the corner and I had a much better idea.

I waited until the last moment, praying I'd get the timing right. I'd have to trust myself. To trust my muscles to feel it.

And they did.

They flung me into the road in front of Rat-faced Weasel and his scooter at the perfect moment. He had enough time to squeal to a halt without hitting me although the distance between us could be measured by a child's ruler. His scooter didn't touch me but I fell to the ground with a scream worthy of a footballer diving when an opposing player had brushed against him. And then I shouted and sobbed until the pedestrians stopped and looked at us.

Rat-faced Weasel had no choice but to get off his scooter and come over to me. I grabbed his arm and pulled myself up, still yelling, then shoved him away, staggering forward a couple of paces myself with the force of the thrust. His turn to fall.

I seized his moped, kicked up the stand and turned the key to 'On', then sped off. Not fast, these machines never are. But quick enough to take advantage of everyone's shock. I turned onto the main road and was fifty metres or so away before I caught sight of Rat-faced Weasel running after me.

Too late, mate, I thought. You'll never catch me now.

But it was too late for me too. I weaved in and out of the traffic looking for the Volvo. I'd been right about the scooter. It was much better for following someone in the city. But only if you could find them. The Volvo must have turned off into a side street while I'd been staging my accident.

Twenty-six

The scooter was a double-edged sword. Brilliant in traffic but it marked me out. Rat-faced Weasel would waste no time reporting its theft to the police so they'd be looking for it as well as Cameron's criminal colleagues – if there was any difference between the two. There was no point making it easy so I turned off the main road and rode through a tangle of residential streets until I came to a railway station. Maybe I should dump the scooter and take a train somewhere. Except where could I go? And how? I had no money with me apart from a few remaining pence in change. And no cards. They were in my car. I only had what was in the rucksack, still on my back, that I'd grabbed when I'd left my room.

I opened the scooter's under-seat compartment. Maybe Rat-faced Weasel had left his wallet. Nothing, except the bottle of water I'd seen him drinking from and a prawn mayonnaise and iceberg lettuce sandwich. I left the bottle where it was. I wasn't thirsty enough to drink from something that his mouth had touched. But the sandwich's packaging was unopened.

It tasted good. A bit warm from its time under the seat but fresh and the lettuce still crisp. There was no bin nearby so I put the packaging back under the seat and noticed a few bits of paper right at the very bottom.

Nothing very interesting. A receipt for the sandwich from Morrisons in Anniesland. Another one from Subway. In fact several for sandwiches and bottles of water. And a parking ticket. Crumpled up. I guessed Rat-faced Weasel had no intention of paying it. The scooter had been parked illegally on a street in the centre of the city for quite a number of hours yesterday. There was a host of innocent reasons why he might have parked there but it was something. No. Not something. It was the only thing I had.

The address was a narrow street north of the Barrowlands Ballroom. Far enough away from the ballroom to be quiet but nevertheless painted with double yellow lines. I thought Rat-faced Weasel had been unlucky with his parking ticket because the road was sprinkled with illegally parked cars and bikes.

I rode up and down it a few times. The street was short and lined mainly by the backs of buildings with entrances on parallel roads. The entrance to a yellow-fronted garage that proclaimed it sold the best-value tyres took up half of one side. It was busy even though it was a Sunday – maybe because it was a Sunday and it was open – but the Happy Snacks café opposite looked as though it hadn't served any snacks whether happy or not for a long time. Had Rat-faced Weasel parked here and gone somewhere else? Because if he'd stayed here for the number of hours the parking ticket claimed he'd either spent most of the day choosing tyres or waiting outside Happy Snacks in the unlikely event the long-gone owners decided to open up.

And then I realised there was another possibility.

An anonymous redbrick building with filthy windows and a dilapidated sign advertising office space to rent by the month also had a couple of entrances on the street. Ones so nondescript I'd missed them until a couple of women came out chatting and walked away. I followed them in the scooter until they stopped at a bus stop on Gallowgate. Just two office workers going home.

I dumped the scooter and walked back, slowing as I passed the entrance they'd come out of. It was the first of two separate office buildings only indicated by the numbers 5 and 7 and I guessed they housed businesses so transient they never got round to putting up signs.

Was this where Rat-faced Weasel had been?

Or was I kidding myself? Clutching at straws? I couldn't imagine why organised criminals would need to rent seedy office space... unless they used it for storage. Were they hiding children here? Unlikely. I thought rapidly. Maybe it was somewhere they brought the children to. To meet clients. It would be deserted at night, once the office workers had left. The building was half-empty anyway and the streets would be dead quiet once the garage had closed.

Time was running out. I had nothing else to go on. I had to hope that whatever was going down tonight was going to happen here. I pushed the door to number 7 casually but it didn't open. A keypad was tucked into a niche by its side. The same at number 5.

I tried the garage next. Went in and asked to talk to someone about an estimate for some tyres. I was directed to an office, constructed out of chipboard and glass in one corner, where a middle-aged woman was patiently explaining on the phone why they couldn't replace only one tyre.

I asked her for a price for various different tyres for a BMW M3, a car whose tyres they wouldn't have in stock and as she searched through different suppliers, I sat on the battered plastic chair and chatted.

I concocted a fake business looking for temporary premises and asked if she knew anything about the building down the road. She didn't. I wondered what it was like inside. She had no idea. And what the other businesses might be. She shook her head. And whether they'd mind me bringing my kids in from time to time. She softened a little at that point. Maybe decided my awful appearance was down to overwork rather than bad hygiene and said she couldn't see why not. I explained that although they were both at nursery, there were always times when they were ill or had doctor's appointments or teachers were on strike. And it was very difficult then. And some of the office spaces I'd looked at had strict rules saying no children. Something to do with insurance, I thought.

I was sure this wasn't true but she accepted it.

And finally I wondered if she'd seen any children going in and out of the building.

She hadn't.

I'd run out of questions.

'Funny you should ask about children, though,' she said as I took the piece of paper she'd written the tyre details and prices down on.

'Why?'

'The other evening, I'd been working late and, when I was going down the street to catch the bus home, I heard a child wail. Gave me quite a turn. But when I looked round there was no one.'

She hesitated. I waited.

'I thought it might have come from that building. The windows on the top floor were open. So maybe someone had brought their child to work.'

Yes! I thanked her and left.

Nothing for it but to keep watch on the building. Except there was nowhere to loiter unobtrusively once I'd spent several minutes peering in through Happy Snacks' window. I started wandering up and down the street, trying to look like a pedestrian passing through each time, then made a circuit via an adjoining street until I noticed an alley ran down the back of the buildings. I explored that. No 5 and No 7 had back yards behind a high wall. There were gates but they were locked. I could get over the wall, though, if I wanted to.

Should I break in? It wouldn't be difficult because ramshackle fire escape stairs ran up the buildings. The fire exits would be locked from the outside but I might find a window I could force. The gadget I'd bought to break Alice's car window would work as well on a normal one. Maybe later. For now I wanted to see who arrived. I carried on circling. Up the street at the front and then down the alley at the back. Evening came. The roads darkened. My legs started to tire and I wobbled a bit from time to time. The garage finally shut and the mechanics disappeared into the night in the illegally parked cars. I supposed someone kept a watch for traffic wardens while they were open. The windows of the buildings I was watching remained dark.

Night finally arrived completely and I regretted throwing away the pink puffer coat. I started to wonder what I was going to do if no one arrived. What if everything had been cancelled because the stupid, stupid police had picked Cameron up? I couldn't give up. Not while there was a chance of finding out what was going on. But neither could I walk up and down all night. Maybe I should climb into the building through the back and hide in there while there was still enough strength in my muscles.

The problem was – which one, No 5 or No 7?

As I stared up at their anonymous fronts, I realised I was wrong about No 5 being empty. A dim glow shone briefly from behind a blind in one of the windows on the top floor. Bluish and cold. Someone was up there.

No 5, then.

I walked round and down the alley to its back wall. Shards of glass had been embedded into the cement on the top and, once again, I regretted the pink puffer jacket. It would have been good padding for my hands. I found a place where the shards were worn and missing, then prepared to jump.

Footsteps came up behind me. I froze for a fraction of a second then walked away, only turning to look once I'd slipped into a doorway. Someone had stopped by the gate into the yard of No 5, the one with the lights on in the top floor. They glanced back the way they'd come then looked in my direction. The streetlight caught their face. It was Tattoo Man.

My heart beat like a John Bonham drum solo. So hard it hurt.

I burst out of the doorway and raced down the alley towards him.

He tensed as I appeared. Went into fight position. Weight balanced on both feet. His hand shot round to the small of his back and pulled something out. I stopped a couple of feet away from him.

'You bastard,' I said.

His shoulders dropped. 'Jen?' It was barely more than a whisper. He thrust whatever he was holding back into his waistband.

'Of course.'

'Shh!'

He stepped forward, seized my shoulders and looked at me. In the midst of the appalling tattoos Nick's eyes gleamed. Nick's dark, smiley eyes.

I thought he was going to say something but instead he pulled me towards him and kissed me. Surprise held me still. For a brief second I was back in the high and deserted mountains above Alajar, with Nick's arms wrapped round me and watching galaxies of stars stain the night sky. Then reality kicked in.

I shoved him hard. He broke off and stepped back.

'You bastard,' I said again. 'Letting me think you were dead.'

I was furious. And some emotion now set his face in hard lines. He'd never looked so unlike the Nick I knew. Or thought I knew. When I'd seen him outside the park, something about the shape of his body and the way he held himself had made me look twice, the second time much harder, then the tattoos had looked familiar and I'd worked out who was beneath them and the shaven head.

I started to speak but he beat me to it.

'Get out of here. Now. Call Duncan. He'll come and get you. But get out.'

'No way. I want to know what's going on.'

'Duncan will explain.'

'No, you can explain.'

He shook his head. 'No time.'

'But there are some things I have to tell you.'

'We know. We know about the Camerons. We know about Basset in France. We know about the children. This operation has been going on for months. And it's about to come to fruition. You should never have got involved.'

I couldn't believe I was hearing this.

'What was I supposed to do? They threatened to seize Rania and Aya. They killed my father. I was told you were dead. And then undercover chasing drug dealers.'

'I'm sorry about your father. I truly am.' He shook his head again. 'I didn't know about Rania and Aya. Look, I have to go. I promise you it will all be OK. But, Jen, please get out of here.'

And with that, he turned, clambered over the wall and dropped into the dark on the other side. It was quietly done but clumsily. He had no climbing skills at all. Never had. And I delighted in showing him how it should be done with a quick leap and swing onto the top of the wall. He didn't see, though, because he was already punching a code into the back door. He disappeared inside. I walked along the top of the wall and leaned against the next-door building, in the shadows, where a casual glance wouldn't see me.

What now? Nick had said the operation was about to come to fruition. I wasn't sure what that meant but I didn't fancy meeting a lot of trigger-happy armed police if they were planning on storming the building. I wasn't leaving, though. No way.

Before I could decide, another figure suddenly appeared below. Short and thin. And very quiet. I hadn't heard them. They unlocked the gate and sped across the yard, punched in the code and went in through the back door.

Was it Rat-faced Weasel? He was certainly thin enough.

A light flicked on from a first-floor window. Then, a few seconds later, a soft crack broke the night. Then silence.

The light went out.

My skin prickled. What just happened?

All the things I should do ran through my mind for less than a second. Like get out of there. Like call the police because I thought the noise was a gunshot. No, not the police. I might be passing on information to the wrong person.

I'd have to do something myself.

I scrambled down the wall into the yard, ran to the building and up the fire escape to the first landing. Tried the fire exit. It was locked. I found the glass breaker in my rucksack, reached over to a small window at the side and used it. The glass cracked and broke.

The noise seemed huge to me, but no lights came on. No sound of feet nor voices. The glass hadn't shattered completely but the jagged hole was big enough for me to snake an arm through and open the window from the inside. I climbed in to a small toilet, opened the door carefully and stepped out into a dark corridor lit only by a fire exit sign.

To my left, two doors. Both shut. No noise from either of them. To my right, a flight of stairs led down to the back entrance and another up to the floors above. A black heap was lying on the floor in between them. I risked a flash of my torch. It was Nick. Lying utterly still. With eyes closed. And blood oozing from a cut above his left eye.

I was kneeling beside him in a trice, ramming the torch into my pocket and reaching out hands to find his pulse. The cut above his eye looked horrible but it wasn't really. Head wounds bleed a lot and the fact that he was bleeding was good news. Dead men don't bleed. And he had a pulse.

And a hole in his sweatshirt. Right in the middle of his chest.

He'd been shot. I was sure of it. Shot right by his heart and bashed his head as he fell. But how was he still alive? I touched the hole. No blood. I pressed a little harder and felt something padded. It went round his whole torso. He was wearing some kind of protective vest. It had saved him. Because he'd clearly been taken by surprise and not had the time to pull out the gun I found in a neat little holster in the small of his back.

A burst of voices came from above. As though a door had been opened and shut. Was someone coming? Back down the stairs? To get rid of the body? I had to get Nick out. If they came close to his body, they'd realise instantly he wasn't dead. And the vest wasn't going to save him from a shot in the head.

He wasn't tall but he was square and I had no hope of getting him down the stairs to the back door without hurting him but the back of the building was lower than the front and the main door was right behind me. I dragged him half out into the street.

No one about. Of course not.

I called 999. I couldn't think what else to do. Begged for an ambulance fast. Told them Nick had fallen down the stairs. Said it was desperate, blood everywhere. Maybe I should have told them he'd been shot but I thought everything would grind to a halt if I did. They'd call the police which might be dangerous. And even if it wasn't, it would all take forever.

They told me to stay on the line.

More voices from upstairs and what I thought was a child crying.

Someone yelled, 'Shut that kid up', and 'For God's sake, go and move Kincaid's body'. Then the voices dropped in volume.

I cut the call, shoved my phone in my pocket, took Nick's gun and left him in the street, shut the front door behind me and started creeping up the stairs. I had some idea it would be easier to stall them if I met them coming down. By pretending to be an innocent bystander. To give the ambulance time to arrive. Besides I couldn't stop myself. I had to know what was going on upstairs and put an end to it. No one else was going to.

Twenty-seven

The landing was dark on the top floor. The fire exit sign wasn't working and the only light came from a door a little way along that was a few inches open. The layout looked the same as the floor I'd arrived on. Two doors leading to offices and two to separate toilets with the stairs at one end. One of the office doors was padlocked. The voices, I'd heard, came from the other office, whose door was ajar. They were no longer raised but quiet and urgent. I crept along until they became clearer.

Two men. One Scottish and one English. I heard their accents first before their words started to make any sense. And the clattering of keyboards.

'Reference 113659. Payment received.' This was the English voice.

'Access granted,' the Scottish man replied.

'Reference 790348. Payment received.'

'Access granted.'

I thought the English voice was Rat-faced Weasel. It was thin and nasal exactly as I thought he'd sound. But who was the Scot? And what were they doing?

'Reference 696352. Payment received.'

'Access granted.'

Only the sequence of numbers changing each time. Otherwise the words were the same. Monitoring payments?

I didn't understand.

'That's all for now.' The Englishman spoke.

'Then go move Kincaid's body. Hide it in one of the toilets and block the door. And check it is Kincaid.'

I held the gun tighter.

'It is.' This was someone new. A woman. Not English. Not Scottish. Stress making her voice harsh and dry. Who was she? 'But we should just run,' she went on. 'Kincaid's been alive all along. The police must know everything.'

'We've got a wee bit of time,' the Scottish man replied quickly. 'If the police are outside, they know Kincaid came in. They'll want to find out what's going on before they storm the place.'

'*If* the police are outside?' The woman muttered something sharp and staccato in a foreign language. 'They must be.'

Shit, I hoped she was right.

'Guys like Kincaid generally work alone. You're completely sure it was him?'

'I told you,' she half-shouted. 'I recognised him at once. But then I always wondered if he was really dead. I told Pierre he should have made sure.' Her voice barely covered over the cracks of panic. 'Besides I suspected something was up when I came through the airport here,' she went on. 'Something about the way the passport officer looked at me. Then your father texted to say he couldn't collect me. He – that's why I came straight here instead. And met Kincaid on the stairs.'

She'd mentioned the airport. And passport control. Someone from abroad? From France. The trace of accent could be French. Another thought whirred in my mind. Could it be Alice? Alice Cameron? Was Alice Cameron French? I thought back quickly. I'd never heard her speak. It could be her. Was she in this too?

And then a child's voice piped up. It said words I couldn't understand. Loud and fearful.

'Mute that,' the Englishman said.

'Not much longer, *Maman*,' the Scot continued. 'The money's pouring in now. I'll tell Pierre five more minutes. Then I'll switch the French feed directly through to the audience and we can get out of here.'

'No. We must go now,' the woman said. Again that slight foreign accent.

'And what are we going to do if we don't have any money? Think about it. You keep checking the road. And Ronnie, go and move the body. I'll come down to help you in a wee while.'

Before I could hide, Ronnie shot out of the door. He saw me straightaway and came to an abrupt halt. Ronnie was Rat-faced Weasel. No mistaking the skinny features, face jewellery and sparse white-blond hair. He already knew who I was. No point pretending. I raised the gun and pointed it at him.

We stared at each other.

I should shoot him.

Except I couldn't. The noise would bring the others out. I couldn't shoot them all. Could I?

He raised his arms slowly.

'What are you waiting for?' the Scot shouted from inside the office.

Ronnie took a step towards me and shook his head. Shit. I'd seen this play out so many times in the movies. *The rookie too afraid to shoot. The bad guy takes the gun.*

But I couldn't do it. Not kill him. I pointed the gun down at his legs, shut my eyes and squeezed the trigger.

It didn't budge. There must be some kind of safety catch on it.

I opened my eyes. Ronnie still stared at me.

And behind him a man with a red beard stood in the doorway.

Xander. The policeman from Nick's funeral. Sandy's son. But, of course. No wonder he'd been so friendly then. He'd been checking me out.

Not so friendly now as he launched himself at me, grabbed the gun and thrust me through the door, then hurled me down on the floor by a large iron radiator. The force of his push knocked the breath out of me and all I could do was gasp at the air as he wound thick tape round my wrists.

'*Putain*. An ambulance.' This came from the woman standing by the window, silhouetted in the dim light from the street as she peered out through a corner of the blind.

'I'm going down to see,' Xander said.

'No.'

The woman stepped forward and grabbed his arm but he shook it off and stormed out. His footsteps thundered on the stairs and disappeared.

The light from a computer screen had caught the woman when she'd stepped forward. I'd been right. It was Alice Cameron. Dressed for a business meeting in dark trousers with a faint stripe running through them and a bottle green polo neck. She twitched from head to toe as though faint electric shocks ran intermittently through her body. Alice was involved. She was the figure I'd seen slip into the building after Nick. She had shot him.

She and Ronnie now gaped at each other as if Xander's absence had removed their ability to do anything.

I looked around the room. The only light came from the streetlights filtering through the blinds and two computer screens. One on each of the desks placed in a V shape in front of the windows. There was no other furniture apart from two chairs, and a pile of boxes against the far wall.

Ronnie broke out of his paralysis, stepped over my legs and went to the screen on the right. But it was the screen on the left that dominated the room. It was huge – the sort graphic designers use – and split into different windows. Several of them showed text, some rolling, some static. And one had bars that shrank and grew. A white face stared out of another window. Someone sitting in front of a computer too? But it was the largest window that caught my eyes and wouldn't let them leave. A group of children sat on a bed and as I watched the picture zoomed in on them and panned across, lingering on their faces.

Where were they? Clearly not here.

I found my voice.

'What is this?'

'Online event.' Ronnie's voice was high with adrenalin. 'We –'

'Don't tell her anything.' Alice cut him off.

'She won't understand.'

But I did. Too well. The name Pierre had given it away. And the mention of a French feed. Pierre was Basset's name. The children weren't in Glasgow. They weren't in the UK. They were still in France. Xander and Ronnie had organised a virtual event. A sort of international Zoom conference for sickos. Why go through all the hassle and danger of transporting children over the English Channel, one of the busiest and most watched strips of water in the world, when you could do whatever you wanted from Calais? And why limit the participants to a few individuals in person when you could reach a vast public via the dark web? Every business was rushing to get online. Why not paedophilia?

I'd got it all so wrong. This was a tight and clever operation. Maybe dreamed up by Alice using her business acumen and Xander's skills. With a bit of help from Shona. A family business. But how did Basset fit into this? Unless… Alice was French. Was Basset related to her? Was that the link between them?

I couldn't look at Xander's screen. Instead my eyes met Alice's. She was staring at me while her fingers plucked at the blind covering the window.

'Who's she?' Alice asked.

'Didn't Xander tell you?' Ronnie broke off from gnawing at

black nail varnish on his skinny fingers. 'We think she recognised Pierre. In France. She must have come with Kincaid. She's been in with him since Calais.'

Alice glanced at him but didn't reply. Her gaze returned to me. She was thinking about me. I was sure of that. Thinking about my presence. Her panic seemed to have subsided because there was a cool intent in her gaze. Then her attention was distracted by the ambulance.

'They're leaving,' she said.

Xander came back up the stairs and into the room.

'They're leaving,' she repeated.

'Kincaid's body's gone too. But they didn't come in.' He crossed over to me and squatted down, seized my shoulders and thrust his face into mine. 'You called them, didn't you?'

The sweat glistening on his skin smelled sharp and chemical. I could see no point in lying.

'Yes,' I said. 'He wasn't dead. And the police are outside.'

He pulled his arm back and clenched his hand into a fist. At that point I had no problem believing he'd killed Pa. And that he'd kill me too.

'No, Xander.' Alice shouted. 'Not now. We need to go. Close the whole event down. Immediately. Everything. Pierre must be compromised too.'

'Calm down, *Maman*.' Xander stood. The urge to violence still throbbed through veins in his temples. 'I don't think the police are outside. They'd never have let her come in.'

'I called them once I was in here.'

'No, you didn't.'

He squatted back down by me and seized my face, squeezing it hard with his hands until I thought my bones might crack. At that moment I had no doubt he would kill me without a second thought.

'My colleagues would never have let the ambulance come in if they were outside. I know she's lying.'

I kept my mouth tight shut. He flung my head back against the radiator. I barely felt the crack.

'Just five minutes,' Xander said. 'The money's pouring in now.'

'*Non.*' Alice darted to Xander's computer. Her voice sliced through the air. '*Pierre. La police est ici. Arrête tout.*' She spoke to Xander and Ronnie. 'No switching. Just shut everything down. Everything. Do as I say, Xander.'

For a second he stared at her.

'Xander. You know I'm right.'

The big window on his computer went dark. He shrugged.

'OK. Pierre's stopped. Ronnie – you know what to do.'

He tapped a few keys, wrenched a desk drawer open and took out a drill. Its rattling whirr filled the room then heightened in pitch as he drove it through the laptop connected to the big screen. He passed it to Ronnie who did the same to his.

'Ach, they'll never get anything off them,' Xander said.

'What about the server?' This was Ronnie.

'They won't find it,' Xander said. 'Needle in a haystack. No, hay in a haystack.'

'Let them come in and get us then. They've got no proof.'

'No,' Alice said. 'They know too much.'

'What are we going to do?' Ronnie's voice was scratchy with fear.

'Escape.'

'How?'

'Oh, we have a way. We've always been prepared for everything. It's why I chose this place.' She turned to Xander. 'Come on.'

He grabbed two long pieces of metal with handles.

'You too,' she said to Ronnie.

'I'll get rid of her.' Xander jerked his head in my direction.

'No. We'll take her. If the police are outside, they won't be so quick to shoot if she's with us. Gag her, though.'

Twenty-eight

Xander slapped a piece of tape over my mouth, then pulled the boxes away from the far wall to reveal a door. Recently installed judging by the new plaster around it. A sharp intake of breath from Ronnie. We went through into another office. This was empty.

Shit. We were in the next-door building. Number 7. They'd rented the office the other side of the dividing wall between the two buildings and created a way through. Would the police be watching this building as well? If they were out there at all. I was beginning to think they weren't. Xander was right. Nick had been acting on his own.

'You rented this place too?' Ronnie was falling apart. His face was beaded with sweat and he wiped his hands on his grimy jeans. 'Jesus.'

The thoroughness of Alice's planning was terrifying and the speed with which she'd made the decision to shut the operation down once she'd pulled herself together.

We sped down a set of stairs identical to the ones in the building next door and out through the back door into a similar yard. Xander wheeled a bin aside to reveal a manhole cover sunk into the tarmac. It was my turn to gasp. I felt the coldness of a gun pressed against my head.

'This gun is very quiet.' Alice's voice had teeth that bit into my brain. 'Make sure I don't have to use it.'

Xander fitted the ends of the two metal rods into the cover. He and Ronnie pulled it out. It came away easily. Doubtless cleaned and greased, ready for escape. A square, brick-lined hole went down into the dark. Alice shone the torch into it. Rusty metal brackets had been driven into the joints between the bricks to make a kind of ladder.

'Down there,' she said to me.

I bleated a bit and waved my hands.

'Go down or I'll push you down,' Xander said.

I guessed it wouldn't matter to them if I broke my neck. I went down, clinging to the brackets with my taped hands and scraping each foot down the bricks until it met the next one. My feet met water. Running water. Not deep, though. It barely covered my feet as I stood at the bottom. And the smell wasn't too bad. Dank and sour. Not sewage. At least I hoped not.

The others followed me down and the cover crashed shut above us. I thought of the quiet little courtyard above our heads. With the manhole cover surrounded by bins. No one would think we'd escaped this way.

It was utterly dark, magnifying every sound: the murmur of flowing water, the drips falling from damp bricks and boots scraping metal. Alice landed beside me with a brief splash and a grunt. Light appeared from a torch in her hand.

We were in a redbrick tunnel with water running over a stone floor. Alice stood on a raised area to one side and pointed the torch upstream.

'This way,' she said.

Xander gave me a push. 'You first.'

I headed into the dark. The shifting light blocked by my staggering body. With no arms to balance me, I couldn't walk as fast as they wanted. Xander repeatedly shoved me forward. Once the force of his push tumbled me into the middle of the flowing water. I struggled to get up. The stones beneath the water were slimy. The others strode on past me and I realised they no longer cared if I was with them or not. I forced myself to my feet and went after them, banging against the walls and tripping in my speed to keep up. I stumbled through a blur of different tunnels, mainly brick but, from time to time, newer stretches were lined with concrete, and once we passed through a sort of tube made from steel pipes. I gave up walking at the edges where the water was shallowest – I was wet through anyway – and splashed through the middle where there was enough height for me to stand.

I remembered Vince talking about rivers running under Glasgow. Was that where I was? But most of the time all I thought about was keeping up with the dancing torchlights that showed me where they were – desperate not to be left behind in the dark.

The torchlights came to a stop and I lurched into a place where the tunnel widened out into a square chamber. They were all in the far corner. Xander feeling around the ground below more brackets fixed into the wall and leading upwards. He retrieved a crowbar from under some fallen bricks and tied it round his waist.

'You'll have to help me get it open,' he said to Ronnie.

'Where are we?'

'Not far from High Street Station. It's normally quiet above but don't hang about once you're out. Go somewhere and lie low.'

'What about my money?'

'You'll get it.'

'Where is it?' Alice asked.

'I've got the crypto wallet with me. The keys are in it.'

'*Bien*. We'll need it.'

'*Maman*, you could stay, you know. There's nothing to connect you to anything. Go home as soon as we're out of here and tell them you know nothing. It'll be rough for a bit but it's better than –'

'No, I tell you they're on to the whole operation. They must know Pierre's my cousin. There's nothing here for me, except debts. Your father's debts. I'm not wasting any more money paying them.'

'He's a bastard.'

She held out her arms to Xander and they wrapped themselves in each other for a few seconds. Alice detached herself first. She pointed to me as I hovered by the end of the tunnel.

'We don't need her now.'

Xander took the gun from her hand, turned and shot me.

I felt nothing although my feet slid from under me as though someone had given me a great shove. I hit the ground once more. Xander shot at me again but this one whizzed past me into the dark and hit the wall. Then a stabbing pain pierced my shoulder and I knew the first shot hadn't missed.

Xander took a few steps towards me. I couldn't run. I was finished.

'Leave her,' Alice said. 'She's not going anywhere. Let's get out of here.'

I lay in the water and watched them climb the wall and disappear into a shaft. I heard the sound of metal hitting metal and a low cursing, followed by a grating sound. A few seconds of silence. A short flurry of voices echoed down, then the grim noise of metal clanging against metal.

They'd gone.

I was alone. Alone in the stifling dark. I had to hold it together. Think what to do. But the noises nibbled at my concentration. The steady gush of water. I could bear that. It was the little unexpected sounds. The sudden splashes echoing down the tunnel and turning into scurrying feet in my imagination. There must be rats down here.

I tried to stand. Pain flared through my shoulder. The tape over my mouth smothered the cry. I tried again. It was agony. Like someone twisting a corkscrew through my shoulder and winding every nerve tight until they all shrieked with pain.

But the pain helped. It took over my thoughts until I could think of nothing but how I wanted to press my hand to it. It helped me force myself to my feet and stagger over to where they'd climbed the wall. To feel around until my hands found one of the metal brackets they'd used to climb. To grind my tape-covered wrists against its corner. The agony ratcheted up a notch with each movement but I dug through it until the tape gave way. Once it had started to tear it came apart easily.

I ripped the tape from my mouth, then swung my arm round and cradled my left shoulder. It was wet. Blood? I didn't know. The rest of me was drenched from my falls in the water. Shakes began to rattle my teeth.

No.

No way.

Must stay focused. If the wound was bleeding badly I had a limited amount of time before…

Don't think about that.

I shut my eyes. Somehow it made it easier. For a while. But eventually fear crowded my thoughts. I hated being here. Hated the dark. Hated the feeling of all those tons of earth and concrete above me. The walls were closing in. Not falling but slowly creeping closer to wrap me in a damp embrace and squash the life out of me.

Stop. Think of something else. Breathe.

Panic receded but it hovered nearby, waiting.

I remembered the tunnels under the Botanic Gardens when I'd thought maybe I'd overcome my fear of dark, confined spaces. But there the tunnels had been wide and high. There'd always been a glow of light and the feeling of air streaming through. And I'd had a torch. The one on my multi-tool. The one I thought was still in my pocket.

I checked.

It was.

I forced the hand of my injured arm to hold it while my fingers felt its surface, found the knob and pressed. A click. Light poured from my hand. I sobbed.

The squared-off chamber hadn't changed. The walls hadn't started closing in. I took a deep breath and looked at my shoulder. Couldn't see much. Except a small hole in my T-shirt with blood staining its waterlogged edges. I gritted my teeth and pulled the sleeve aside.

Not as bad as I'd thought. It looked as though the shot had hit my shoulder at an angle and come out on top of my arm. The hole there was horrible. I could fit a thumb in it. Not that I was going to. It was bleeding too but not wildly.

I peeled away some of the torn tape still hanging from my wrists and covered the wounds. My shoulder shrieked with pain when I pressed it but I felt better once the wounds were out of sight.

What next?

Get out of here, of course. Not here, though. I'd never open the manhole cover above. Xander had needed a crowbar and Ronnie's help.

Downstream would lead to the Clyde. I didn't want to end up in its waters. Upstream the river would eventually have to come out into the open.

Upstream then. I set off, clutching the torch in my good hand. The tunnel shrank quickly. The water flow became sluggish and soon I was wading through silt with stalactites hanging off the walls. Then crawling. The passage came to an end in a small chamber with water entering through a narrow pipe. Too narrow for me to fit through. Even if I'd wanted to.

I turned round and retraced my steps. I was cold now and I focused on putting one step in front of the other. On not falling.

On not moving my left arm. On not wondering how long the battery in my torch would last.

I arrived back in the chamber with the manhole cover. My watch told me half an hour had passed. The Camerons and Ronnie would be long gone from above. Maybe I *could* open the cover or make enough noise to attract a passer-by.

I grabbed the first of the brackets fixed into the wall with my good hand and hauled myself up. It was slow and painful.

Finally my good hand hit the manhole cover at the top. I dragged myself as far up as I could and started pushing at it. First with my hand and then with my head as well, my legs bent and forcing me upwards. I tried pressing against the centre, against the edges. I tried short sharp shoves. I tried to slide it up and out. Nothing worked. And finally I tried screaming.

A metallic crack answered my yells. Someone was banging the cover. I screamed some more, then pushed at it again. This time it shifted. A crack appeared round its edge. I shoved harder and the gap grew as the cover lifted. Someone was forcing it open from above. Glimmers of street lighting cast shadows on the dark bricks. The same someone rammed a piece of wood through to hold the lid open and fingers appeared and started pulling.

Fingers with bitten black nail varnish.

Shit. Ronnie!

I wrenched at the piece of wood and pulled it into the tunnel. The cover fell with a clang, swiftly followed by Ronnie's shout smothered by the layers of metal, as it crushed his fingers.

I scrambled down, leaned against the bottom bracket for a few seconds and thought. They knew I was alive and functioning now. Would they come after me? No time to wait and see. I ran.

Downstream this time.

And as I splashed and stumbled, a rasping crunch broke through the rushing of the water. They were lifting the cover again. I sped up, hurtling down the tunnel despite my shoulder.

The sound of bigger water met my ears. I didn't remember this. I must have passed the point where we'd come down. Was I nearing the Clyde? Was this the sound of the outfall pouring into the open air?

I sped up even more, lurching from one side of the tunnel to the other in a desperate effort to keep upright. Turned a corner and discovered what the noise was.

Another river. Another buried river running under the city. And mine was only a tributary flowing into this larger one. At the junction, it poured over a low wall with a pillar supporting the roof.

Shit, shit, shit.

Same decision to make: upstream or downstream. A rat stared at me from the opposite side. I hissed at it and it scurried off downstream. Right. I'd go the other way.

The bricks of the tunnel I'd come down suddenly glowed red. Torchlight flickered over them like a flame. They were closer than I'd thought. And now I heard the splashing of feet running through the water. They'd be on me in seconds. I should flee except the tunnel ran straight in both directions from the junction. As soon as they got here, they'd see which way I'd gone. I couldn't run in the dark.

I shone my torch round. Looking for something. Anything. And found it. A side drain also led into the river at this point. A little arched opening beautifully built with a narrow channel leading upwards. It might do. I leaped into it, turned off the torch and squirmed up as far as I could. My shoulder screamed with pain but I forced it on.

And stopped when I could ram my body no further up.

I thought my feet were hidden. I hoped they were. I prayed to the goddesses and powers that Ma believes in. All I could do was wait. Wait an age. In the dark. With only the smell of old brick to tether me to reality. Unable to hear what was going on because my body wedged tight was a sound barrier and the only noises reaching me were the muffled gush of water and the pounding of my heart. I counted to two hundred and then to five, trying to time it to my heart. Two beats per count. I stopped at six hundred. That was ten minutes.

I wriggled out backwards. My shoulder hurt dreadfully. It didn't matter. Nothing was stronger than the fear hands would grab me as I emerged. But I came out to nothing more than a gentle splash as I landed in the water. I stood up and looked around. It was pitch black now. Pitch black apart from a faint flash of torchlight downstream. They'd gone the same way as the rat.

Unless they'd split up…

I pushed the thought away and headed upstream, only turning on my torch once the glimmer of theirs had long gone. The tunnel rapidly became lower even though the river was deeper here and faster running. I walked bent double with my hand clutching my shoulder as much as I could. The pain had changed. It was no longer a fire radiating along my nerves but a stabbing deep in my shoulder every time I jarred it. And I knocked it a lot as I blundered against the curve of the tunnel roof and the bits of pipe and stone that stuck out.

The roof dropped suddenly under a square block of concrete running over the river. If I wanted to go any further, I'd have to crawl. And in the dark. I'd need the hand holding the torch to take my weight.

I used another piece of torn tape to attach the torch to my head. I didn't want it to get wet. Turned it off, though. Its light wouldn't be useful and I might as well save the battery. Then I shut my eyes – they were useless anyway – and felt my way forward. And shut my mind to everything except concentrating on moving forwards.

The ground was slimy under the water and I had to use both hands to crawl. The pain sickened me. I'd only got a few yards in when a roaring started in the distance away to my right.

Twenty-nine

My mind reeled. What was the roaring? A storm drain sending a torrent of water rushing down on me? The tunnel collapsing? A dragon?

It came closer and closer.

I crouched down, hugging myself tight and waited.

Nearer and nearer. A great clattering boom that reached me then exploded over my head in a long rattle of thunder and rumbled away to my left.

A train? Yes. The rhythm gave it away. I must be under a railway line. An underground one. It wasn't a concrete block cutting through the roof above me but another tunnel. And somehow knowing that helped. Real life was out there. Rushing towards morning. And also it meant this overhead tunnel was probably only the width of a couple of railway lines.

I crawled on through the dark and after a while, when I lifted my head to see if the roof was still low, it met nothing. I stood cautiously until I was upright, then reached for the torch and switched it on.

The space I was in was almost beautiful.

The builders or the architect had inserted a run of arches in the roof here. Their soft curves gave the place the feel of a cathedral crypt. I wanted to stop. Spend a little time here. Let myself rest.

I knew it would be a mistake so I didn't.

But the thought of resting increasingly dominated my thoughts as I made my legs take one step after another. I started promising them that we'd take a break after the next hundred paces. Then telling them we needed to do another hundred.

If only I knew where I was. I had visions of myself wandering forever through a network of water-filled tunnels.

I hunted for other things to think about.

What was going on up above me? The ambulance had taken Nick away. I hoped he was awake and organising a rescue for the children sitting in a line on a bed in Calais. Waiting. Waiting. I hoped he knew about the children. And organising a hunt for the Camerons and Ronnie.

What was Sandy Cameron's part in all this? It struck me he might be an innocent bystander. Maybe not totally innocent. His gambling created the money worries that soured Alice Cameron's life. But it looked as though he was the only member of the Cameron family not involved in the child-trafficking and abuse. Neither Xander nor Alice had mentioned him. Plus he clearly hadn't told them Nick was alive.

And that brought me back to Nick.

I had to get out. So I could tell him how the Camerons had escaped.

Besides, if I didn't, I'd never know how this ended.

I came to yet another tunnel running overhead. I'd have to crawl again. But a closer look showed it was nothing more than a pipe and I went to duck under it. The jerking movement was my undoing. My feet slipped from under me and I landed heavily on my wounded shoulder. The pain was a white flash that blinded my senses to anything else and cocooned me in hell.

I made myself breathe. Reached over and felt my injured arm. It was still there. I couldn't bear to touch the shoulder but I levered myself upright and opened my eyes.

It was pitch black.

I'd dropped the torch.

And after fumbling around I knew I wasn't going to find it. I'd lost my bearings in the dark. I could no longer even find the pipe that cut through the roof of the tunnel. Anger flickered inside me. Anger at my own stupidity. I should have been more careful. I should have realised I was dangerously tired. And now I was lost and in the dark. I didn't even know which way to go.

An angry voice in my head told me to stick my hand in the water, to feel the flow and follow it upstream.

I did as it said and off we went. Me and my poor battered body, bumbling through the water and banging against the walls. My eyes tight shut against the dark as though I could make myself believe it wasn't real. Accompanied every faltering step by the nasty voice that blamed me and cursed at me. It wouldn't let me stop. It told me to stop being a wimp every time the horror of the dark undid me. It made me sing to frighten away the rats. It drove me on and on for what felt like years.

And then my fingers met something different. Strands of something rough and almost hairy. I screamed and snatched my hand away. The air moved around me. Full of different smells. I should open my eyes. But if I did and they met nothing but impenetrable blackness. Endless night. I wasn't sure I could bear it.

I did, though.

It was dark.

Shit, shit, shit.

But maybe… maybe not as dark as before. Parts of the black were grey. Different shades of grey. Light and dark. I blinked and stretched my hand out to a dim shape coming out of the wall beside me. It was a fern. I could see it was a fern. That was what I'd grasped.

Plants needed light.

Even ferns.

I took a few stumbling paces forward and the black lifted. It became the shadows of a city night where light stains the sky and bounces off the edges of wet surfaces. Water dropped on my upturned face. I realised it was raining.

I'd done it.

I was outside.

In the open air.

In a cutting with high walls adorned with plants growing up to the railings that lined it. Above me the night sky glimmered and the occasional noise of a car broke the quiet.

I'd done it.

I'd never climb the walls with my shoulder in the state it was. I yelled. And screamed. Shouting came from the tunnel behind me. I whirled round, slipping and falling yet again. More shouts. In the distance, darting beams of light came closer. And the sound of heavy footsteps pounding through water.

They'd caught up with me. Caught up with me when I was so close to escaping.

I looked around. Climbing out was impossible. But at the far end of this short section above ground, the river poured out of another tunnel. It was the only way out of here. For me.

But I was finished.

I'd rather die here, I thought. Out in the air. With the sky above me and green things clinging to life.

I made one last effort and heaved myself upright, then stood, leaning against the wall and clutching a fern.

They tore out of the tunnel. Two of them. And, like me, came to a sudden halt as they realised they were out in the open air.

Their swinging torchlight caught me straightaway and pinned me. After hours in the dark the beams burned. I was blinded. Their torches seared bright blobs on my closed eyes.

'Jen, thank God.'

I recognised that voice. I'd have recognised it anywhere. How was it possible?

Hands grasped mine.

I yelled with the pain.

'What is it?'

'My shoulder. Xander shot me.'

And I no longer cared if this was a mirage. I opened my eyes.

It was Nick. Under the tattoos, his face grey and strained with the pain of each rasping breath. He'd never looked more like the lizard I often thought of him as. A chameleon drained of colour in the fading dark.

'Shouldn't you be in hospital?' I realised my mind was escaping.

'Probably,' he said. 'Are you OK?'

'I don't know.'

And behind him I saw Ronnie shouting into a phone.

Nick saw the shock hit my face. He turned.

'He's police,' he said. 'Ronnie's police.'

'He's in the police?' Rat-faced Ronnie with the scabby nose filled with studs and chains and black nail varnish was a police officer?

A thousand questions fought each other to be first out of my mouth.

'The children?' I asked. 'Are they safe?'

'Yes. I called for support as soon as I came to.' He stopped briefly as a spasm of pain locked his chest. 'French police... working with us. Much bigger operation at their end. Waiting outside Basset's building. Stormed it as soon as I... The children are fine. Everybody's been picked up. The Camerons too. All picked up.'

'Everybody?' I interrupted him. 'You're sure you got everybody. Shona, too?'

'Yes. The police on Malta arrested her first of all.'

I breathed in and out quietly as I let his words sink in. Rania and Aya were safe. I was safe.

'It's over,' Nick said. 'It's all over.'

A black van appeared at the top of the cutting's vertical sides. Men called down. Nick and Ronnie called back. Our rescuers had arrived.

I looked at my watch. It was two. Two in the morning. I'd only been in the tunnels for a few hours although it felt like weeks. I still didn't understand everything. But, for now, it didn't matter. All I wanted was to get out of here. The rest could wait.

Thirty

They took us to hospital after hoisting us out of the cutting. A series of unsmiling men oversaw the operation. They knew what they were doing. And they had all the kit. All the very latest kit. I'd have hung around and chatted to them if the paramedics hadn't bundled us into ambulances and raced off through the night.

We got the full works on our arrival at A&E. Groups of medical professionals clustered round our trolleys talking at each other as they wheeled us into separate cubicles. Ronnie was the first to disappoint them. He was in the next-door cubicle and I heard them tell him he could go and sit in the main reception. A nurse would come along and dress his fingers. Nothing was broken. If he wasn't up to date with his tetanus jabs, he should remedy that immediately.

They took a little longer to decide that I was equally unworthy of full-blown emergency treatment. The bullet had passed through the flesh on my shoulder. A low-velocity bullet as the damage was minimal. Minimal as far as they were concerned, but it still hurt a lot. The bored-looking nurse sent to clean and dress the wound told me they saw much worse on a daily basis. I told him I didn't need the details and he shut up. Once he'd finished, I was told to come back to an outpatients clinic in two days, then sent to the main reception to wait for a prescription for antibiotics.

Ronnie was still there.

'Bloody NHS,' he said. 'I think I'm going to be here for hours.'

'No priority treatment for police, then?'

'I don't think they know I am.'

Fair enough, I thought. He didn't look like a police officer. His cover was good. If it was just cover. Part of me thought he might be like this in real life.

'I guess I'm too well,' he added.

The people in the waiting area did look much more ill than him. Someone over in the corner by the drinks machine had been in a fight judging by the blood pouring out of his nose and the cut above his eye. Behind us a grey-faced woman held a baby and tried to keep another infant from crawling all over the floor.

'Shouldn't some of your colleagues be here? Assisting you?'

'It's better I keep a low profile.'

'Where's Nick?'

'Who?'

'Jamie Kincaid,' I said. 'Or whatever name you know him as.'

'Kincaid's being scanned.'

'Why?'

'Broken rib and possible internal injuries from being shot.'

'I thought he was wearing a bullet-proof vest.'

'Bullet-resistant. No such thing as bullet-proof. He's probably OK, though. Just bruised. But you're supposed to go and get yourself checked straightaway after being shot, not go racing around underground looking for – anyway, he wouldn't.'

A nurse came out with a piece of paper. We all stared at her hopefully. But it was the turn of the mother and two children.

'So tell me what's been going on,' I said. 'And don't give me any of that shit about it being secret.'

'Well, it is.'

'No one's paying us any attention.'

'I mean secret from you.'

'Don't be stupid. I know enough to be dangerous. I could go and tell lots of people what's been going on. Like journalists. Or put it all over social media.'

He looked very uneasy.

'If Nick… Kincaid was here, he'd tell me.'

I wondered if this was true. Nick hadn't always told me everything.

'OK,' he said unexpectedly. 'What do you want to know?'

'Are you really a police officer?'

'Well, yes. Sort of. I mean I didn't get into this by the usual route. I was more recruited, you could say. It was this or prison really. The MOD don't like being hacked.'

'I see.' And I thought I did.

'This was my first time out in the field. Up to now I've been strictly a back room operative.'

He told me how he'd been working undercover with Xander and Alice to set up their online business. He skirted round its content, which suited me just fine. A lot of the time I couldn't follow him. He was fond of talking about the tech and used terms and explanations that were beyond me but I got enough to understand he'd helped them set up secure networks and links and paywalls as well as advertise discreetly. I figured I'd get more out of him by letting him follow his own route. And it was clear he wanted to talk.

And as he opened up, I realised it had been a truly massive, international police operation. Via the Camerons they'd hoped to pick up huge numbers of paedophiles all over the world and infiltrate scores of other rings.

'It was a genius idea of Alice's in the first place,' he said, unable to disguise the admiration in his voice. 'And while she didn't know how to set it all up, she understood how to organise it, how to sell and market it. And once she'd started it just grew legs and started running. More and more perverts turning up every day and signing up.'

I wondered if the success had caught Ronnie's bosses by surprise too. It sounded as though they'd thought it a small operation at first. Something suitable for a youngster like him to cut his teeth on. It was only as the operation progressed, they'd realised how much of an opportunity it was.

Just as all the months of hard work were about to come to fruition, both for the Camerons and for Ronnie's undercover operation, and the Camerons were getting ready to go live with their first event, a battered and unconscious Nick had been captured and brought to Basset.

He owed his life to Ronnie's quick thinking. To Ronnie, who had been sent over to sort out a last-minute problem with the Calais links while Xander handled the Glasgow end. Not that he knew who Basset was at that point.

'No names, no pack drill,' he said to me although I suspected he had no idea where the phrase came from. 'I didn't know Basset's last name then. I didn't know he was a gendarme. And I worked on his computers in an anonymous hotel room. I only knew he was called Pierre. And there are a lot of Pierres in France.'

Ronnie was supposed to be secreting a tracking device into something belonging to Basset. Instead he'd slipped it into Nick's jeans' pocket so that he could be picked up as quickly as possible after he'd been dumped, alive, into the Channel. But the ramifications of Nick's presence had been huge.

Ronnie's department no longer had any way of identifying Basset. They had Ronnie's description but they couldn't do much with it. They'd been relying on following him.

And the ever-cautious Alice Cameron shut the operation down while they waited to see if Nick's presence meant they'd been discovered.

'It was very helpful that the Camerons knew Kincaid,' Ronnie went on. 'They knew he worked undercover. It meant they'd connect his supposed death at Calais to the man they thought they'd killed. All I had to do was confirm the picture they showed me of Kincaid was the man Basset had thrown in the water. Which was the truth.'

The only true part of the story.

So Ronnie's department had identified the first suitable dead body as Nick. Organised a funeral. Primarily to ensure the Camerons believed Nick was dead but also to provide an opportunity for someone to hint to Xander that Nick had gone rogue and fallen for a woman he'd met while undercover. That he'd broken every rule in the book and no one knew what he'd found out.

'I suppose it was quite useful that I came to the funeral then,' I said.

'Very useful,' Ronnie agreed. 'It backed up our story. Especially as you looked so fierce and sad. And you played a blinder with Xander. Trying to find out what he knew without revealing anything about yourself. You couldn't have handled it better if we'd briefed you.'

I got up and went to the drinks machine. Hit it a few times. People were always smacking them so my actions barely raised more than a couple of glances. I thought about walking out. I hated the way they'd used me to create a story, but I wanted to know the rest of it and seeing what loose-mouthed Ronnie could tell me was probably my best chance. I went back and sat down again.

'So why all the stuff with Sandy Cameron? I gather he wasn't involved with what Alice and Xander had planned.'

'That was clever,' Ronnie said but a little less enthusiastically than before. My attack on the drinks machine had made him uneasy. 'A really smart piece of thinking. No one knew how deep in Sandy was. Word was he was on the payroll of a couple of the big Glasgow families but nothing for sure. And there are always rumours. But we needed to know if he was part of the paedo thing. So my, er… department resurrected Nick and got him to spin Sandy a story about drugs arriving via Calais. If Alice and Xander heard about it then we'd know Sandy was involved. And it would be fine because drugs were nothing to do with them. If they didn't hear, we'd know Sandy was –'

'Playing for the right team,' I said. I couldn't quite keep the note of sarcasm out of my voice.

'Well, not quite.'

'And I don't suppose Nick – I mean Kincaid – went anywhere near anyone to do with the drugs trade in Glasgow.'

'No.'

All that time I'd spent hunting for Nick. All the time I'd spent thinking – or trying not to think that he was in great danger.

I shook my head.

'Kincaid went back to Spain until –'

'He went to Spain. Does Angel know he's alive, then?'

'Who's Angel.'

'His cousin.'

'The one you went to Calais with?'

'Yes. Never mind. You said he went to Spain until… until what?'

'He came back when you went missing and insisted on being part of the operation.'

Ronnie told me that after my trip to Calais with Angel, Alice Cameron had felt comfortable enough to start up again. Apparently Angel and I had struck just the right note of grieving friends or lovers desperate to know how their loved one had died.

I blocked the rage simmering underneath.

But then I'd turned up in Glasgow again, making a great fanfare of my presence through my exploits at the film shoot. And this had been a problem. For the Camerons who were concerned I knew something. And for Ronnie's department who were worried my presence would make Alice once again call a halt to the operation. Determined to keep an eye on me, Xander had despatched Ronnie to steal my phone and hack it. He'd seen his opportunity at the gym but he'd set the phone up so he could spy on me as well as Xander.

'But why did you try and steal my phone afterwards at the Botanic Gardens?'

'Because I needed to talk to you. We needed to talk to you. And without Xander listening in. You'd downloaded a picture and an article about Basset and since that point Xander had been glued to your phone, listening in to every word you said and monitoring your texts and calls. But you hit me and ran off and then your phone died so Xander didn't know where you were and neither did I.'

If I hadn't been so angry, I'd have laughed.

'It was only later when Duncan contacted us that we knew you'd gone to see him.'

'So my phone died before I met him? No one knew I'd told him about Basset.'

He shook his head. 'Downloading the photo and the article was what gave it away.' He paused. 'I maybe shouldn't –'

'Shouldn't what?'

He shook his head again and started fiddling with one of the studs in his nose.

But I'd put two and two together. Or, at least, I thought I had. It's wonderful how pure rage clears the brain. Ronnie had said he'd used the tracker meant for Basset in Calais to save Nick.

'You didn't know who Basset was until I identified him for you. Until Angel called you.'

He grinned. 'Maybe.'

It was enough.

'But why didn't Duncan tell me how much danger I was in?'

Ronnie hesitated before he spoke. 'We'd only shared essential information with him at that point.'

Which translated as *we'd told him very little and most of that was false.*

I'd have liked to say something pithy and ironic. But words were never my strong point. Equally I'd have liked to spit on the floor in disgust like the old men in Angel's bar did but the receptionist who'd been casting glances at me ever since I'd smacked the vending machine might have chucked me out and I wanted to get the rest of the story out of Ronnie while he was being so forthcoming.

And forthcoming he was. I learned I'd been right about a lot of what I'd worked out. Xander had known I'd found Leila. Getting together and sharing information had been a death sentence for us both.

'I'm sorry about your father,' Ronnie said. 'We had people watching the Gardens for you. No one thought your father was in danger. Xander just lost it when you didn't turn up.'

The nurse came back out and called my name. Which was a good thing. Because a host of feelings were threatening to break my composure. I wasn't going to let Ronnie see them. No way. I walked over to her slowly, giving myself time to push them back down. There'd be time to think of Pa later. The nurse handed me a prescription and a container with a couple of tablets in it. I was to take them this evening if I didn't make it to the chemist.

'Hopefully I'll be next,' Ronnie said, when I came back. And then, 'Anything else you want to know?'

He'd enjoyed telling me everything, I thought. And he'd enjoyed the operation. It was still a bit of a game to him. And I didn't like it. I didn't like the way the people he worked for played with people's lives. I didn't like the shadowy world they lived in.

Was there anything else I wanted to know before I left?

'Down by the Clyde,' I said. 'The night Cameron went gambling. What were you doing there?'

'We were keeping a very discreet eye on Cameron. So when he set off late on Saturday night, I went down to see what he was up to.'

'Did you recognise me?'

'Not at first. Your hair is, er… something else!'

'But you did recognise me and follow me. You shopped me to the police, didn't you?'

'Yes. But it wasn't a question of shopping you. I am the police. We needed you out of the way especially as you seemed to be getting so close to Cameron. You spoke to him, didn't you?'

I remembered the mad impulse that had come over me and nodded.

'Anyway, you didn't stay long enough the first time you went back to your room. Kincaid was furious with me for not stopping you myself rather than waiting for back-up.'

'But your colleagues were waiting for me when I came back.'

'You got away, though.' There was admiration in his voice. 'No one was quite sure how you'd done it. It would have been better if you'd been picked up. You'd have been safe.'

Would I have been safe? I wasn't so sure. I thought Ronnie's view was overly simple. Who knew what strings Xander could have pulled once I was in a police station.

'And Sandy Cameron? What happens to him?'

'He'll be quietly retired. We think he knew nothing but we can't be sure.'

'Will you get them?' I asked. 'All the people logging in to watch, I mean. You and Xander drilled through your computers.'

'No.'

'No?'

'No. Drill through a hard disk and you'll never get anything off it.'

He fell silent for a few seconds.

'It was supposed to be just Xander and me there,' he said. 'Quietly raking in the cash and the identities of the perverts at the same time. And then once they were all in, Kincaid and I were going to… neutralise Xander. With two of us he wouldn't have been able to destroy everything.'

So it *had* just been Nick and Ronnie. No back-up ready and waiting to storm the building. I suspected Nick would have handled most of the neutralising. Ronnie didn't look capable of overpowering a flea.

'Except Alice turned up,' I said. 'And shot him.'

'Yes. So it all went wrong. We could have picked up Xander and Alice and the French lot weeks ago. Discovering the identities of the people who paid to view was the whole point of the op. It would have taken months to unpeel the layers of encryption they'd hidden behind but we'd have tracked them down eventually. Arrested some but used others to find out more.' He paused. 'At least Kincaid got out of it alive. Thanks to you. I didn't know what to do when Alice said she'd shot him.'

I was sure that was true.

'And the children have been rescued,' I said.

'Of course. But there'll be more children.'

He looked away from me and out through the window into the night but I could see his reflection. He looked older and more serious. Maybe he was beginning to realise the reality behind the game he'd been playing.

'We'll never get anything off the computers. Xander made sure of that.'

'What about the ones in Calais?'

'There's nothing on them of any use. Xander and Alice trusted no one. The whole thing's been for nothing. Just a massive shit show.'

I wished I was too tired to care. But I knew the faces of the future children we hadn't saved would haunt me. I knew I was going to spend hours wondering if I could have acted differently so the operation wouldn't have failed.

'Unless we can find the server,' he added.

I remembered him asking Xander about a server. It must have been some last ditch attempt to salvage something from the mess.

'Xander had a server somewhere. We needed a lot of processing power to run and store everything and somewhere secure to house it. He always knew he might have to destroy his laptop. We've looked everywhere but we can't find it. If we could, it would be game on again.'

I thought for a minute.

'In Alice's office?'

He shook his head.

'What about underground? Xander and Alice seemed to know a lot about what's under the city.'

'No. A server needs guaranteed power, a reliable network connection and a controlled environment – preferably cool and dust-free and certainly not damp. It could be anywhere, though. Not even in this country. Hiding in a server farm somewhere remote. You know what they are?'

I nodded. I had a vague idea and I'd seen pictures of rows and rows of computers, stacked high in racks, an array of dark grey metal and flashing green and red LEDs. Surprisingly peaceful really.

'Although I think,' Ronnie added, 'Xander had it somewhere he could physically access.'

A nurse came out and called Ronnie's name. He stood up.

'Will you still be here when they've finished with me?'

'Unlikely.'

I was sick of it all.

Nothing had been what it seemed. All the things I'd thought were true had turned out to be false. No one was who they'd claimed to be. And I'd got it all wrong.

I hated it all.

I'd hated being undercover. Hated being immersed in a different personality. It had stretched me out of shape, thinned the barriers in my head between good and bad until they became porous and leaking. 'In fact, no,' I said. 'I'm going in a minute.'

He hesitated.

'Unless you want to try and stop me.'

He shook his head.

'They'll probably want to talk to you.'

'They?'

'You know who I mean.'

'Fine. I'm sure *they'll* be able to find me.'

He shrugged and followed the nurse out of reception.

I hung around for a while. Wondering what to do. Where to go. Night was starting to pale into dawn but it was still too early to call Ma. Or go to Fergus's. I looked at my phone. Dead. Being submerged in the water had done it no good.

I had another phone. In my car. I tried to remember where the car was. A few roads away from the room I'd inhabited for the last few weeks. It wasn't that far from the hospital. I'd go there first.

But as I headed for the door, Duncan rushed in. And straight past me to reception. The white light emphasised the worry on his face. He asked for Jamie Kincaid. The receptionist sighed. He flashed what I guessed was his police ID and she looked a little livelier, said something to him and disappeared. He turned round and surveyed the waiting area.

I went up to him but he stared right through me.

'Duncan. It's Jen.'

He looked harder. Recognition flashed across his face.

'Jamie?' he said. 'Is he OK?'

'I think so. They're just scanning him as a precaution.'

Some of the tension left his shoulders.

'What's been happening?' he asked.

How could I answer him? How could I sift through the tsunami of things I'd learned and sort them into something that made sense. Especially as I wasn't sure I'd finally been told the truth anyway.

'I heard someone had called in the firearms unit,' he said. 'Someone from outside Glasgow. I thought it might be Jamie so I rang a few colleagues. No one knew for sure but they said something big was going down.'

'And there you had it in a nutshell, I thought. How difficult it was to run anything covert without news of it leaking through the local police force instantly. No wonder Nick and Ronnie had been acting alone.

'I think Jamie will have to tell you what's been going on himself,' I said.

'I did pass on the note you left to Jamie's department. I'd been in touch with them since you told me about that French gendarme.'

'I know.'

'They said it was safe for you to come in. That Sandy wasn't a threat although they were about to pick him up. That...'

'That I was a huge nuisance?'

I took his silence as a Yes.

Poor Duncan. He'd been used as much as I had. Lied to. Or, at least... what was it Ronnie had said? *Only essential information had been shared with him.*

The receptionist returned and told Duncan that Jamie Kincaid was back from the scan and he could go through and see him.

'You coming?' he asked me.

'No,' I said. 'I need a wash and some food and some sleep. I haven't been clean for days. I'm leaving.'

I headed for the door.

'Jen,' he called after me.

'Yes.'

'Any message for Jamie?'

'Tell him...'

What should I tell him?

That I'm confused.

That right at this moment I can't bear to see him.

That I'm not going to pretend I don't care about him. I'm sick of pretending.

But the world he's part of sickens me.

'Tell him I'll be in touch.'

Thirty-one

It was a longer walk from the hospital to my car than I'd anticipated. And probably not what the doctor would have advised for someone with a gunshot injury. But with no money, no working phone, no transport and only the filthy and torn clothes I was wearing, I didn't have a lot of options.

I almost enjoyed it, though.

Despite the early hour, morning had arrived. The day was bright with the promise of sun but still cool under the pale, blue sky. It felt wonderful to be walking without the ever-present fear that someone might snatch me. A police car went by in the distance, its sirens raking the cool air. And I laughed.

The first thing I was going to do when I got to the car was call Ma. Call Ma to tell her everything was sorted. They could all go back to Tregonna. And I'd be back soon, too. As soon as I could. I'd get the talking to the police bit over first. I didn't want them to come to Tregonna. Especially if they were the police from Nick and Ronnie's secretive department. Their presence would sully the place. Ma and I would have to do some sort of cleansing ritual after they'd gone. Burn a few herbs and suchlike.

Shit. I was starting to sound as nuts as she was.

But the thought of the forthcoming police interview stayed with me. The walk gave me time to come up with a plan. A way forward out of the morass of deceit and trickery I'd been wading through. A way of sorting out a couple of problems too, even though it meant dirtying myself by trading with the game-players again.

Strangely enough no one had stolen my battered little car and I still had the key rammed deep in a jeans pocket. I called Ma and told her it was all over. Told her they could go home. It was safe. Told her I was fine and I'd be home in a couple of days. Told her I wasn't up to talking about what had happened yet.

'Of course,' she said.

'Where are you?' I asked.

'In the outskirts of London. With some old friends who live in a community of the diaspora. Some of them knew Rania and Aya's mother. People come and go all the time here so we don't stand out.'

'It sounds good.'

'I knew I could trust them.'

'Of course. I'm sorry you've had to look after the girls on your own. You must be exhausted.'

'Not really. Everybody shares in the work here, so no one is overloaded. It is a true community. Actually we might not go home straightaway.'

'Just let me know what you're doing. I'll call you later. I need some sleep. Give Rania and Aya a hug from me. And Yasmiin.'

'I will. But listen to this before you go.'

I waited while Ma walked into another room. Quiet voices broke the silence. Quiet but childish voices.

'No,' one of them said. 'It doesn't go there. It's blue. It must be sky.' I recognised Rania's voice. Jigsaw, I thought.

'Yes, it does.' The voice replying to Rania was almost unknown. Forceful and defiant but much younger than Rania's. 'Let me,' it added and gave a little cry of annoyance.

'Aya?' I said to Ma.

'Yes. Not all the time and not every day but she's finding her voice.'

'And Rania? How is she?'

'Being here has been good for her. Talking to people who knew her mother. And being with children who've been through similar experiences. She's made some friends. It will take time but her feet are on the right path for her.'

Tears prickled my nose but I wouldn't cry. Not yet. There were things I had to deal with first.

'And you, Ma? Are you all right?'

'I am now. I wasn't for a while. Because of Peter.'

'I'm sorry. I wish –'

'No point. It's in the past. Don't let it poison the future.' The jingle of her bracelets told me she was shaking her other hand. As though to free herself of the memory. 'I might invite some people here to come and stay at Tregonna for a while,' she went on.

'Good idea.'

'And Kit wants to speak to you.'

'You've been in touch with him?'

'Yes. Should I not have been?'

The gulf between Ma's world and the one I'd been living in never seemed wider.

'I didn't tell him where we were, you know,' she added. 'Only that we'd gone to stay with friends. He wants to speak to you. He's left you lots of messages. He was quite upset you hadn't called him back.'

'I'll call him. I always wanted to, you know that.'

And I had. And I did. He'd been the first person I'd wanted to speak to after Pa died.

'Give him this number. It'll be a few days before I can resurrect my old one.'

'I will. Now go and sleep.'

I drove to Fergus's. And parked illegally. The roads around his flat were residents' parking only. I'd get a ticket or the car would be towed. I didn't care. I'd happily never see the heap of grime again.

I collected all the stuff I'd left in it. A couple of spare phones and hats. Some cash under the front seat. Nothing much because I'd kept anything essential in my rucksack which I'd lost at some point last night. I couldn't remember where. The contents of the wastepaper basket from Alice's office were strewn on the floor in front of the passenger seat. I'd never had the time to look at them properly.

I unscrewed and read them. The receipt from the builders for cement made more sense now. She and Xander must have used it when they made the doorway between the two buildings near the Barrowlands to create an escape route. The report on the jewellery business was dull and wordy and much of the language beyond me but I forced myself to read every word. Alice thought their range of products was too unfocused to 'stand out in a crowded marketplace'. The second to last page was a SWOT analysis which I did understand a bit. Kit and I had been asked to do one by a business adviser he'd brought in when he was thinking of selling the business he used to run. What did it stand for? Strengths, Weaknesses, something beginning with O and Threats, I thought. Kit had said it was actually quite useful at the time. I flicked over it before turning to the last page. Another SWOT analysis. This time handwritten and Alice had written the headings in full. O stood for opportunities.

The handwriting was scrappy and difficult to read as though it had been dashed off quickly. I wondered if it was the rough version of the typewritten one for the jewellery company but the notes that I could read were completely different. Strengths included '*a product very much in demand*' although she didn't specify what it was. And '*in-house expertise*'. Threats were impossible to read apart from two words. *Police/Gendarmes*, they said.

What was I looking at?

Had Alice done a SWOT analysis on her paedophile business? Had she finished the one for the jewellery company and decided to fill in a free moment.

I looked much harder. She'd scribbled a few items in the Opportunities box: *sell photos/videos for post event follow-up; special requests; VIP invitation only events*. I felt sick but I forced myself to read on.

Not much under Weaknesses. *Pierre*, she'd written and then a note: *Manage him*. Then an illegible one-word scrawl followed by another note: ~~Needle~~ *Hay in a haystack*. Someone had used that phrase recently. I tried to remember but it eluded my tired brain. Maybe later.

I shoved everything into a carrier bag and went to the flat.

Fergus was up and dressed when I arrived. And relieved to see me.

'Is it over?' he asked. 'Is that why you're back?'

'Yes. Nearly, that is. But there's no more danger. Can I have a bath? I can't shower. I mustn't get my shoulder wet.'

The police would arrive. I was sure of that. I hoped it would take them a while but if they came soon I wanted to face them clean.

Tam came out of her bedroom as Fergus ran the bath, rubbing sleep out of eyes that snapped into focus as soon as she saw me. She moved forward to hug me. I stepped back.

'I'm filthy and my shoulder's injured. And I'm only just holding it all together.'

Fergus called that the bath was ready.

'But I'm OK, Tam. Or I will be soon.'

'Shall I put your hair back to its normal colour?'

The decision was almost beyond me.

'Does it mean dyeing it?'

She nodded.

'No,' I said. I didn't know why. 'It'll grow out and I can cut it off. If you could tidy it up later, that would be great.'

The bath was good despite having to keep the dressing on my

shoulder dry. I didn't linger, though. I wanted to be dressed and ready if they came... when they came.

And afterwards, wearing some of the clean clothes I'd left behind when I went undercover, I called Angel.

'I need to make this call,' I told Tam and Fergus. 'But it will be short. And then I'll tell you as much as I can.'

Angel answered straightaway and spoke before I could say a word.

'Jen?'

'Yes. How did you know?'

'I've been waiting for you to call. Hoping you'd call for days.'

'You know he's alive then.'

'Yes.'

'How?'

'It was a couple of days after we came back from Calais. He sent a postcard from Sevilla. Of the church of Saint Nicholas. I knew what it meant. So I went straight down and met him. You called while I was gone. My phone was turned off. In case it had been... *pirateado*. I don't know how you say that in English.'

'I understand.'

'I took Nico back to my house and I was going to drive him to a cabin in the Sierras. A quiet place where he could stay hidden. I listened to your message though, when I got home. About coming to see me. Nico wanted me to call you and tell you to come straightaway but you never answered. He rang someone. He wouldn't tell me who. They told him you'd gone missing in Glasgow. So he went back. Forced them to let him get involved.'

'Did you do his tattoos?'

'Me and a friend. Why?'

'They were very like yours. That was what made me look closely enough to see through his disguise. He reminded me of you, I think. But then you're very like him in a lot of ways.'

'Yes.'

'It confused me when we were together in Calais, you know, Angel. When we both thought he was dead. It didn't mean —'

'I know, I know. I knew it meant nothing. I always knew that.'

I wondered what else to say. Nothing really. Since Ronnie told me Nick had been in Spain, I'd thought Angel must know, but I had to be sure. I couldn't leave him grieving.

'Are you OK, Jen?'

I thought a bit more.

'Yes and no. I need to sleep now.'

I gave Fergus and Tam a brief account of what had happened and headed to bed but before I could crawl under the covers, my phone rang. I reached out to silence it and saw the number was American.

Issy?

It went to voicemail as I hesitated. I waited then listened to the message.

Jenifry, it's Issy. Her voice crackled at the edges although a seam of iron still ran through it. *Your mother gave me this number. The police told me definitively that you had nothing to do with Charlie's death. So I guess I should apologise for accusing you. I am sorry. Really. Please don't call me. I don't know what's been going on and I don't care much. I've learned a lot about Charlie since he died and I don't like most of it. I'm going home and I won't be back. I've spoken to your brother and told him the funeral and everything is up to you both now. The police will release Charlie's body soon and I've sent all his stuff here on to Kit. There was a plastic bracelet thing Vince said was yours.*

So Pa had found my bracelet. It was all he'd found in the tunnel. I'd been seeing hiding places for children everywhere in Glasgow when they'd never even left France. What a mess he'd left behind. I wondered what Issy'd do about their grand lodge at Yosemite. Hopefully the insurers would pay up. I did think about calling her back. I couldn't face it, though.

*

Tam woke me a few hours later.

'The police are here.'

I came to with a jerk. My brain was surprisingly clear. My thoughts all lined up in a row, ready to be ticked off. Plus I'd remembered who had used the phrase *Hay in a haystack* and I had an idea what it might mean.

'OK. I'll be out in a minute.'

'Ach. Take your time. Dad hasn't let them in. They don't have a warrant or anything official.'

But I got Fergus to let them in as soon as I was dressed. It took a short while to convince them I wasn't going to a police station. They'd have to arrest me and I knew they had no grounds.

'Tell him,' I said. 'He'll have to come here if he wants to talk to me.'

'Tell who?'

'The man waiting for me wherever you were planning to take me.'

'Who is the man waiting for you?' Fergus asked after they'd gone.

'I'm not quite sure but we'll find out. You don't mind if I talk to him here?'

'No.' He smiled. 'I'd like to know how this is going to end.'

It didn't take long. Half an hour tops. Then a taxi drew up outside and deposited a man in a smart suit with razor-cut blond hair. Looking out of Fergus's window, I could only see the top of his head but I knew if he looked up I'd see a bony face, sharp with angles, and a stupid smudge of a moustache on his upper lip. Unless he'd shaved it off.

'Is this who you were expecting?' Tam asked.

'Yes. He's the man in charge,' I said. 'Everybody's boss. I'll have to talk to him alone. I'm sorry.'

'You sure you'll be OK.'

'I've met him before. I'll be fine.'

And this time I would. Last time in Calais, after he'd had me picked up by the French police, I'd still had some belief he was on the side of the angels. I didn't believe in angels any more. At least not within the police. I was sure he'd had Peter killed on a whisper of suspicion that he might betray Nick.

'I'm just trying to rescue something from this whole affair,' I added.

Fergus let him in and hovered in the doorway to the sitting room.

'I'll be fine,' I said to him and shut it gently.

Nick's boss spoke immediately. 'I suppose you won't agree to come somewhere more private?'

I shook my head.

'And you won't ask your friends to leave?'

'It's their flat. Their home. I wouldn't dream of it. Besides this won't take long. Just tell me what you want.'

I wondered if he was capable of a straight answer.

He surprised me.

'I'd like you to make a witness statement. Tell us everything you saw and heard in the office with the Camerons. And also in Calais with Capitaine Basset.'

'Why? Ronnie was there too.'

'It would suit us if Ronnie didn't have to appear.'

I understood. It would be far better for them if no one ever knew of Ronnie's involvement.

For the first time a flash of expression lifted his blank features. But it was unidentifiable.

'Maybe you could return the compliment and let me know what you want,' he said.

I was ready.

'Permission for Yasmiin Noor to stay indefinitely in this country with full rights and a guarantee that if she chooses to apply for British citizenship it will be granted.'

He didn't even bother to think about it.

'We can do that.'

The next was trickier. I'd spent a large part of my walk this morning going over most of the things that had happened over the last few weeks.

'And a guarantee that Leila Samaan will not be prosecuted nor otherwise prevented from resuming her life here.'

'So she is alive, then? And presumably home?'

I kept my mouth shut and my expression closed. He'd answered one of my questions, though.

He sighed. 'She may be dangerous. Have you considered that?'

I had but I wasn't going to discuss it with him. At heart, Leila was full of contradictions. To me, at least. Although I thought she was to herself as well. The naive and ardent youngster she'd been before she went fought with the wary and tough woman she'd become. Her experiences in Syria and since had shocked her. Shaped her. But whatever they'd created wasn't clear yet.

Bottom line, though, she'd tried to help me. Plus I owed her a life. She'd saved Rania's in Calais. Besides, I thought Nick had reached the same decision. His boss hadn't known Leila was alive which meant Nick hadn't told him.

'If you want me to help, that's the price. You already owe me. You'd never have known Basset's identity in Calais if I hadn't recognised him. It's a good thing for you I was involved. Despite what you think.'

I wished I knew what was going behind the cold eyes staring at me. I didn't let myself look away. Of course he'd be able to read me.

I knew that. I'd never be as adept as him at deception and double-dealing but I didn't care. In fact, I was glad. A memory stirred.

'No accidents,' I said. 'No convenient accidents.'

Again a glimmer of something crossed his face. This time I thought it was irritation.

'Ever,' I added. 'I know enough to make life very difficult for you.'

Was that true? I wasn't sure. Probably.

He thought for a couple of minutes longer.

'We can fulfil your request.'

'No prosecutions? No restrictions?'

'No.'

'OK, then.'

I suspected they'd watch Leila all the same. Maybe they'd have done that anyway. Maybe he'd worked out it would be a better solution while he'd been considering my demand. I realised I'd never know.

'Is that all?' he asked.

I thought about asking him to thank me for identifying Basset for them. But what was the point?

'Yes. That's all I want.'

He tapped his fingers together for a few seconds.

'Give me a couple of days to get the paperwork together – I'm assuming my word won't be enough.'

'You're quite right. It won't.'

'As I say, it will be done in a couple of days, then please report to Glasgow City Centre Police Station.'

'Will you be there?'

'No, I don't think so.'

'Good. I'd prefer not to see you again.'

This time the flash of expression resolved itself into a chilly smile.

'Believe me, Ms Shaw, the feeling is entirely mutual.'

He headed towards the door. Was I going to tell him what I thought I'd worked out? I disliked him. I disliked everything he stood for but he was the person best-placed to make use of the information.

'One more thing,' I said.

He stopped and turned round, his face a blank.

'I gather the... the participants in this event are untraceable. Without you finding the server Xander Cameron used.'

Not one muscle of his face moved, but he waited.

'I have an idea where it is.'

It was my turn to wait. Pathetic really but I wanted to make him ask me even though I knew I'd tell him eventually, because I too desperately wanted them found and stopped. It was all that mattered.

'What is it? Your idea?'

I handed him the page with the SWOT analysis on it and explained what I thought it was. His face hardened but he listened and looked as I pointed to the Weakness section.

'I've heard this phrase before. *Hay in a haystack.* Xander used it when he said no one would ever find his server. And I think this first word may be *servers.* I wondered... I know he works, worked in cybercrime. I'm guessing that might need a lot of computing power. Is it possible he could have somehow used his department's servers? I don't know, maybe partitioned something off or hidden another computer in the racks.'

I remembered once again the pictures showing stacks of anonymous metal boxes quietly flashing lights and whirring away. *Hay in a haystack.*

'Sounds unlikely.'

He left but he took the SWOT analysis with him.

Thirty-two

'It's all over,' I said to Fergus and Tam as soon as he'd gone. 'For me, anyway. But I've managed to squeeze some good out of the whole affair.'

'What about the man you were trying to find?' Fergus asked. 'You didn't mention him earlier. Did you get to him in time?'

I didn't know how to answer this.

'He's alive,' I said in the end. 'And that's good.'

Nick was the last box on my list waiting to be ticked. Or crossed out. My gut told me which it had to be and that was probably why I'd left it till last.

Because I really didn't want to do it.

'I think I'll go for a walk,' I said to them. 'I ought to find a chemist as well.'

I avoided the Botanic Gardens, turning the other way and found a chemist on the main road, then wandered into Kelvingrove Park. My mind was a blank for most of the time but as I walked past the museum, I remembered Duncan telling me how he and Nick used to visit the stuffed elephant there. I thought about going in myself. But it was closed. Of course. I'd slept most of the day and my body clock was seriously out of rhythm. It probably had been for days.

And that brought me back to the recent past.

And Nick.

And I found I'd made my decision.

I trudged back to Fergus's.

A text arrived. From Kit.

Ma gave me this number. Said not to call you. Yet. You OK?

Yes. But can't talk.

OK. Am at Tregonna. Call when you can.

A couple of seconds later.

Needed to spend a bit of time here. On my own.

I understood. Tregonna was full of memories of Pa. Mainly good ones. The times before he left.

And then another text.

Ma not back for a bit. Maybe you could meet me here?

I'd like that. Need a couple of days tho.

OK.

It would be good to finally have time to think about Pa. And to do it with Kit.

We need to talk about Tregonna, anyway.

Why?

It's ours. Or will be. Pa left it to us.

Of course, he had. I texted him straight back.

What about Issy?

She'll get the insurance. She's OK.

Ma should be part of the discussion.

Of course.

I reached the steep road up to Fergus's flat as another text arrived from Kit.

She's going to fill Tregonna with her friends.

I guessed Ma had told Kit where she was and how she might invite some of the people there to stay.

Would that be so bad?

I guess not. There's a postcard for you here BTW.

I wondered why Kit was bothering to tell me.

Very strange. Doesn't say who it's from. But it's St Matthew's lighthouse.

St Matthew's was the lighthouse down the road from Tregonna. Why would anyone send me a postcard of it?

Message?

Just says, *Reminds me of a lighthouse in France.* **No name.**

I knew then.

St Matthew's was where I'd met Nick for the first time. And the lighthouse in France was the one near Calais where we'd concocted the plan to rescue Rania.

A host of memories swirled through my head and my eyes stung as if I'd been chopping onions. At least Nick had tried to let me know he was alive. Secretively, though. Because, of course, he couldn't just tell me. I understood why he couldn't. He was in hiding. There was too much at stake. And so on and so on and so on. But it was a problem. His life was always full of other imperatives. It was the nature of the game he was involved in.

The slope up to Fergus's flat seemed steeper than ever. I was out of breath and my shoulder hurt when I buzzed for him to let me in.

'I'm on my way down,' he said. 'Wait there.'

I waited and got my breath back. As soon as the bullet wound had healed, I was going to devote some serious time to getting fit again.

'Thanks,' I said as Fergus opened the door.

'Before you go up,' he said. 'There's someone waiting for you.'

'Ah. A man with a shaven head and tattoos?'

'Some tattoos, aye. The rest I can't tell. He's wearing a woolly hat.'

'But you let him in.'

'Aye. I thought you wanted to talk to him.'

'I guess I do.'

'Tam's out and I'm going to a meeting, so you've the place to yourself.'

He pressed the keys into my hands and went.

It was Nick, standing by the window. And he was wearing a woolly hat, which covered his head and made him look more like the Nick I'd spent time with in Alajar. But not enough to change my mind. I'd always known he was a shapeshifter. A chameleon. It was part of his job. His shitty, shitty job.

We said Hi.

Him over by the window and me hovering by the door.

Him holding out his hands and me trying to ignore them.

It was awkward. I guessed he got some inkling this wasn't going to be the happy ending he'd thought it was because he dropped them.

'Fergus made you tea, I see.'

'Yes.'

'I'll get one myself. Why don't you sit down?'

'If I do, I'll never get up. Your friend's sofas are very low. Alice's gunshot cracked a couple of my ribs.'

'No other damage?'

'No.'

'That's good.'

I sidled into the kitchen area and put the kettle on.

A few minutes, I thought. Let the kettle boil. Make the tea. Then I'll ask him to leave. Explain that there's no future in this. Him going away all the time. Me never knowing where he is. Or if he's alive. That would be enough. I didn't need to mention how much I hated what he does. My eyes and nose stung again. I was probably going to cry. But it didn't matter.

'What's wrong, Jen?'

He'd moved towards me while I was focused on the kettle and now leaned on the counter that separated the kitchen from the sitting room.

'Nothing. Did your boss tell you where I was?'

'Hendricks, you mean? No. I haven't seen him.' He paused. 'Ronnie told me this was the last place you'd been before you disappeared. He was going through the police's cybercrime computers. Hendricks told him to look. He thinks he's found Xander's server. A box in the racks that shouldn't be there. It took some finding apparently. He's a clever boy.'

I wondered if either of them knew I'd suggested it to Hendricks. Probably not.

'I hoped I'd be luckier finding you now,' Nick said. 'You were very good at evading us, you know.'

He was trying to be lighthearted but I couldn't do it.

'I hated every minute of it. It played tricks with my mind.'

Silence.

'It does,' he said eventually.

'I'm never doing it again.'

'I hope not.'

I took a deep breath. 'Nick. I –'

'Neither am I.'

'Neither are you what?'

'Going undercover again.'

I looked at him properly for the first time. He looked tired, really. Shadows under his eyes and pale face under the tattoos. The colour, whether fake or from the Spanish sun, that had darkened his skin when he was playing the role of Brahim in Malta had faded.

'You've moved up the chain of command then. Is that what you'd call it?'

'Probably. But that's not what I meant. I've resigned, Jen. I resigned before the fiasco in Calais. And confirmed it afterwards.'

The kettle boiled and switched itself off.

'Of course,' he went on when I didn't say anything. 'It's never as easy as leaving a normal job. I knew that. I had to go through with my death scenario. Too much depended on it. Then they got me to set Sandy Cameron up. Then you went missing in Glasgow.' He took a ragged breath. 'I thought the Camerons might get to you before we did.'

I couldn't look into his face any more. Because of hope, you see. Hope is a wicked thing. It makes you think you've found a shortcut up a face and then you discover it's led you astray. But I couldn't stop myself. Hoping, that is.

I pulled a piece of kitchen paper off the roll and blew my nose.

'Are you going back into the normal police, then?'

I sounded politely interested. Or at least I hoped I did.

'No. I've resigned completely. Handed in my badge and my gun, so to speak.'

I let the words sink in.

'And,' he went on. 'I was… I was hoping…'

That wicked word again.

'What were you hoping?'

'I'm not sure what I'm going to do but I was hoping we might think about doing it together.'

He paused as though hoping I might speak then carried on when I didn't.

'It doesn't matter where,' he added. 'Cornwall. Spain. Or London. Or anywhere.'

I found my voice.

'I'm not sure what I'm going to do next either.'

'OK.'

'But I guess I'd be up for giving it a shot together.'

EPILOGUE

Alajar, Andalusia, Spain.
Five months later…

'Green or black?' Nick called.

I looked up from the pastry stall, where I was patiently queuing. Today, with Christmas so close, the Thursday morning village market filled the square with colour and noise as people shouted over the makeshift orchestra playing Spanish carols outside Angel's bar. Guitarists strummed and an army of percussionists banged tambourines, chimed triangles and played *zambombas* – a weird Spanish drum that produced a noise halfway between a wail and a gasp when the musician pumped a rod through a hole in its membrane.

It was magic.

I shook my head at Nick. He knew I didn't like olives.

'For your mother.'

Did Ma like olives? They hadn't been a feature of childhood in Cornwall.

'Green,' I called and hoped he wouldn't buy too many.

Ma bringing Rania and Aya to Alajar for Christmas was a big experiment. Aya had made huge strides, but none of us knew how she'd cope in a totally strange environment, surrounded by a different language. Ma had said they'd go back early if the little girl hated it.

Rania was desperate to go climbing with me.

Nick bought the olives and slowly pushed his way through the shoppers to the pastry stall. He stopped every two seconds to embrace a friend or answer a question from one of the head-scarfed, basket-clutching women who thronged the square. He'd not spent much time in Alajar as he'd been at Seville University for the last three months, only returning here for the occasional weekend, while I had snatched visits to Spain when life in Cornwall with Ma and the girls permitted. It had become easier since Ma had, in Kit's words, filled Tregonna with people who had nowhere else to go. I'd even managed to go away for some work briefly.

The syrupy, spicy smell of the pastries wafted over as I stood and watched Nick's slow and smiling progress.

I'm happy, I thought. This moment is a good one. We're together. We're going to buy cakes with strange names like *borrachuelos* and *polvorón* because it's traditional here at Christmas, although none of us will actually eat them because Ma is secreting a Christmas pudding in her luggage. And after we've bought them, Nick and I will wander over to the bar and talk to Angel about nothing much, then we'll go for a drive up into the back country because the sun is shining today. He'll take me somewhere interesting and tell me all about its history, and afterwards I won't remember any of it. These two weeks together will blur into a memory of days spent lolling around and laughing, reading quietly in front of the fire at night and waking up in the morning next to each other.

Nothing very exciting. But it was enough for the moment. More than enough.

Acknowledgements

Gone To Earth is my fifth book and I'm still not much wiser as to how they get written. Somehow I manage to go from sitting at my desk with a few random ideas buzzing around my head to sending around 90,000 words of hopefully coherent prose to my editor – albeit months and months and several drafts later. One thing I have learnt, though, is that I couldn't do it without a lot of help, and what follows is a small attempt at thanking some of the people who have been involved in the process of getting a book in front of readers.

First and foremost, Jenna Gordon, my editor at VERVE, who, as well as being endlessly patient with my procrastination and love of agonising over the word order of a single sentence, is wonderful at helping me see what I'm actually trying to write as well as giving me lots of ideas about how to make my book work.

Friend and brilliant author Fiona Erskine also read an early version and sent me a list of all the bits that were rubbish – sounds harsh, I know, but I have known Fiona since our joint writing infancy and we don't need to sweeten our advice to each other. She also sent me a couple of brilliant suggestions as to how to put some of the rubbish bits right – the rest she sadly left me to work out for myself! You can find out about Fiona and her brilliant books at fionaerskine.com.

Input from other authors and readers is pure gold at any stage of the writing process and I'm also grateful to my sister, Nikki, who is always the first person (and often the only one) to read an early draft of my books. Also, to fellow author Nicky Downes, who kindly read a late-stage version and reassured me no end.

You'd think when I came to write this, the third book to feature climbing ace Jen Shaw, that I'd be an expert climber myself or, at the very least, extremely knowledgeable, but the sad truth is that it doesn't work like that. In the gaps between books, I seem to forget the little knowledge I've acquired. So, early on in the process of writing *Gone To Earth*, when I was tearing my hair out over an intractable climbing problem, I put a plea for help on the UK Climbing Forum. I was surprised by the welcoming response from this wonderful community and I was lucky enough to meet Stuart Halford there. Stuart worked with me to shape the climbing parts of *Gone To Earth* and checked all the later versions. He also introduced me to East Greenland, which sounded so exciting I had to include it. I even have an idea for a book set there as well! You can find out more about Stuart and his work at greenlandexpeditions.com.

I also have only a layman's knowledge of policing and urban exploring, so I rely on experts to help me. I'm very grateful to Michelle Kiedron, who patiently answers all my queries about policing and is kind enough not to point out all the bits I've got wrong when she reads the books. There are some things I don't dare ask her because I'm sure the answer will get in the way of writing a good story!

My interest in underground Glasgow was first sparked by a tour through the tunnels under Glasgow Central Station with Paul Lyons (www.glasgowcentraltours.co.uk). It was a fascinating trip and one I'd recommend to everyone with an interest in history. Paul kindly offered to show me round the abandoned tunnels that the excursion didn't visit but I didn't take him up on it as I'd decided to use a different set of tunnels in *Gone To Earth* – honestly, it was nothing to do with all the rats he warned me about.

For the rest of my knowledge of underground Glasgow, I owe a lot to a group of people I've never met but who have posted descriptions, pictures and video footage of the disused tunnels underneath the city. I'd particularly like to thank Ben Cooper for their detailed description and pictures of the underground Molendinar Burn. They were a wonderful resource and inspiration.

Big thanks to Oliver for putting me right on all the IT aspects of *Gone To Earth*, although he assures me his knowledge of the dark web is purely theoretical.

Glasgow plays a large part in *Gone To Earth*. I love the city and I hope I've done it justice. *Gone To Earth* is a thriller so, out of necessity, I've focused on the problems that plague all large cities, but vibrant, creative and friendly Glasgow is much more than that. A note to eagle-eyed readers: I have invented a few of the places in *Gone To Earth* and played around with the details of a couple of the real ones. This is a work of fiction, after all!

Huge thanks to the team at VERVE Books: particularly to Ellie Lavender, Lisa Gooding, Sarah Stewart-Smith and Demi Echezona. It's always a pleasure to work with you and I look forward to it every time!

I'm so glad I met my wonderful agent Amanda Preston at LBA books when I did. Thank you for all the wise advice and for working so hard on my behalf!

I've met some lovely people since my publishing journey started and I discovered what a fantastic community book lovers are. A massive thank-you to all the reviewers, bloggers, podcasters and cheerleaders who do so much to promote authors. A big hug to all the authors who have shared their experiences with me and patiently listened and offered support when I've droned on about some problem or other of my own.

Almost finally, a huge thank you to all my friends and family – particularly my husband, Alex – for all their love and support.

And finally. Thank you to all of you who have read this book. It still feels incredible that there are people who don't know me who've bothered to pick up my books and read them. Even more incredible is when people write to tell me how much they've enjoyed them. I think I might say this every time, but when I write the books, squashed into a little desk in the corner of our sitting room (it has a view over the sea, which makes the squashing bit worthwhile), I often think about the person who might read them. I hope that they'll be led astray by the red herrings I've inserted, or that they might smile at something I've written or be unable to put the book down at certain points. Both Jen and her mother, Morwenna, arrived on the page without me having to do any work to create them. Sometimes characters do that. I've loved writing about them and I hope you enjoy reading about them in this, their (probably) final outing.

If you'd like to know more about me and my books and hear about new releases, visit my website (Jane-Jesmond.com), where you can also sign up for my newsletter, or follow me on Facebook at JaneJesmondAuthor.

About the Author

Jane Jesmond writes crime, thriller and mystery fiction. Her debut novel, *On The Edge* – the first in a series featuring dynamic, daredevil protagonist Jen Shaw – was a *Sunday Times* Best Crime Fiction of the Month pick. The sequel, *Cut Adrift*, was selected as a *Times* Thriller of the Month and a *Sunday Times* Book of the Year upon its publication. Jane also recently published *Her*, a speculative standalone novel, with Storm Publishers. Jane's latest standalone mystery, *A Quiet Contagion*, was published by VERVE Books in 2023.

Although Jane loves writing (and reading) thrillers and mysteries, her real life is very quiet and unexciting. Dead bodies and dangerous exploits are not a feature! She lives by the sea on the northwest tip of France with a husband and a cat and enjoys coastal walks and village life. Unlike Jen Shaw, she is terrified of heights!

Also Available from VERVE Books

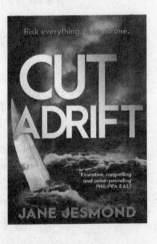

VERVE BOOKS

Launched in 2018, VERVE Books is an independent publisher of page-turning, diverse and original fiction from fresh and impactful voices.

Our books are connected by rich storytelling, vividly imagined settings and unforgettable characters. The list is tightly curated by a small team of passionate booklovers whose hope is that if you love one VERVE book, you'll love them all!

WANT TO JOIN THE CONVERSATION AND FIND OUT MORE ABOUT WHAT WE DO?

Catch us on social media or sign up to our newsletter for all the latest news from VERVE HQ.

vervebooks.co.uk/signup

📷 **f** 🐦 ♪ **@VERVE_Books**